BOOK ONE

IN THE TEMPLE SHADOWS

KELLY O'HEARN

Global Entanglement, LLC

Paperback ISBN: 979-8-9905798-0-4
Hardcover ISBN: 979-8-9905798-2-8
Ebook ISBN: 979-8-9905798-1-1

Written with Kate Hensler Fogarty
Cover design: Pure + Applied
Cover photo: Tomb Relief of the Chief Physician Amenhotep and Family, c. 1279–1257 B.C.E. Cleveland Museum of Art.
Interior design by Jess LaGreca, Mayfly book design

Library of Congress Catalog Number: 2024909197
First Printing: 2024

For the three great loves in this life:

My two boys
I would be your Mom in a million lifetimes.

And You.
It's always been You.

PRESENT DAY | **SARAH** | **HARRY**
EGYPT | SARRAH | HASIM

ABOUT THE ARCANUM SERIES:

Five souls, inextricably connected, traveling through time and crossing paths until they finally find "happily ever after." These are the stories that came to me, a seasoned intuitive channeler, when I turned my attention from reading others' energies to my own inner self, and asked the tarot cards about my past lives.

Soul mates come in many forms: lovers, friends, guides, villains. The five souls in Arcanum take the form of a different

MAX	LEYLA	KEN
METI	LILU	KHUFU

character in each of the books, propelling the story forward. The series is best enjoyed in order.

If you've ever met someone and felt like you've known, loved, or feared them before, then you've experienced the spark that lit the Arcanum series.

—Kelly O'Hearn

She has been here before—but when? Everything is intimately familiar: the musk of wood smoke and horses, earth and sand, leather and sweat, rain-soaked roses. Distant battle cries, whispers of longing, desperate pleas in the darkness uttered in languages she shouldn't be able to understand but does—Arabic, Norse, Italian. Sensations: the brush of coarse linen against her thighs; her ribs constricted by a boned corset; a man's warm hand on hers as she takes a sip of chilled champagne.

The centuries spin around her as if she were faint, but the crispness of each tableau never dulls. She has never felt more alive. The cerulean hue of the Nile from aboard the Pharaoh's royal vessel; a powdered wig heavy atop her brow as the carriage hurtles down the *allée*; hiding for her life in the shadows of St. Peter's Square; shivering, snowdrifts deep around her handmade boots, lips set ablaze from a stolen kiss; the wet wind on her face, her glove on his knee, as the E-Type dashes through the rolling Sussex hills.

CHAPTER ONE

New York City, October 17

Sarah turned over in her sleep, hoping to feel the presence of . . . reality? Or some reality? She was awake enough to be wholly present in *this* reality, the cool sheets rustling around her feet, the soft breathing of her husband beside her, and the distant siren of a cop car heading down Fifth Avenue. She pressed her palm against her cheek to prove to herself this was real.

Please be real.

They're just dreams, she tried to tell herself. Just a jumble of random associations that her subconscious was trying to expel or sort through. But then why did they feel *so real?* She took a sip of water and drifted back to sleep—or rather, to those other worlds, those other dreams.

But as she passed through that misty territory of half-waking and half-dreaming, she understood the truth.

She knew what dreams were.

These were not dreams.

Somehow Sarah had always thought her life would become . . . *more*, with layers that would build upon each other and create a deeper, more meaningful existence. Like the way a fragrance evolved and intensified as you breathed it in, with some scents intertwined, some revealed over time: the light, alluring top notes; the headier heart notes; the truest base notes . . . She didn't *want* for anything—it wasn't "more" in that grabby sense of the word. She just. . . .

Oh, screw it. She got out of bed and padded silently through the darkness, avoiding the dresser and trailing her fingertips along the wall as she guided herself out of their bedroom. Carl never had trouble sleeping, no matter how much he had going on or how many people he had depending on him. Every night he got into bed, turned out the light, and just like that, he was asleep. She used to admire it, thinking he must have the world's clearest conscience, or have achieved some level of inner peace. But now she just thought he was, well, really self-centered. So utterly self-centered that none of those other people or obligations or thoughts, even, ever intruded on the *him* he'd created.

She padded quietly into the kitchen and made herself a cup of tea, trying not to feel like a cliché. So what if she couldn't sleep because her hot husband was a bit of a selfish prick some-times? So what if her beautiful life felt a bit empty at four in the morning? Maybe she was ungrateful. (She could totally hear her mother saying that.) Maybe she was unappreciative of how much life was offering her. (Ditto.) Maybe she needed to medi-tate, or be an untamed love warrior. Whatever the hell that was.

The tea warmed her hands. She picked up the blanket draped over the back of the club chair and made her way out to the balcony that ran the length of the living room. She settled into a loveseat and looked out over Central Park.

And waited. Waited for the world to open again.

What she'd originally cursed as insomnia, she now welcomed as her favorite part of the day. Quiet. Emerging. Promising. New. *Hers.*

Twelve years ago, when they were deciding where they wanted to live, she and Carl had gone back and forth about whether they should buy a place on the East Side or the West Side of the Park. Morgan Stanley was in Midtown, so it didn't really affect his commute either way. She traveled for work constantly, so as long as there was a doorman to hail a cab to the airport at any hour, she had no preference. They didn't have kids yet but were thinking ahead to schools, and there were good options in both neighborhoods. They both knew they wanted to be on the Park, not a block or two away—not close to the Park, but open-the-door-and-walk-into-the-Park on the Park.

But this morning, since she was giving herself permission to pick apart her perfect life, she realized she never should have agreed to this apartment, even if it had seemed like a dream come true twelve years ago. The apartment had needed a ton of work, but it was what they could afford without having to borrow money from her parents. It was up high enough that they wouldn't hear a ton of street noise. But it never *felt* right to her. It never smelled right. It didn't face the right way. Or something. As detail-oriented as she was, she'd never paid much attention to feng shui, but maybe the ancient Chinese had a point. Hell, maybe *she* didn't face the right direction.

Twelve years ago was also back when she and Carl actually listened to each other. He'd known she was having some reservations about the apartment, and he'd wanted to hear them. But since she couldn't put them into words—and because she of all people thought inarticulate hunches weren't worth losing sleep over—they ended up buying this place.

And it had been a great choice. Really.

The irony about losing sleep wasn't lost on her.

Again, poor little rich girl alert. She took a sip of her tea and shook her head, trying to shake away this stupid line of thinking that had her combing over every tiny detail of her life story until she'd red-lined any goodness whatsoever. Her life was good, dammit. In fact, it was great. It was just that . . . it all seemed to be going in the wrong direction.

She and Carl had worked their asses off to get where they were. Yes, they'd had a brilliant head start—supportive parents, great schools—but they'd taken every one of those advantages and then put in the effort. When she started her fragrance company, she was one of the first women in an industry that had been male-dominated for literally centuries to raise that amount of venture capital. A decade later, she was still one of very few female leaders in the field. She had paid back every penny she'd ever borrowed, and then some. She made her own money. She managed her own money. The kids and Carl were great. Or rather the kids were great, and Carl was great most of the time. She was living the dream.

Wasn't she?

Then why didn't it feel like it?

Taking another sip of tea, she looked out over the rooftop of the Metropolitan Museum of Art and let the truth sink in. She was forty years old today. It was bound to be a doozy. But all that trip-around-the-sun nonsense that everyone posted on social media these days just made her more annoyed with herself. She knew it was only a number, an arbitrary marker. What was a year? What was a day? What were forty of them? Or fourteen thousand? It was all so haphazard.

All she wanted was to have a plain old Saturday: go for a run in the Park, maybe take the kids to a movie and then have a burger around the corner. When she'd told Carl a few months ago that that was how she wanted to spend her fortieth birthday, he'd just laughed and said, "Of course, deep down you want a party—you're just getting emotional about the big four-oh."

That was the type of Carl comment that was starting to make her crazy. After all their years together—fifteen since they were married, twenty since they'd met in college—it was all making her crazy. If she were being honest (and why the hell couldn't she be honest with herself when she was alone at dawn?) it wasn't all of her life that was making her crazy, it was pretty much everything about *Carl* that was making her crazy. "For richer, for poorer" was a vow he would probably not swear to these days, that was for sure.

Her mind circled back to what she'd been thinking about in the darkness of her bedroom an hour earlier. Weren't the different layers of her life supposed to *enrich* it? Wasn't marriage supposed to be about building a life together? Growing? Deepening? The two of them had been building their lives, but not with each other. Was there even a "them" anymore? She was starting to feel like a ghost, or an actress walking around performing her life. Tonight would just be one more performance, with a trailer in that movie voiceover voice—*The Fortieth Birthday Party*, starring Sarah Fuller as the poor little rich girl who wakes up to realize that she's no longer in love with her husband and needs to get over herself.

She sighed and tried not to take any of the fortieth-birthday baloney too much to heart. At least tonight it was only going to be her parents and a few friends in the private room at Papilles.

As rays of sunshine made their way through the concrete canyons behind her and gleamed on the top of the Egyptian Wing of the Met, she let all those petty thoughts float up into the sky. She didn't need to be in love with her husband every minute of every day; that wasn't what marriage was about. He was a good person (most of the time), and she needed to focus on that good person. She decided she'd spend an hour or two in the Egyptian Wing that afternoon to clear her head, stare at a mummy, decompress. She never felt more grounded than when standing by the sandstone Temple of Dendur, that prize of ancient Egypt, staring out at Central Park through the gallery's glittering, triple-height window wall. It was as if she were at once suspended between antiquity and modernity, and the overlapping layers felt harmonious rather than jarring. It was that same time-bending spell that she tried to conjure in her fragrances.

As she took the last sip of cold tea and felt the day's warmth rising, she heard the first rumblings of the kids shuffling to the kitchen and looking for her.

"Mom?"

"Mom!"

"I'm out here." In a few seconds, arms and legs and sleepy heads were scrambling over her and bare feet wiggled their way under the blanket with her. "Happy birthday, Mom!" The twins gave her kisses and hugs, and she took a deep breath and pushed aside everything except the joy of these two loving creatures that she had somehow managed to bring into this world. It was the best part of the day, when she didn't feel like a stranger in her own body. She squeezed them tight and exhaled into them.

———

The whole "It's Your Day" thing proved to be not quite how things happened. After snuggling with the twins until their lengthy rendition of "Are ya one, are ya two" hit "Are ya forty," Sarah threw on some leggings and went for a run. The smells of Central Park always inspired her—the crisp air and freshly cut lawns, the roasted-chestnut vendors, even the errant waft of marijuana. When it came to aromas, she was an equal-opportunity employer.

Back at the apartment an hour later, she took a quick bath and changed into jeans and a long-sleeved T-shirt. As she walked from her dressing area back into the bedroom, she noticed a red-and-gold Cartier box on her pillow. Carl was leaning against the door frame between their bedroom and the hall, clad in his

Brooks Brothers pajama pants and looking like a preppy *Playgirl* model.

He cracked one of his half smiles.

"Open it."

She'd always liked him best when he was a little bossy. It gave her a warm feeling, the way he stared at her and willed her to do his bidding.

"Birthday girl," he added, then took a sip of his coffee.

The hinged box opened with a satisfactory pop and a pair of spectacular diamond earrings flashed up at her.

"Ice for my ice princess. Love you, babe." He winked at her and turned back toward the kitchen.

Ice princess. It was a nickname she had liked early in their relationship. She didn't want to be soft or gooey or emotional: she wanted to be tough as nails. She wanted to be powerful, in the boardroom and in the bedroom, like some feminist powerhouse from the '80s—or at least in the '80s movies she'd seen.

But now it just made her feel cold. She supposed it wasn't really Carl's fault. She felt something deep and scary changing inside her, and she was almost physically overcome with the feeling of loss and emptiness starting to seep out of some dark place in her gut, the place where she'd shoved everything— every worry, every care, every inarticulate hunch. God, Carl could be so charming, but it was usually at her expense—literally. How much had these earrings cost her?

She definitely wasn't going to sail through this day the way she'd hoped.

Breathe.

Sarah steadied herself by retreating into her dressing room and sitting at her grandmother's vanity. Its mirrored top was crowded with crystal bottles, some as old as the 18th-century table itself. Naturally her grandmother had left her this vanity; ever since Sarah was old enough to peer over the tabletop, they'd shared a passion for fragrance that was almost their own language. *That was probably thirty-five years ago!* she thought to herself.

The Venetian glass stopper felt heavy in Sarah's hands. As she brought it to her nose, she could still detect the potent blood-orange citrus of Tarocchi, her grandmother's prized scent, though the bottle had long been empty. The fragrance itself had been discontinued decades before Sarah was born, she'd been told by her grandmother—who'd chosen it not only for the scent but for the unusual bottle, engraved with an image of the tarot card known as the Wheel of Fortune. Her grandmother had dabbled in tarot and other mystic arts as well as fragrance, and she delighted whenever she turned over the Wheel card in doing a reading for young Sarah.

Um, back to that bling! Sarah took one chandelier earring and put it on, then the other. They glinted in and out of her long, dark hair when she looked in the mirror. At least she didn't *look* like a woman on the verge of a nervous breakdown. And the earrings were stunning.

She wasn't accustomed to spending much time in front of the mirror—it was just something she did to make sure she looked presentable. But now she stared at herself a little longer, pulled her shoulders back, assessed a few wrinkles around her mouth, and then looked into her own eyes.

For a few seconds Sarah didn't even recognize herself; instead, she saw flashes of all the women she *might* have been, all the versions of herself that she could have been. Her stomach flipped, and she felt as if she *had* been those women, not just some alternate versions of the woman sitting here in a Fifth Avenue apartment—that she'd experienced their entire lifetimes, passions, lovers, tragedies. She felt it in that deep place again and unconsciously put her palm over her womb. It wasn't as scary to think about looking into that dark, powerful place as it had been a few minutes ago. Then she'd felt like she was breaking, but now it felt like a revelation, as though everything she'd ever needed was already there, or here, buried so deep that she'd only known it as a rumble, a glance, a hint, like a river at the bottom of the ocean.

Then, as quickly as that feeling had come, it was gone.

Sarah put the earrings back in their elegant box and walked into the kitchen with renewed interest in this birthday thing.

"Anyone want to go to the Met with me for a couple of hours?"

Sam shook his head and didn't divert his gaze from his Gameboy. Alexandra looked up, mouth full of cereal, and mumbled "No thanks" as a bit of milk dripped back into her bowl.

"I've got a squash match at 10:30," said Carl, swiping through emails on his tablet with one hand and holding his Wharton MBA coffee mug with the other. "Let's all meet up for lunch later. Dina can watch the kids when you and I go out tonight."

She stood looking at the three of them, then smiled. "Sounds good. I'll meet you all here around 12:30." Alexandra was the only one still looking at her. Sarah mouthed "Love you," and Alex mouthed it back.

As Sarah climbed the steps to the Met, she felt a rush of familiar pleasure coupled with the promise of something new. She took the stone steps two at a time as she got closer to the top and said hi to the guard as he waved her in (no bag to look through). She emerged from the revolving door into the Great Hall, then flashed her member card to the woman at the admissions desk. God, the seasonal flower arrangements on the desk were always insane, she thought, as she breathed in the heady autumnal roses, the ginger-leaved katsura branches.

Medieval Art? Nope, no churches today. Arms and Armor? She was dragged there often enough by the kids. The American Wing? No, today she was feeling especially ancient. This was her day, and she was going to spend it winding through the Egyptian Wing. Unencumbered and unhurried by the kids' pleas to hit the gift shop (and bored Carl), she was going to take as long as she wanted to pore over every label. The mummies, of course, the mummies were cool. But she was drawn to the objects of daily life and the handwrought artifacts that millennia ago had been the picture of modernity. The intricate neck collar of Princess Sithathoryunet. The glass mosaic inlay. The sky-blue faience crocodile amulet. A copper mirror engraved with the emblem of the goddess Hathor—how fine the handiwork four thousand years ago! The power and wealth of the pharaohs had yielded earthly delights that still seemed timeless and priceless. Ancient Egyptian people were passionate about life, about their land. They thought themselves the luckiest people on Earth. Their technological advances were unreal: construction, irrigation, shipbuilding. The *wheel,* for god's sake. She marveled at the forged iron surgery tool, the toothbrush, the beer mug, the bowling ball. They really knew how to have a good time! Was there anything that this ancient culture hadn't conceived or foretold?

Her birthday brain sated, she wandered down the hallway toward the *pièce de résistance,* her home base—the Temple of Dendur. As she neared the familiar glass doors, she saw that they were shut. On a Saturday? "THE GALLERIES ARE TEMPORARILY CLOSED," the sign said. She knew she was being churlish, but really? A guard standing by the closed door politely let her know that someone had rented the gallery for the evening.

Sarah sighed and smiled at the guard. "Oh, what a shame. . . ."

"Sorry. It should be open again tomorrow."

"I guess some rich asshole's having a party?" she kidded. "Thanks anyway. You have a good day."

"You, too," the guard said, smiling.

What kind of douchebag rents the entire wing for a private party? she thought. *Okay, fine, if the Dendur Society wants to fete the President or some deep-pocketed tech guru, then exceptions can be made. But just some rich asshole shutting down a public treasure for a silly party? Ugh.* As Sarah's mood plummeted, she headed down the main stairs and out into the October sunlight. It was a gorgeous day, and she refused to let some—

Her cell phone buzzed when she was halfway down the stairs. Her face lit up as she hit the green button.

CHAPTER TWO

“Hey, stranger! How was Mauritius?”

“*They say it’s your birthday!*” Max sang into the phone. “*It’s my birthday too, yeah!*”

Sarah laughed. “I wish it really *was* your birthday, too, yeah, so I didn’t have to trawl through this stupid day like a mopey fourteen-year-old.”

“By the way, you were never a mopey fourteen-year-old. I was there, remember?”

“Yes, thank god you were there. How would either of us have survived our childhoods without each other?”

He gasped. “It’s too horrible to contemplate.” She heard him take a sip of something. “Anyway, why are you moping? It’s autumn in New York, you’re probably on your way into the Met, I bet you have burger-and-fries plans with your handsome husband and two rascally children, and most importantly you get to have dinner with *me* tonight . . . and we all know I’m the hottest ticket in town.”

Sarah walked out of the Met and skipped down the steps, forgetting all the trifling annoyances that had dogged her earlier in the day.

“You’re right, I have nothing to mope about. I’m so glad you’re back in town. But it’s not fair that you still get to gallivant all over the globe while some of us have to stay put and create a stable environment for little humans. Wouldn't they be stable if I took them to Mauritius? It's just so *unfair!*"

"Yes, your life is one unfair setback after another, I know." He was panting slightly.

Oh. He's calling me from a treadmill, she thought. *Classic Max.*

"Hey, I meant to tell you, I met this amazing guy there," he said. "He was there on business, but we hung out at the resort—which was fantastic, by the way. You have to go when you're done creating stable environments, or something. Fucking spectacular. Seriously. Anyway, this guy—"

Sarah wound down a pathway into Central Park and smiled as she listened to her dearest friend ramble in his inimitable manner. Max was some miraculous combination of confidant, comic relief, a shoulder to cry on, and the brother she'd never had. They'd kissed once when they were sixteen, then simultaneously wiped their mouths with the backs of their own hands.

Never.

Gonna.

Happen.

Which turned out to be the best possible turn of events. They never quarreled, never got on each other's nerves; they just knew each other down to their bones and loved each other anyway.

"Why are you telling me about some guy? Is he for you or for me? Who has business in Mauritius?"

"Very funny. Get your mind out of the gutter—he's this brilliant entrepreneur who was flabbergasted to learn that I knew 'the one and only Sarah Fuller.' He's actually in your business. Apparently his company sources and supplies rare essential oils from all over the globe, but never have the two titans met. He was visiting some 'artisanal frangipani grove' in Mauritius. 'Do you really know her? Would I mind making an introduction—' I'm not used to being used for access to *you!* I told him he should see how the one and only Sarah Fuller dresses when she's not being Sarah Fuller!"

She glanced down at her shabby T-shirt and jeans. Maybe Max was right; now that she was forty, it was time to get an actual weekend wardrobe! "No way, is it what's-his-name who's 'Manhattan's Secret Bachelor' or whatever the *New York Post* is calling him?"

"His name is Harry Aiken and yes, he's that guy. From what I hear, he got married young, but his wife passed away many years ago and he's been married to his work ever since. Took a while for the *Post* to find him out! But I swear he's good people, not pretentious at all, works his ass off—his very fine ass, I might add—and I think you should really talk to him about being on the board of your do-good-thing."

"You are impossible—it's not my *do-good-thing*—"

"I know, I know. You're going to save the trees now that you've made millions of dollars off their flowers and bark and stuff. It's just so exhausting for the rest of us—"

She burst out in laughter. A woman pushing a stroller toward her on the path looked startled, then smiled. Sarah smiled back.

"You should talk," she said. "How many companies have *you* created now? Five, seven?"

"This has nothing to do with me, and you know it. Anyway, let's pick a day next week for you to meet Harry."

"Oh, it's *Harry,* is it? Your new BFF?"

"I only have one BFF, and it's you. So, let's get back to why you were moping before I swooped in and saved you from yourself. Talk to me."

She sighed, then looked for the closest bench, and sat down overlooking the ancient Cleopatra's Needle monument behind the museum. At least she could look at that if nothing else. "It's so petty, but I just wanted a regular old Saturday, and Carl's gone and made it all birthday-y."

"Like, 'cause it's your birthday, maybe?"

"Like I said, totally petty." A couple of dogs frolicked on the grass. "Some rich asshole has rented the Temple of Dendur for some private party full of rich assholes, and all I wanted to do was sit down quietly for an hour in there this afternoon and let all this stupid shit go and . . ."

"And . . . ?" he waited. She loved how he waited.

"Carl's driving me fucking nuts." The words just fell out. That was sort of the way it always was with Max and her. No filter.

"Well. That's . . . something."

Maybe she should get a dog. Or two dogs.

"What are you thinking right now?" he asked. "I can tell you're thinking something dangerous—"

"Maybe I should get a dog . . . or two dogs?"

"Right, because *riiiiiight*, two dogs will definitely solve the whole potential I'm-not-sure-I-love-my-husband-anymore situation."

"I didn't say anything about not loving him."

"You didn't have to, sweetheart."

Sarah hated when he did that. Amid all the banter and fun and joking, Max would call her *sweetheart* and she knew he saw right through her, more than anyone else—more than her mother, way more than Carl. And not even *through* her; he saw *into* her.

"I hate when you do that," she whispered.

"Oh my god, are you going to cry? I'm so sorry. I really didn't—"

"No, I'm not going to cry. Not now, anyway. Soon, probably. I've been on thin ice ever since I woke up."

"At three o'clock this morning?"

"Four, actually. And I get it, I really do. It's a big milestone and I need to process whatever it is that's making me feel like such a malcontent."

"Listen, please go home and hug your kids and enjoy your day. I'll see you at dinner and we'll have the best time. And then we'll talk through all this other stuff over a boozy lunch on Monday, okay? Don't do anything rash—"

"Like run away," they said simultaneously.

"I'm never going to live that down, am I?" Sarah smiled. "That was seriously twenty-five years ago."

"But it was so priceless! As if getting on the train in Southampton and hiding at your cousin's Park Avenue apartment could ever be construed as running away. You thought you were such a tough cookie!" His deep laugh made her feel so good.

Sarah stood up and started to head back home. "I can't wait to see you tonight. I've decided I don't like it when you're away. I lose my sense of humor—I think *you* are my sense of humor."

"Ditto, kid. Enjoy the rest of the day, and I'll see you at seven."

"Sounds good. Love you."

"Hey, wait—"

"What?"

"I forgot to ask, what are you wearing?"

She looked down at herself. "A long-sleeve T-shirt and jeans. Why?"

"Not *now!*" he roared with laughter. "Tonight, of course!"

Max had better taste in clothes than most women she knew.

"Oh, who cares. Black pants and a silk top, probably."

"Oh my god, you are totally killing me! Don't make me come over there. You are not wearing black pants to your fortieth birthday party for fuck's sake. It's a party, okay? Not a PTA meeting."

"It's just dinner at Papilles. What would you have me wear, a ball gown?"

"*Totally!*" Max sounded genuinely delighted. "Oh my god, if only you would wear a ballgown, my life would be complete."

"Well, I'm not wearing a ball gown."

"Will you at least wear something sexy? Come on, if nothing else you deserve to feel hot on your birthday."

She sighed.

He laughed. "You don't need to make it sound like a chore, Sarah. Get in the spirit. Hey, I know! Why don't you pretend it's *my* birthday! You always have fun and look great on my birthday."

She started laughing again. "That's such a good idea. I already feel better. Why is that?"

"I don't know. You can talk to your shrink about why you don't think you deserve to be happy on your own damn birthday, but I'm here to tell you, you do!"

She entered her building and waved to the doorman. "Okay, fine, I'm going to look like a sex goddess tonight, thanks to you."

"Hoo-fucking-ray! Mission accomplished!" The phone clicked, and he was gone. Must be done with his workout. Max was not one for lengthy farewells.

Sarah tapped her phone and glanced at the screen as she got in the elevator. She scrolled through a few emails and replied to the one from Alex's class mom, saying that she'd bring gluten-free, sugar-free, egg-free cookies (what *could* they contain?) to the fifth-grade bake sale next Thursday.

———

Max was right, as usual. The rest of the day had been just what she wanted. She and Carl took the kids to their favorite burger joint over on Third Avenue and then to a matinee of the latest Marvel movie. It had been mindless and entertaining and exactly what she'd needed. They were home by late afternoon, so she had plenty of time to pamper herself before dinner.

It wasn't quite a ball gown, but she'd definitely erred on the side of glam, especially for a small dinner party. The dress was deceptively provocative, with a high neck in the front and a revealing dip at the back. The cut was pretty straightforward—a sleeveless sheath—but the material was liquid gold. The word *slinky* came to mind, especially since she wasn't wearing anything underneath. She unhooked the tag; of course, she'd never worn the dress before. It had hung in the back of her closet since an ill-advised tipsy stroll n' shop with Max down Madison Avenue a few months ago.

Sarah sat down in her dressing room to slip on a pair of barely-there stilettos with narrow gold straps that wound around her ankles. They were surprisingly comfortable for heels that looked like they could double as weapons in a spy movie. She stood up and surveyed herself in the full-length mirror. Not bad for the big four-oh. Her hair was pulled up into a messy chignon, and the new diamond earrings glinted between strands of curls that softened the turn of her jaw. Suddenly she felt like her forties were going to be the best decade of her life. Her twenties had been consumed with work. Her thirties had been focused on her kids—and more work. Maybe her forties were going to be . . . hers.

Now: which fragrance to wear? That decision wasn't usually up to her: the lab was always sending a sample of this or that test scent, or the marketing department would send her a competitor's latest best-selling product, or Uncle Pierre would send some vintage formula he'd recreated, or a rare essential oil. Sarah looked at all the bottles and pipettes and prototypes on the vanity and picked up Tarocchi. There was barely a drop left, but she wanted her grandmother's spirit around her tonight.

She did a little turn in front of the mirror to make sure everything looked okay from behind, then slid the door open and walked into the bedroom.

Carl was fastening a cufflink as he regarded his face in the mirror: first right profile, then left profile. He turned to watch her walk into the room and let out a low wolf whistle that seemed utterly without irony. A thrill of pure sexual electricity ran down her spine.

"Babe." He shook his head.

"Good?"

"Better than good. . . ." He moved toward her with a prowling gait and a predatory look in his eyes. "Do we really need to go out?" He kissed her neck, and she let her head tilt back.

"No," she whispered. "Please, no?"

He nearly growled, as his finger trailed down her spine to where the satin pooled at her lower back. "This is indecent. . . ." His fingertip dipped beneath the fabric to the low of her back and he moaned a little, pressing himself against her thigh. Sarah felt the supple Italian fabric of his suit pants through the thin layer of her dress, and the heat of him, the urgency of him.

This was the Carl she had fallen in love with. Focused. On *her.* Not the rest of it—the clubs, the parties, the Joneses. She laughed, low and sexy, then he pulled away. "Back to reality, baby. Time to go to your birthday dinner."

"That *you* insisted on having!" she added.

"If I'd known you were going to look like that, I'd've made other plans." He smiled at her, kissed her again on the cheek, and turned to give himself another look in the mirror. He flicked his fingers through his hair and shot her a wink. "Ready?"

"As I'll ever be." She caught his eye in the reflection and smiled.

They kissed the kids goodnight and let Dina know they'd be late coming home. Alex told her mother that she looked beautiful. Sam gave her a thumbs-up and said, "Hundred percent!" They were already in their PJs, cozied up on the couch. She kissed them again on the tops of their heads and then reached for Carl's hand as they left the apartment together.

As they stood in the elevator, Carl looked at his watch. "We're running early. Do you want to go to the Met Roof Garden for a few minutes? It's closing for the season in two weeks."

"Sure," Sarah replied. She loved the roof garden, especially at sunset. And she loved that the museum stayed open late through early fall weekends, so they were able to enjoy it.

A cool autumnal wind was picking up, and she pulled her black cashmere wrap more tightly around her as they crossed the street. The Met's fountains and banners were awash in up-lighting as dusk descended on the facade. A few people still sat on the front steps but most of the tourists had gone for the day, and this stretch of Fifth Avenue felt quiet and homey.

Sarah lifted the fabric of her dress at the knee so she didn't trip on the hem as she ascended the stairs. Carl held her other arm and she looked up to the main entrance.

She was suddenly overcome with heart-pounding exhilaration. She tried to catch her breath, but her chest was hammering furiously.

"You okay?" Carl asked quietly.

"Yeah, just, wow . . . isn't this so beautiful?"

He looked at her, then looked up. "Yes. . . ." Then he looked back at her more carefully. "You sure you're okay? You're trembling."

They'd reached the top of the steps, and she inhaled deeply. "This day has been so weird. I promise I'm fine. It's probably the high heels—and the pound of Twizzlers I ate at the movies." She hoped he'd believe her levity, because now was certainly not the time to tell him she was completely overcome with premonitions and omens and *feelings*.

They went into the Great Hall, and Carl started to steer her to the right.

"Where are you going?" she asked.

He leaned in, conspiring. "I was thinking we should try to crash the asshole party at the Temple of Dendur." Sarah had told him that afternoon how annoyed she'd been that it was closed, and he'd laughed and called her spoiled. He was right, but she was glad he remembered and wanted to remedy it somehow.

"Oooh, I *love* the idea of crashing someone's party!" She slid her arm through his and matched his pace.

"We are obviously dressed for the occasion. I'll totally talk my way past the guest list minion." His voice got lower as they approached the entrance. A woman in a black pantsuit with a security earpiece and a tablet looked up and smiled.

"Welcome, may I see your invitation please?"

Sarah could hear the telltale clinking of glasses and the murmur of festive voices, but she couldn't see inside the hall. Black velvet curtains had been hung inside the massive glass doors, concealing the vast space beyond.

Carl patted his chest pocket, then his side pockets. "Damn, I forgot to—"

"Langmore," Sarah said, without missing a beat. Max was on every guest list known to man, and he was always fashionably late.

The woman tapped her earpiece and mumbled a security code of some sort. Then she looked down at her screen and scrolled to the Ls. "Max Langmore, plus one?" she asked, looking up with a courteous smile.

"That's the one," Carl said, enjoying the ruse.

Sarah appreciated the frisson of mischief that ran through her as the glass door opened and the sounds of the party swelled. When was the last time she'd crashed a party? Being naughty was fun!

As a door attendant began to draw the heavy velvet curtains, Carl pulled her close, kissed her neck, and whispered, "Happy birthday, babe." He pulled back a few inches and looked into her eyes.

"Please don't hate me."

"Why would I hate—"

CHAPTER THREE

As the hall came into view, the entire crowd erupted into a frenzy of "Surprise!" "Happy Birthday!" "To Sarah!" "Cheers!" Before she knew what was happening, her mother and father were there hugging her and someone had taken her wrap. Max was there, partially visible in the throng. He was smiling and shaking his head and giving her a thumbs up, mouthing the words "sex goddess." Her best friends from college were somehow there—one of them lived in St. Louis, what was she even doing in New York?—along with the moms from Sam and Alex's school, the ones she actually liked, and the cousins she thought had gone to Vermont for the weekend, and old work colleagues. . . .

She started trembling again, as she had on the steps, but now it felt like a tsunami that she wasn't going to be able to control with any number of steady breaths or shoulder relaxation techniques or anything—

Then Max was suddenly by her side, with a flute of champagne and a steadying hand. "Drink this right now. You're going to be fine." Under his breath he muttered, "Fucking Carl and his bright ideas."

"I don't want to cry in front of all these people," Sarah whispered close to his ear, with a weird fake smile, so it looked like she was thanking him for being part of the whole thing.

His grip tightened just above her elbow. "This party is not a big deal. Start walking with me and stop smiling like you're unhinged."

She laughed: it was short and dry, but she did laugh. The tsunami retreated. "Thanks, Max. I needed that."

"What the hell is going *on* with you?" he asked in that low, serious-Max voice. "You've been the center of attention before. You've spoken in front of thousands of people. What is it?"

She smiled at a friend and lifted her champagne flute, cocking her head to gesture that she'd be back in a sec. "Something's been happening to me all day, I don't know how to explain it, but it's like I'm . . . breaking open."

"Okayyyyyy . . . we've covered a lot of terrain together, but this is new. Like you're having a break*down?*"

They walked behind the Temple of Dendur, and she started to calm down. She rested her free hand against the temple wall. There weren't any guards back here. She knew full well she wasn't supposed to touch the wall, but she needed the solidity of ancient sandstone beneath her shaking fingers.

"No, it's not a breakdown . . . I don't feel depressed or . . . I don't know. It feels . . . powerful. Like I've been keeping something hidden away, deep down, and it's not going to stay hidden any longer."

She pressed her hand harder against the stone and felt something like energy calming her and empowering her all at once.

"I'm okay." And she really was. She looked from her hand into Max's concerned face. "I just want to find a quiet spot to regroup for a few minutes—"

"You are not going to run away from your own damn party!"

"No, I'm not, I promise. Just cover for me. Ten minutes tops, I swear."

Max looked skeptical, but he took her glass and walked with

her to the back entrance. He kissed her on the cheek. "Okay, fine. I'll cover for you, but seriously, ten minutes is all I'm giving you. And don't go far." She watched until he turned the corner and went out of sight.

The back door to the American Wing was manned by a lone guard. It just happened to be the same young female guard as earlier in the day; they both did a double take. The guard looked her up and down, dress and diamonds and heels, then smiled conspiratorially and asked, "So *you're* the asshole?"

"Yep. I guess I am," Sarah shrugged. They laughed.

"May I step out for a few minutes?"

The guard opened the door slightly, checking to see if the coast was clear. "We're on reduced staff tonight, so please don't go beyond the atrium."

"I promise." Sarah slid through the partially opened door and followed the path she knew by heart. The sound of her heels against the stone floors echoed quietly. She nodded at another guard as she turned into the atrium. "I'll only be here for a few minutes."

He nodded back silently.

She stood in the large space and felt the joy of being relatively alone in a place that was usually thronged with people. She closed her eyes and let it wash over her.

The birthday party is not the problem.

All of a sudden she felt an invisible ripple along her spine, a jolt of something. Her eyes flew open, and she saw a man standing about five feet in front of her.

"Holy shit," she blurted. "I didn't realize anyone else was here."

"Other than the two hundred people hobnobbing in the Temple of Dendur?"

"Yeah, other than those jerks."

His smile was a knockout. If she weren't happily married . . . scratch that. Tall, dark, probably of Middle Eastern descent?

Gorgeous tux. Crooked smile. She'd have to be dead not to find him . . . attractive.

That was one word for it. *Hot-as-fuck* might be another.

"Harry Aiken." He held out his hand.

Was her mouth agape? Sarah settled herself. "Of course you are . . ."

She took his hand in hers, and the two of them stood there for way too long. Maybe it was only a second or two, but she felt—well, she felt *everything*. The power of his grip, the warmth of his skin, the clean smell of him, the slight bristle of the hairs on the back of his hand, his eyes—but beyond all of those sensory, well, pleasures, really, she felt like he was definitely part of whatever gut-roiling recalibration or transformation was going on inside her today. He was somehow in on it.

She released his hand and backed away a step, as if he had burned her.

Or could.

And then she started breathing again.

"Weird day." She shook her head and started walking slowly around the atrium.

"Do you want to be alone?" he asked.

"Not necessarily. I just didn't want to be in a room with hundreds of people."

Harry put his hands in his pockets and walked alongside her. "Same. I left right before the guest of honor arrived. Just all a bit too much for me, you know."

Sarah realized his clean, buttoned-up smell was just a top note. Sandalwood, tobacco, myrrh: this man was into expensive fragrance of some sort or another, and their heat had brought it to life. A deep, masculine scent. Her mortal weakness.

"You've never *met* her?"

"No. I'm not really even sure why I'm here. I met this hilarious guy named Max—"

She couldn't help smiling. "Yeah, I know him."

"Right? I met him last week. Turns out he's best friends with the CEO of this company I do business with whom I've been trying to meet for years. She's got a firewall of assistants around her. Max is a great guy and all, but he was like, 'You should totally come meet Sarah and learn more about her new foundation, yadda yadda . . .' and I was like, 'Great, I'd really appreciate the introduction.' and then he's like, 'I got you on the list to her surprise party Saturday night' and I'm like, 'Well, that's a little weird to show up at someone's fortieth birthday party uninvited, if I've never even met them, don't you think?' But he's kind of persuasive and funny, and it all seemed like a good idea last week. But now I'm just like a fish out of water . . . and now I'm babbling—"

When he turned to face her, their eyes caught again, and held, like they had when they'd shaken hands. "I'm not usually nervous, but hell, you've caught me off guard," he said.

Sarah just gave herself permission to stare at him. Why not? It *was* her birthday, wasn't it? And maybe he was her gift. Her lip must have lifted slightly on one side when she thought that, because his glance darted to her mouth and his pupils dilated.

Then, as if realizing that what he was doing could be construed as creepy, his eyes flew back up to hers.

Her smile widened.

You can look at my mouth anytime you like, she almost said—but caught herself before she did something . . . regrettable.

"So, is this going to be like some Cinderella story?" he asked, his voice deeper, stronger, if that was even possible. "Are you going to introduce yourself, or am I going to have to enlist the cavalry and ride my steed throughout the kingdom tomorrow to find out your true identity?"

Harry Aiken on horseback, commanding an army. Wheeling his horse around with perfect control. Mastery. Smoke and leather and the clang of ancient weapons and still, always, his eyes on her, always on her. Tracking her, minding her, loving her.

"I could see that," she whispered, then turned to walk back toward the party. "I guess it is a bit of a Cinderella story," she continued, forcing her voice to take on a more carefree tone. "Because I'll definitely turn into a pumpkin if I don't get back to hobnobbing."

He reached for her left hand and grabbed hold of it, coaxing her around to face him again. "Let's skip the party. Let's just get out of here and go talk for hours and figure out what this is." He looked down at her hand in his. She wasn't wearing any jewelry other than her diamond earrings. No wedding ring. Whoops. She was completely naked, except for this sliver of fabric that separated her body from his, and from his hands and his . . . control.

She looked down and realized he was rubbing her ring finger. Whatever it was between them, it was real, and it was coming on fast and strong. She knew those hands; she knew that touch. She knew that smell. She felt the warmth of sexual awareness spreading between her legs and had to shift her thighs. He saw every bit of it. Of her.

"Are you married?" Harry asked bluntly.

"I am."

He squeezed her hand one last time, then released it. Released her.

Something vanished.

"That's a shame." He shook his head, chiding himself good-naturedly. "I can't believe I just said that out loud."

Sarah didn't have any words, none that she was going to say out loud, at least. Because it did feel like such a shame. Why hadn't she met Harry Aiken when she was twenty?

And why did she feel like she *had* known him all her life? In every life?

Her breathing faltered. "Nice to meet you, Harry Aiken."

She turned back toward the hall and booked it back to the party, walking as fast as she could in her perilously high heels. She could sense his stillness behind her, the energy radiating off him, and then she felt it receding as the distance between them expanded. He wasn't going to follow her—not now, at least. Because maybe he'd followed her too many times through the river of time, and now it was her turn to face him, to invite him. To finally be his.

What in the hell am I even talking about? Am I ever going to get a break from this crazy day? River of time?

"*There* you are!" Max was hustling around the corner at the end of the hall. "It's been eleven minutes and I was starting to worry." He turned on his heels as she caught up with him. "You've got a party to slay."

She was in her own world, and she was going to revel in it for as long as she could. Not her own world, precisely, but the imaginary one she shared with Harry Demigod Aiken.

"*Hello?* Are you in there?" said Max.

Sarah firmed her hold on his forearm. "I'm definitely in here."

"Good." He was skeptical. "Have you been drinking? You're all flushed."

"No, I really haven't." She put her palm against her cheek and felt the heat emanating from her skin.

"Okay . . ." He looked at her again, not quite convinced. "You sure you're ready to face the music?"

"Totally. I just needed a moment to collect myself." She felt ready for anything, honestly. It wasn't as if meeting Harry had empowered her, exactly; it was more like the chemistry between the two of them had created some unique energy that was hers to harness.

"Bring it on."

CHAPTER FOUR

The party and dazzling venue had been entirely Carl's idea, but there were telltale Max touches everywhere. He didn't get to be New York's most in-demand event-planner-turned-luxury-travel-concierge for nothing. The two of them must have conspired. Take the tarot card reader, seated at a low round table set atop layered antique rugs, the seats velvet ottomans: that was signature Max. Carl couldn't even set a table properly, much less conceive of the ultimate "guest experience."

Sarah took in the room for the first time. God, it looked amazing. *I wonder how much this is costing me,* she thought as she wove through the crowd, receiving a quick hi or hug from one guest or another. She wandered nearer to the little group surrounding the fortune teller. She wasn't in the mood—but her mother was just getting up from her own reading. This should be interesting!

Sarah's mother had frowned at her own mother's passion for the tarot, at any musings about past lives, at basically any idea of magic in the world. When Sarah was growing up, every so often she and her grandmother would hover conspiratorially at her vanity table. She'd watch as her grandmother reached into a drawer and thoughtfully selected one of her many decks of tarot cards, as precious to her as her fragrance collection. Then she'd cut and release the cards in that curious manner of hers and have Sarah pick several. She'd set them in a pattern on the mirror-topped table and read what they foretold for Sarah in a way a ten-year-old could understand. It never felt scary or dark; it made her feel tingly, grown-up, *special*. Her mother would call from the other room: "She's a *little girl*, for god's sake, Mother. All she cares about fortune-telling is whether Santa's bringing her Malibu Barbie for Christmas."

But tonight was different. Though she was as WASPy and buttoned-up as they came, her mother was especially charmed by this woman, who had basically told her everything she wanted to hear—that she was a wonderful wife and mother, loving and patient, if maybe slightly judgmental (but as her mother loved to say, "That's just *discernment*, dear."). Her father was now seated at the table, letting the soothsayer read his palm. He laughed, and Sarah was surprised to see how much he was enjoying himself.

Two hostesses walked the room, gently ringing brass bells to signal that it was time to sit for dinner. Guests were seated at intimate candlelit tables scattered in front of the Temple, the hall's reflecting pool edged with dozens of flickering votive candles. Darkness had fallen outside, and all that was visible through the window wall were the streetlamps lining the Central Park pathways.

They sat down to dinner. Almost immediately, Carl stood up and tapped his wine glass with a spoon, and everyone quieted down.

"I promise I won't bore you with a long-winded spiel about how brilliant Sarah is—"

The room was peppered with a few shouts of "Oh, come on!" and "Please do!" Sarah blushed and looked down at her plate.

"I just want to say that it has been an honor and a privilege to spend the better part—the *best* part—of my life with such an incredible, talented, beautiful"—he glanced down at her appraisingly, and she wanted to crawl under the table—"and loving woman. To Sarah!" He was looking out over the crowd, clearly pleased with himself. Not at her, of course.

She shook her head and smiled, trying to be gracious and not parse every nice thing he'd said about her. Reaching for her wine glass, she scanned the room.

And caught Harry staring at her. Dazzling in the candlelight, he raised his glass a fraction, narrowed his eyes, and his mouth curved into a knowing, wistful grin. He might as well have ripped her dress off in front of the entire room for how naked it made her feel.

She gulped down a swig of cabernet and closed her eyes, letting the acidity and the warmth hitting her insides distract her for a moment. When she opened them, Harry had turned back to his dinner companion, and she started breathing again. If she didn't know better, she'd say she was jealous . . . of the wine glass in his hand, of the woman sitting next to him, of the wool stretching across his muscled back. . . .

"You look happy," Carl whispered low and close to her ear, pushing aside a lock of her hair and kissing her cheek.

"I am," she said absently, not taking her eyes away from Harry's profile, focusing on that hint of skin—somehow both masculine and tender—just above the crisp collar of his shirt, beneath his jet-black hair. She slipped her hand under the tablecloth, onto Carl's leg. Was it cheating to let her husband believe she was happy because he'd planned this lavish party in her honor? Well, there *were* worse forms of cheating . . . and she didn't have a hard time imagining what they would be. She squeezed Carl's thigh and turned to him. "It's a beautiful party. Thank you."

"Of course. You deserve it." He kissed her again, politely, and turned to speak to her mother, sitting to his right.

Dinner passed in a blur of wine selections and some kind of chicken dish and a few champagne toasts. Fortunately, the "birthday cake" was a gold-dusted chocolate mousse set at each place, so she was spared the song and dance. The band started playing a great selection of swing music, and soon she was on the dance floor with Max, free of her ridiculous stilettos and genuinely enjoying herself.

After a few numbers she begged off and was catching her breath when Max, bright-eyed and sweating slightly, jacket off, dragged her over to the snake charmer.

"She's not a snake charmer, Sarah! You're such a stick-in-the-mud. If you don't believe in it, then what do you have to lose? It's just a bit of fun. She's leaving soon."

By the time they reached the table, Sarah had cooled down a bit after all the dancing. Maybe it *would* be fun after all. "Okay, fine. I'll try to keep an open mind."

The woman was just finishing a reading with one of her mother's best friends. "Oh, Sarah, you're just going to love this!" she said. She'd obviously had a healthy pour of her favorite gin.

"I'll try," said Sarah.

"Okay, I'll leave you to it," said Max, who was scanning the room, probably looking for Harry. Sarah settled onto the tufted chair, feeling surprisingly relaxed.

"Hello, I'm Leyla," said the card lady, extending her hand.

"Nice to meet you."

They held one another's hands longer than expected—nothing like the bolt of megawatt electricity she'd experienced with Harry earlier that night, but. . . .

And then, there it was again: a fragrance that took Sarah back to a memory, a feeling, some kind of weird familiarity or *déja vu*—whatever it was that had been dogging her all day. Leyla's perfume or essential oils were what you might expect—patchouli, vetiver—but more elevated. Her dark curls were behaved, not frizzy. She was dressed in gold bangles and a flowy tunic, but Sarah recognized both as expensive, the real deal. This was no Actor's Equity type.

"Ah," Leyla nodded and smiled slightly, as if to herself. "I've been wondering why I was here tonight, and now I know."

Normal Sarah would have rolled her eyes, but now she was curious.

"I'm Sarah."

"I know."

Sarah tilted her head, as if to say, *You deduced that already?*

"I heard your husband's toast. I'm not a mind reader, just an energy reader," she laughed softly. "Do you have something specific you'd like to look at, or do you want to take a more comprehensive approach?"

Leyla had several card decks before her on the table. It took Sarah back to those precious moments with her grandmother, just the two of them, dreaming together about her future and what had honestly been quite a charmed life up until now. *Oh, how I wish she were here tonight!* she thought.

"I'm sorry, I'm just a little emotional," she said, eyes shining. "I haven't had my cards read since being in my grandmother's dressing room when I was a girl. In fact, I'm wearing her favorite fragrance tonight for good luck—Tarocchi."

"Oh!" Leyla smiled knowingly. "The medieval Italian form of tarot, how fitting! So you have a deep family history with the tarot. You probably know all about it. How wonderful."

"No, actually I don't," Sarah said. "I was young, and my own mom didn't really approve of that kind of thing, so I never pursued it. Though she seemed pleased with whatever you saw in her cards tonight! I'd like for you to talk me through the reading."

"I would love to," said Leyla. "The tarot is a language, and the way the cards fall forms a narrative. That's why I'm called a reader. I translate the language of the cards in relation to the question or topic being explored. The tarot is a deck of seventy-eight cards with four suits, just like a deck of playing cards. But the four suits of the tarot align with the four parts of what it is to be human—physical, mental, emotional, and spiritual or energetic. There are also twenty-two high-vibe cards called Major Arcana. I promise that I will explain everything as we go. The first step is for you to pick one of these decks."

"Arcanum is the name of my fragrance company," said Sarah, weirdly proud. Why did she feel eager to impress this woman? Was it the wine, or did she feel a genuine intimacy with her?

"I chose Arcanum to honor my grandmother. She didn't live long enough to see me found my own company, but I felt her guiding me every step of the way. I remembered the word from her tarot card readings, and I just sort of liked it. Sounded ancient, momentous, high-end." *Okay, why don't you let her do the talking. Pick a deck!*

She reached for the deck that appeared to have the oldest design. "How about that one?"

"Great," Leyla smiled. "I love this deck." She picked up the cards and shuffled them, not absently but intentionally, as if she were communicating with each card as it passed through her fingers. Then she spread them out in an arc on the table.

"Now please pick ten cards, and we'll do a Celtic Cross."

Looking down at the cards, Sarah randomly chose ten of them—nothing earth-shattering. She sat back and watched as Leyla dispensed with the other cards and began to arrange the ten in a loose cross pattern. Occasionally she would pause and let her fingertip rest on a card for a few seconds.

As a server passed by, Sarah asked for a glass of water, then returned her attention to Leyla, observing her concentration.

"You've got a lot going on," Leyla blurted, without looking up from the cards. "I'm not really sure where to begin. . . ."

"Start at the very beginning," Sarah half sang. "A very good place to start. . . ."

Leyla looked up and took a deep breath. Her brown eyes shone bright behind her reading glasses. "This is truly amazing."

Sarah burst out laughing. "I promise, I'm not all that interesting!"

"You can keep telling yourself that."

Sarah's laughter died away. "Well . . ." She took a sip of water, grateful that the waiter had returned so quickly. Leyla was still staring at her.

"Okay," Leyla slowly continued. "The beginning. . . ." She pointed at a card showing a figure that looked like the Grim Reaper. "Death . . . it's not what you think."

"That should be on a T-shirt," Sarah joked.

"It should!" Leyla laughed. "I'm glad you have a sense of humor about this because, seriously? I'm completely overwhelmed."

"Just tell me already—am I carrying the second coming of Christ?"

Leyla smiled again. Sarah liked her smile. She seemed like a nice person, not some woo-woo crackpot.

"Death is the card that indicates an end of one phase of our lives, but invariably that paves the way for something new. So it can feel like we are breaking . . . but not breaking down, more like breaking open."

Sarah choked on her water. "*What* did you just say?"

"Breaking open . . ." Leyla was still looking at the cards, seemingly deep in thought. "The fact that this card is at the center of the cross tells us that this break, this change, whatever this is, is at the center of where you are right now. You are in the eye of the storm." She looked up.

"But a *good* storm! A storm that could be clearing away the detritus of the past."

Sarah shook her head. "Your choice of words is simply uncanny."

"I've heard that before. Do you want me to go on?"

"Yes, of course. It's wonderfully entertaining."

"The strange thing for me is that I usually read, well, pretty literally, if that makes sense. I tend to see the energy of the cards as an overview—where one has been, where they are now, where they're heading. But these cards. . . ." Leyla touched the next card over, the King of Cups. "This one, for example, because of its placement, it's almost like it—*he*—is deeply connected to your past, even though he's not in your present. But he is present now . . . yet intrinsically tied to your future. I can't quite describe it, but he's a powerful presence in your life, even though you may not know him yet."

Sarah felt the blood rush to her face. Of course she was talking about Harry Aiken. Had Leyla seen them together in the atrium before she returned to the party? Or was that just the type of thing you said to a woman at her fortieth birthday party—that there was a tall, dark knight in shining armor in her future? And then suddenly Harry was standing beside the table, looking down at the cards and then at Sarah, holding his wine glass the way she wanted him to hold her: possessively.

"I didn't picture you as the tarot card type," he said.

"How *did* you picture me?" Sarah asked without missing a beat. *Naked, I hope.*

"Touché." Harry took a sip of wine and kept his eyes on her over the rim of the glass.

Leyla cleared her throat. "Sarah, would you like to continue while your friend is here, or. . . ."

"Oh, yes. Definitely. Harry Aiken, this is Leyla—"

"—Sullivan," Leyla finished for her. She reached out her hand to Harry. A perfunctory handshake. Nothing. Leyla barely looked at him. Her attention returned to the cards almost immediately. *Okayyy, so she didn't see us together. . . .*

"Moving on from the King, we can read a lot into the Nine of Pentacles, which indicates a vast amount of material success—not just money, but accomplishment in the physical world. You thrive on achievement. You're good at things." Leyla looked up. "Obviously."

"Obviously," Harry said at the same time, and Sarah started laughing again.

"Why am I so *obvious*? I want to be mysterious, damn it."

"Well, hold on! You're in luck," Leyla continued. "The High Priestess represents a cloud of . . . unknowing . . . but also an up-leveling of an intuitive understanding of life events. Combined with the Two of Swords and the Tower, I would venture to say that your feeling of breaking open is about to get switched into high gear. In other words, with the Death card at the center, it probably means that all uncertainty and ambivalence and indecision is going to get blasted to bits." Leyla's smile was infectious. "That storm's a-comin'!"

"Don't know why . . ." Harry began to sing.

"There's no sun up in the sky," Sarah continued.

"Stormy weatherrrr . . ." they sang together, never taking their eyes off each other.

"Since my man and I ain't together, " Leyla continued, in a moment of levity. But then she got serious again. "There's that King of Cups." She stared right at Harry.

Sarah's heart was pounding. It didn't take a psychic to see she was about to start hyperventilating. Leyla nodded slightly at Sarah, took one last look at the cards, then swept them up and piled them neatly in the stack with the rest of the deck.

"Isn't Leyla the best?!" Max mercifully burst in. "I knew you two would hit it off, even though you are the *worst* skeptic, Sarah!" He turned and saw Harry standing there and gave him a pat on the shoulder. "Oh my god, I can't believe I haven't had a chance to introduce the two of you yet. Harry, this is Sarah Fuller. Sarah, this is Harry Aiken. Isn't he fabulous?!"

"Leyla, it really has been a pleasure," Sarah said. "Do you have a business card? Or does Max have your contact details?

I'd love to stay in touch." And bizarrely, she meant it. Whatever this—*storm*—was, it was only just beginning, and Sarah welcomed the idea of having someone like Leyla to shelter with. Someone not at all like her controlling psychiatrist, or her perfectly fine husband, or her judgy mother, or her whirlwind best friend. A guide.

"Absolutely. Max has my info. I'd love to see you again."

Sarah nodded, then stood up. Harry was right there, too close . . . or not close enough. Just there. "So nice to meet you, Harry." They shook hands (again), and she tried to don the mask of a casual acquaintance, but Max was no dummy.

"Wait! Did you guys meet already? What's going on?"

"We did, actually." Harry finally let go of her hand and turned to face Max. "And you were right. Turns out we have a lot in common. I look forward to learning more about your foundation, Sarah. Let's schedule a time to meet soon."

Her stomach flipped. "Sounds good," she agreed, trying to sound casual.

"Oh, that's perfect!" Max crowed. "I totally knew you two would hit it off. Headline reads: *Overachievers Unite!* I won't bother trying to horn in, because you'll be too busy nerding out about climate change and botany and saving the world."

Harry took another sip of wine and hummed something that might have been construed as agreement, but Sarah felt it like a strum across her lips.

"There you are," Carl said, walking over. "Sorry to be the bearer of bad news, Sarah, but the sitter just texted that Alex is running a fever."

"Oh, poor thing—"

"I'm happy to go home and be with her," Carl offered, "but she's asking for her mom."

"It's totally fine, I want to go," Sarah said without hesitating. "You should definitely stay and say thank you to everyone for me. It was a lovely party, darling." She leaned in and kissed his cheek.

"If you're sure. . . ."

"I'm absolutely sure. Go chat up my parents and tell them what a devoted mother I'm being. They'll love that."

Carl traced his fingertip along the curve of her shoulder and down her upper arm. "Okay, see you later." Then he was gone.

She turned to see Harry watching her, retracing the cold thread of Carl's touch with his eyes. She saw that Harry's grip had tightened so fiercely on the stem of his wine glass that it was apt to break.

"Well, gentlemen," she said, "It looks like dreams really *do* come true, and I get to leave my own party after all."

Max slid her arm into his and called to Harry over his shoulder. "Come on Mr. Prince of the City, let's walk the Queen home."

CHAPTER FIVE

Memphis, Ancient Egypt, late flood season

Sarrah reached for her Uncle Khufu's forearm. He looked down at her hand and shook his head almost imperceptibly, a gesture only she would notice. She let go immediately; she knew better. Khufu was presenting her to the inner court of the Pharaoh for the first time. At the ripe age of eighteen, she knew this was not the time to appear cloying or desperate. Shifting her posture slightly away from her uncle, she instead used her hand to lift the hem of her long tunic, hoping the gesture gave her an air of confidence. She wanted to project femininity. Elegance. Wisdom. Power.

These were not just projections. She *had* those qualities. She'd had them for as long as she could remember. And her Uncle Khufu had sensed them in her. He'd watched her grow and mature, an exotic flower that had outgrown its pot. She'd always been perfectly comfortable with her family, but there had been an undercurrent of something more—some path that would lead her far beyond the small house with the carefully swept dirt floor and the goat and the warm fire and a mother who loved her. Maybe she should have had more respect for the comforts and safety of that home.

But that wasn't Sarrah's nature.

She was a seeker. Even when she knew—felt, believed? it was all the same to her—that her wandering might lead to danger, she couldn't resist. Not out of a lack of willpower. She had that in abundance. It was the pull of power. *Her* power—that needed to be unleashed.

———

"Heka," cooed baby Sarrah. Her first word was a prescient one. Heka, the god of magic and medicine, was the most important god in Egyptian mythology. Well, weren't magic and medicine one and the same? Who was to say whether it was the physician-priest's spell or his salve that cured someone's burned hand?

Heka wasn't just a god; he was a life force, a concept, a presence so magical that he was believed to be the generative power that other gods drew upon to create the universe. And no one could deny that more than a little of Heka's supernatural energy emanated from this bright-eyed infant.

It was true. Mystical powers ran in her mother's bloodline. They hopped and skipped around through the generations, but when a six-year-old Sarrah comforted the weeping childless woman in the village by telling her she'd have a baby when the rains came—and then she did—her mother knew her only daughter had the gift.

Sarrah had always had a passion for flowers. As soon as she could toddle through its rows, she was her mother's favorite helper in the garden. Her brothers were useless; they would pop more figs into their mouths than into their baskets. Uncle Khufu argued that they should replace the flower patch with more rows of vegetables, but her mother refused. Flowers were beautiful and fragrant, and they enlivened the rooms of their simple mud-brick house. But they also had powers, many of which were well known—and many more that were the secret property of mystics.

Take the lotus, which flourished in the shallow waters at the banks of the Nile. The gods believed that the lotus flower symbolized the innocence of childhood; a bouquet of lotus was believed to be the perfect gift for a new mother. But Sarrah's mother taught her that the flower had practical powers as well. She would dry the amethyst-hued petals to make a tea to help the infant sleep and also to heal the mother's postpartum inflammation. This tea sachet was tucked into the gift bouquet, a covert offering between women—along with a whispered incantation to bring mother and baby good health.

As Sarrah was growing up, her family and most of the people in the village worked on the massive farms of noblemen and royalty. But their personal gardens were their masterpieces. After all, this home would also be their home in the afterlife. This rich black soil, this small pond, this palm tree, the exact view outside one's window—this would be one's view for eternity. It was instilled in Sarrah and every Egyptian child to appreciate their surroundings, and to take pride in their homes and their stations in life. This view of the afterlife seemed to be appreciated and even celebrated by everyone Sarrah knew. So why wasn't this nearly enough for her?

Sarrah's mother taught her about the properties of the lotus flower and other blooms: narcissus, violets, camellias, chick-pea flowers, lilies, belladonna. Together they milled leaves of paper from papyrus. Sarrah pressed specimens of each blossom between two leaves of paper, then stitched them into a book. She made notes next to each dried flower about its capabilities (good and evil)—but in her own made-up hieroglyphics. Not only had she no idea how to read or write, but she didn't want anyone else to be able to decipher her notes.

It was true that Sarrah could share the extent of her intuition with only a few others. When she was very little, she hadn't understood that not everyone had visions or could read thoughts. She sensed them as easily as she smelled, saw, or tasted, and she assumed that everyone else did as well. But her mother began to shush her tiny fortune teller. "Be careful. People will want to use your powers to their advantage—especially bad people."

So yes, occasionally Sarrah would help find a lost child (tangled in the tall reeds by the pathway to the Nile) or decode what her best friend Nour's dream meant (the boy from the next village *was* flirting with her). But sometimes Sarrah was ashamed to admit that she used her gifts to her own advantage. Who wouldn't like to read the mind of the boy one liked, then please him by cooking his favorite treat for him? Or outwit her brothers to avoid chores? She liked the feeling of control.

Her mother noticed this tendency also, however. "Watch out, Sarrah," she said. "You've been given a gift by the gods, but you are certainly not one yourself. The gods will punish you for your selfish intentions. Just look at your Uncle Khufu. He has had the gift of intuition all his life—not as strong as yours, it's true—but he has *nothing*."

Uncle Khufu was a talented urban planner who had helped the Pharaoh expand Memphis from a dusty trading post into a majestic and modern city with roads, temples, and a sense of order. But whatever gave Sarrah a sixth sense about the powers of the natural world also gave her the creeps about her uncle. The way he looked at her made the hair on her neck stand on end.

While working as a laborer on one of Khufu's massive building projects, Sarrah's father had tragically died. It was such dangerous work—limestone boulders that took twenty men to carry; rickety, rope-lashed ladders propped against looming temple walls; razor-sharp axes and picks, oppressive heat, vats of molten iron, white-hot tempers flaring. . . . Sarrah wasn't the only child in her village who'd lost a father in the service of the Pharaoh and mother Egypt, and she would not be the last.

Sarrah couldn't even remember her father—she had been just three years old when he died—but she knew her mother's fastidiousness was meant to honor him. When reunited with her husband in the afterlife, Sarrah's mother wanted everything to be as pristine, as fresh, and as fertile as the gods allowed so that they could enjoy it together, free of the cares of this world. Singing ancient incantations as she moved about the house and garden, her mother labored tirelessly and humbly to create an enduring home for her family for this life and the next. It was enough.

Her mother certainly didn't need Uncle Khufu's help. But there he was, sleeping in his own room in their modest mud hut while the rest of them crowded together on pallets in the other room. After her father died, Khufu had insisted on moving in with them; and of course, he had no family of his own. Sarrah's mother had protested—she didn't need her domineering, ruthless, ambitious older brother to boss her around in her own home as he had when they were children. But Khufu "felt terrible" about the accident. She "needed a man in the house." It "wasn't safe." Well, it wasn't long before he was seated at the head of their table, helping himself to the best and biggest slice of lamb, the ripest peach, an extra spoonful of her mother's prized honey.

He didn't give two bits about Sarrah's brothers, but he did keep a careful eye on his niece. He took note of Sarrah's intelligence, her intuition, her ambition—despite how carefully her mother had tried to cloak them. Sarrah could sometimes feel him behind her, watching her sketch flowers, plant small clippings, carve amulets, share her secrets with her girlfriends. She knew—and he knew—that unlike the others, the two of them could communicate on an extrasensory level. As if there were a door inside her mind, Sarrah could feel Khufu knocking, trying to introduce his thoughts and ideas and sinister plans—but she didn't open it. Khufu's psychic powers veered toward the darker arts.

It wasn't just control over city architecture that Khufu craved. It was the ear of the Pharaoh on all matters—military, governmental, personal. Khufu was ambitious, successful, and cunning. Not many Egyptian boys ascended from bricklayer to urban planner to becoming the Pharoah's most trusted advisor. In fact, many people wondered how he'd gotten to that place. But Khufu was ruthless. The burial ground was filled with co-workers, dignitaries, and architects who had stood in his way on his rise to the top over the years—and some of those graves were fresh.

Fortunately, after ten years Khufu was invited to live within the palace walls, and he moved out of Sarrah's home. He had proven himself worthy (or forced himself?) to be part of the Pharaoh's inner circle. And in the years since, his visits to their home had dwindled. He had little use for them now—except for his niece. On each visit he made sure to find time to have her show him her latest garden project or her newest painting, or to play the lyre for him. And she could once again sense that mental knock on the door—but she still didn't respond. Khufu never once invited their family to the palace, or to tour his latest architectural feat or walk around the city markets with him. He was too important for them now. And ingratiating oneself with the Pharaoh was competitive and exhausting work. Scores attempted it, but Sarrah had to admit that very few reached Khufu's position of authority. And whatever the cost, there would be no. Going. Back.

———

From their village, Sarrah could see the temples and monuments of Memphis in the distance across the vast fields stretching between here and there. For the most part, visions of the city only swirled in her imagination, in vivid dreams of winding down cobblestone streets or past sparkling fountains, or ascending palace steps clad in fine robes. Of a secret rendezvous in a verdant garden, its well-tended rows stretching as far as the eye could see.

Sarrah had actually visited Memphis only a handful of times, on much-anticipated festival days. She and her brothers would clamber onto the back of a horse-drawn wagon with the other village children. While most of them buried their faces in their robes to shield themselves from the brick-red dust clouding into the wagon bed, Sarrah would peek out between the slats as they traveled into the city along with hundreds of other commoners. At first all she could see were endless fields of einkorn wheat and barley. She heard the familiar songs of laborers—just like her own family—wielding scythes under the merciless sun. She saw stands of small mud huts, naked children playing, outdoor markets with fruits, grains, and slaughtered animals piled high. She breathed in the smells wafting from bread ovens, roasting goats, crackling fires.

As the wagon drew closer to Memphis, the dirt road turned to gravel. The mud huts turned to thick clay-brick structures, and servants carried kitchen water and waste pots to sewage drains that lined the roads. Closer still, the homes seemed to be constructed by experienced builders, not the inhabitants themselves. They were sturdy and stately enough that the roofs were used as outdoor rooms, decorated with plants, seating, and torches. These noblemen's animals lived in barns that were nicer than Sarrah's own home!

As they neared the city, the horses clop-clopping on the cobblestone streets, the children unburied their faces and grew giddy with excitement. Crisp scarlet and gold flags flapped against a lapis-blue sky. The sounds of music and merriment grew louder, and crowds walked on foot into the city alongside the wagons. Many wore fine tunics woven with metallic threads, elaborate jet-black wigs, and hammered gold neck collars and jewels. Sarrah's mouth watered with the promise of street vendors' meats, honey cakes, and fruits, along with a crisp sip of her mother's beer to wash it all down. Oh, to be an Egyptian on a day like this. Praise the gods!

After these rare visits to Memphis, back in the village and busy with mundane tasks, Sarrah felt especially restless. This home, this garden, this view—when she thought about these remaining the same for this life and future lives, she couldn't imagine that it would be enough. She prayed to Heka for patience, gratitude, satisfaction, but her heart and her mind were filled with dreams of palaces, power, pharaohs. Why couldn't she be happy with her own lot, just as her mother and others were?

Sarrah told no one of her ambitions. Sadly, the only person who seemed to recognize the extraordinary nature of her gifts was Khufu. If anyone could get her in the presence of greatness, it would be him. On his visits, she began to ask him more about what he did and what he saw in the courts, palaces, and streets of Memphis; she was certain that no one else ever bothered to do so. Khufu had no social skills, not to mention friends, family, or even lovers. She was sure he took full advantage of his access to the hetaerae now that he was an official of the court.

Yes, she knew all about the courtesans. Everyone did. Occasionally an older woman dressed in elegant linen robes draped a little too close to her body—her pale face painted in a glamorous but impractical fashion, her hands supple and laden with gold rings—would visit Sarrah's village seeking introductions to girls around twelve or thirteen years old. Some mothers were anxious to present their daughters to her, but she took only the most beautiful, the brightest, the friendliest. Who *wouldn't* want their daughter to live within the palace walls, wear fine clothes, eat and drink her fill, and consort with noblemen? To have an easier life? But Sarrah's mother wouldn't allow it.

Sarrah's friend Nour, a bright-eyed, shapely, bubbly girl, had packed her few belongings and traveled back to the city with the woman five years ago. Sarrah missed her terribly. The next time Nour returned to the village, she had been transformed. She was still beautiful, but now she looked like a woman of means. Her eyebrows were threaded, her hair arranged in braids. She smelled of jasmine and rose oils—and her hands! Her hands were no longer like Sarrah's, rough and tanned from washing clothes in the Nile and working in the garden. Her ivory hands were exquisite.

The two girls walked down to the riverbank as Nour told colorful tales of life in the palace. First the hetaerae had removed her clothes and scrubbed every inch of her body, then doused her in oils. Brushed her hair until her scalp hurt. Cleaned under her nails and taught her how to rim her eyes in kohl. She had been measured for gossamer robes and soft leather sandals. But that wasn't the end of it. They taught Nour how to play the flute and converse about history and observe court protocols. But they also taught her how to please a man—up, down, and sideways! Because when it came down to it, the job of a hetaera was to stroke rich and powerful men's egos but also to stroke their bodies. They showed her how to track her blood flow cycle (she would be excused from having intercourse with visitors on certain fertile days) and how to use a paste ground from acacia dates and honey as contraception.

The hetaerae lived in gorgeous quarters in the palace and never went hungry. But on any day, every day, if the soft entry bell rang, someone would have to answer the call. As the newest in the fold, even if the sun had set hours beforehand, Nour would have to quickly wash and dress herself and greet the general or whoever was at the door. She would remove his sandals, wash his feet, sate him with food and wine, and then please him with whatever he wanted, for as long as he wanted—into the dawn or even into the next evening.

Nour tried to look happy, and it was hard not to envy her jewels and curls, but Sarrah knew that life as a hetaera wasn't easy. Sarrah had learned through stories told by the elders around the village fire that Nour would be safe with the hetaerae—so long as she remained beautiful, pleasing, and willing. But after a few years, a decade at best, she would be transitioned to a job as a nursemaid or palace attendant. Or they would send her right back home. None of these rich and powerful men she'd lain with would ever marry her, and back in the village it was doubtful that she'd find a husband, either. There was no shame in Nour's being a hetaera, but men were jealous types. Most likely her hands would once again be roughened—and she would most likely move back in with her mother.

Uncle Khufu's visits became more and more frequent. Sometimes Sarrah didn't mind the attention—it was interesting to hear about the machinations of the court, the history of Egypt and the region, and the political landscape. Often such lectures got her excused from her chores. Sometimes her feistiness and inquisitiveness got her in trouble with her mother, but Uncle Khufu didn't seem to mind—in fact, he welcomed it. Khufu could sense that Sarrah's psychic powers—otherworldly wisdom, healing hands—outmatched his own. But he also knew that her powers of human connection outmatched his as well. She had the ability to commune with the gods and then communicate their wishes to others in a way they found comforting and appealing—as opposed to making them feel threatened or suspicious, as he seemed to do.

The current Pharaoh, though as revered as a god, was admittedly not the nimblest this civilization had seen. Sensing Khufu's intelligence and caginess as he rose through the ranks, the Pharaoh had enough smarts to keep Khufu close, trusting him to an almost unnerving degree. But what the Pharaoh did *not* recognize was that Khufu was disliked by almost everyone else in the court. True, he was unparalleled as a city planner, but his unbridled ambition and his craven gamesmanship seemed almost a mortal rebuke of the powers of the gods.

It came to Sarrah in a vision: the young Meti, son of the Pharaoh, in a palace chamber lit with candelabras, listening quietly to a discussion between his father and Khufu. His hands were gripping the sides of his chair. She could actually feel his tension, his rage, his suspicion of Khufu's false warmth and deference. *Oh, Meti has a temper!* she thought. She had certainly never been in Meti's presence. She only vaguely knew what he looked like from depictions in sprawling murals on her rare visits to Memphis. But Sarrah could already intuit that the boy Pharaoh was repelled by Khufu. The gods had brought her these visions for a reason, and she kept them to herself.

Because she knew that Khufu sensed it as well. And she knew that he considered her his secret weapon to ensure that the Pharaoh's son would someday be as dependent on him as his father was. No virile Egyptian male would be able to resist his bright-eyed niece if Khufu played it right. She was beautiful and alluring, and she knew the potencies of flowers and incantations. And he knew that Sarrah herself was an ambitious person. She had marveled at his elegant robes and the delicacies, fragrant oils, and fowl he brought as gifts from the palace when he visited their humble home. Khufu intentionally gave Sarrah numerous glimpses of the luxuries that would be hers if she relied on his counsel—and she took the bait.

CHAPTER SIX

Today, the seventeenth day of the tenth month, was Sarrah's eighteenth birthday. Uncle Khufu had come to their home—unannounced—for the afternoon meal. Afterward he presented her with a hammered gold arm cuff. It was a masterpiece, engraved with the lotus flowers she loved so much and inlaid with colored glass and carnelian. "This bracelet was made by the royal jewelers themselves," he said, self-importantly.

"Put it on, along with your best robes," he said. "I want you to look nice, as I'm taking you on a very special errand. Pack a bag with your belongings, as we will be gone for some time. I will tell you about it on the way."

Sarrah understood that her mother knew what Khufu had in mind but was powerless to object. She gathered the few items that were actually hers—her book of flowers, her robes, her brush and vials of oils. Her mother hugged her extra tight as she left, and she whispered, "My dear daughter, I have taught you what I could. I know what you are capable of and the breadth of your gifts. My brother shares these gifts, but he is filled with pride and does not always honor our family or the gods with his actions. But you will. Remember that what you sow in this life, you will reap in the next. And—be careful."

Sarrah nodded, looking into her mother's eyes. *I may never see her again,* she thought. She looked around, committing the house, the garden, the view to memory. Her world was about to break open. She hoped that the forces of good within her would prevail—for her family, for the gods, and for Egypt.

————

The driver cracked the whip on the horses and took the wagon not on the road toward Memphis, as Sarrah expected, but down to the banks of the Nile. She was surprised to see an elegant wooden vessel waiting at the dock, outfitted with low, cushioned benches and a billowing sail in the royal scarlet and gold. Two sailors scurried to hold the boat still and help them down from the dock, taking care to keep their eyes lowered. "Get in," Khufu said.

Sarrah had never been on a boat before, but she knew that sailboats this grand were rare. A small crowd of children and other onlookers had gathered by the shore, curious about who in this humble village could possibly be transported on this vessel. As they sailed toward Memphis, with the two of them as the only passengers, Khufu told her of his plans while she listened carefully.

"I have the ear of the Pharaoh. *No one* gets to him without going through me—except his son. Meti is a cunning young man, much brighter than his father," he sniffed. "In fact, he is a little *too* headstrong. He has no interest in me or my advice."

He looked directly at Sarrah, eyes blazing. "I need you to honor our family and Egypt, and become Meti's counselor and advisor. I have told the Pharaoh of your talents. This is a role of absolute trust. I have put my life on the line for you—and I promise you, if you even *think* you can cross me, you are wrong. Your view for eternity should you do so would not be the palace halls but the prison cell you would die in."

Khufu knew who Sarrah was. He knew the fire that burned in her veins. He'd always known how to leverage her impertinence to his advantage, subtly (and not so subtly) cultivating the seeds of her innate ambition and hunger for power. She pushed her tongue against the roof of her mouth, the way her mother had taught her. "You may not be able to stop your thoughts," she'd often said, "but you can certainly stop your tongue." Now Sarrah nodded to Khufu in silent agreement, and as they sailed toward Memphis he continued to sketch out her future—or his vision of it.

———

It was dusk when they arrived at the palace. Sarrah tried to hide her awe at the sweeping view before her: a dock and landing made not of wood but of marble, shaded with canopies and lined with servants awaiting their arrival. A sprawling mosaic of the Pharaoh's likeness was beneath their feet, and royal banners hung from the palace roof. Soldiers stood at posts along the shore, scanning the water for intruders, Egyptian or otherwise.

A torchlit walkway led to steps up to the palace. As per Khufu's plan, Sarrah knew that her first stay would be in the quarters of the hetaerae. Yes, she knew many things about this world and the spiritual realm—but she'd not yet known a man. In fact, men had never interested her much at all—too much risk of their standing in her way. Yet she knew from observing them that they were relatively simple creatures. Developing her feminine wiles would be another arrow in her quiver.

The chambers of the hetaerae were the most elegant interiors that Sarrah had ever seen. Women with perfumed robes, delicate sandals, and kohl-rimmed eyes seemed to glide across the rooms, feminine and poised. There were books on the shelves and wine and bronze platters of food on the banquet table. One hetaera strummed a mandolin; another arranged camellias in a lacquered vase. It was as Nour had explained to her; these women were there for sex, to be sure, but they were also well-educated, witty, artistic, and good conversationalists. Often they enjoyed long-term relationships with powerful men—to the dismay or the delight of their wives, Sarrah wasn't sure.

Sarrah was hungry for books. Khufu had taught her to read over the past few years. She picked one up and leafed through it—and was surprised to see drawings of a naked man and woman (or sometimes several) in a variety of acrobatic sexual positions. *Wow,* she thought, *I've only seen animals mate, and it didn't seem this complicated!*

"Like what you see?" one of the women asked, a saucy smile on her tinted lips. She pointed at a particularly tangled duo. "If you want another gold bracelet, I suggest you try this move on your next encounter.

"And if you want to have a little fun yourself," she said, nudging Sarrah and pointing at another drawing, "show him how to do this."

"I pray you, take it easy on her," she heard from behind. She turned to see Nour, happy and smiling. "This is my childhood friend, Sarrah. She told me this day would come. Let's welcome her." The two of them embraced warmly. Then Nour walked her over to an older woman sitting at a table, sipping tea and writing in a book. Sarrah recognized her as the hetaera who routinely visited the village.

"Sarrah, this is Amunet," said Nour. "She is the mother hen of us here. She knows all."

Amunet looked Sarrah up and down. "Usually no woman enters these doors unless I've specifically invited her," she said. "But I have heard from Khufu of your many talents. Whatever it is you need, we will share it with you."

"Thank you, that is so kind," Sarrah said demurely, bowing her head to the matron. "Uncle Khufu is just a proud uncle. I am sure that each of you here has special gifts."

She looked around for her uncle. He was nowhere to be found; he was probably behind one of those locked doors working his way through the sex manual. Or being worked *on,* more likely.

She turned back to Amunet. Nour and the others had gone on to the baths to prepare themselves for the evening's festivities.

The older woman took a collection of what appeared to be a game or miniature paintings from a lacquered box. "Do you recognize these tiles?"

Sarrah looked at the images on the tiles. She recognized the star of Sirius; the water bearer Isis; Set, the god of darkness. "I—some of them I do, but I'm not sure what they mean."

"Take a seat," said Amunet. She spread out the tiles across the table, face down.

"These are representations of the seventy-eight leaves of the papyrus of *The Book of Thoth.* This book contained all the mysteries of magic as recorded by Thoth, the god of writing, but it has been lost for centuries at the bottom of the Nile. Images and descriptions of this book have been painted and inscribed on the tombs and sarcophagi of the Pharaohs. It is believed that into these likenesses one can read the intentions of the gods and the fates of men."

She looked at Sarrah, her face softened by the candlelight, and pointed at the tiles. "Pick ten."

Sarrah did as she was told. Amunet turned the tiles face up and was riveted as she arranged them into a pattern. Without raising her eyes, she spoke.

"As I expected. I knew you were brought here for good and not for evil. You will not be in this place very long, but whatever you learn here will serve you well. There is much that you know, my child, but stay humble, wherever your fortunes take you." She looked up at Sarrah. "That, I cannot see."

As the others began to return from the baths, Amunet gathered the tiles and put them back into the box. "While you are here, you will be treated like anyone else. This conversation is our secret."

Sarrah nodded. "Thank you. I'll return to the others."

She understood why she had been brought to this place, and she wasn't afraid of what she would learn here. The hetaerae had something she wanted—the ability to dominate men, not to mention knowledge of the pleasures, both physical and pragmatic, that came along with it. If she could learn what they knew, when she combined it with her mystic and curative gifts, intelligence, and beauty, no goal would be out of reach.

———

One year later

So here she was. Walking up the blindingly white marble steps of the Palace of Memphis, the most glorious residence in all of Egypt—or possibly anywhere, ever. She was a pure descendant of the people of southern Egypt who had built this city, this masterpiece of language and culture and art and urbanity, she thought with pride. Soon the heir to this kingdom would be under her spell. Or would he? Khufu would do his best to manipulate Meti through Sarrah, using all the talents he'd developed in her, rendering her just a potent means to an end.

Sarrah had stayed in the chambers of the hetaerae for the low-water season. When she thought of her mother and her brothers, toiling in the fields in the blistering sun, she sometimes felt guilty. Here in the palace interiors she had no idea where her meals came from or who cooked them. Her robes were sewn by seamstresses she'd never met. When she stared in the looking glass, she barely recognized herself. She was still attractive, but in a more refined way. She looked down at her hands; already they had grown softer, the skin paler, the nails cleaner. Every day she dabbed a little of the fragrant oil she'd made in her family garden behind her ears, to remind herself where she came from.

Sex was no longer a mystery to her. At first she'd watched the other hetaerae from behind the heavy curtains, observing them in their acts of massage, foreplay, intercourse. It was the drawings in the manuals come to life. Sometimes the men were handsome and young, but often they were round and old. She'd seen plenty of naked men, but she'd never actually touched one before. Sometimes she could tell that the women enjoyed the sex, but more often—like the men themselves—they were more interested in the men's pleasure.

After a few weeks, she began to join in with another hetaera, and they'd both have sex with a man. How strange it felt! Usually her mind was half in the spirit world, half in her body, but these acts were fully mortal. She had no feelings for these men; she catalogued in her mind every moan of pleasure, every welcomed touch, every stroke. If the men wished, the women would have sex with each other. Finally, then, she'd feel the warm waves of pleasure in her loins that she had heard and read about! *One day I will teach Meti to do the same,* she thought, smiling to herself. While the Pharaoh came occasionally to the chambers of the hetaerae, she had yet to see his son Meti enter.

Once the rains returned and the mountains, fields, and farms of Egypt literally dripped with bounty, Khufu came back to retrieve Sarrah. "Amunet is pleased with your education," he said. "And the young Pharaoh grows more and more restless. It is time to present you to the court."

CHAPTER SEVEN

She'd lived in the palace for many months now, but Sarrah had never been to the hallowed inner court of the Pharaoh. The baths, dining halls, gardens, bedrooms, yes—but not the inner court. Even if she'd been curious, the guards would have barred her from entering. Few women were welcome here.

Sarrah's eyes adjusted quickly to the dimly lit palace court chamber. Her gaze traveled up the marble steps to rest on the two men standing on the dais before jeweled thrones. She was momentarily caught off guard by the young Meti next to his father, the Pharaoh. How could someone just seventeen years old exude so much power?

She might as well ask herself the same question, she thought, and stood a little more confidently.

Meti had been told from the cradle that he would become the Pharaoh. No, that he *was* the Pharaoh. She reminded herself that he was the reason she was here. He was hers to mold and guide. Not hers to keep, she knew. But in that split second, she grasped that their lives were inextricably bound together.

"Your Majesty." Khufu bowed his head only slightly, indicating his high rank.

Sarrah knelt down and bowed until her forehead nearly touched the marble floor. She would remain so until one of the men chose to speak to her directly. She could remain in that posture for hours if need be—Khufu had made her practice just that.

Several minutes later, after Khufu had reported on several urban planning and treasury matters while ignoring Sarrah altogether, the elder Pharaoh barked, "Tell the girl to stand up. Let me have a closer look."

The Pharaoh would never deign to address Sarrah directly; she'd been prepared for this as well. She rose slowly and revealed herself at her full, statuesque height. She looked just past the Pharaoh's right shoulder out of respect; it was certain death to look him directly in the eye.

"She is a beauty, I'll give you that, Khufu. But does she have the requisite skills to be the great teacher of Meti?"

"Indeed she does, Your Majesty. She has been trained in all the essential arts. She reads, plays the lyre, converses on history and military matters, and has a remarkable knowledge of herbology. But more importantly, she holds an innate wisdom, an ability to see past this world." Khufu made a sweeping gesture with his right hand. "She sees deeply."

Sarrah kept her posture and her gaze fixed as she felt their eyes upon her. She relished the sexual power she held over them, even the young Meti. Especially the young Meti. She could feel his hungry adolescent gaze scalding her. Oh, the talents she would teach him. Sarrah allowed the tingle in her breasts to blossom and felt her nipples brush against the soft linen of her tunic. She knew they all noticed; she wanted them to.

"And she is the pride of the hetaerae. Amunet says that she is a quick and enthusiastic learner, and she has been taught all the skills of pleasure."

"I want this one, Father."

Ah. He speaks. Meti. His voice was surprisingly smooth and promising, like molten steel—steel that she would forge into the greatest tactical mind of this century. Perhaps the greatest of many centuries.

Her heart pounded—not from a lack of control, but from the proximity of wielding control. Her throbbing body was going to be the most powerful weapon in her arsenal. She understood that this was a kind of war, and that she was going to triumph.

There was some sort of commotion to the left of the dais where the Pharaohs were enthroned.

"Khufu," a man muttered with perfunctory deference as he brushed past her uncle. He barely bent a knee to the Pharaoh before launching into a report about the latest skirmishes with the rebels in the northern desert.

Sarrah stared shamelessly. While her uncle and the elder Pharaoh and Meti had been bathed and oiled and scented by their servants, this . . . barbarian . . . appeared to have washed at the edge of the river, if at all. He had removed his breastplate and sword and laid them near the entrance. His wrap was gathered tightly across his waist and thighs, secured with a hook made of brass and horn. His tanned, bare chest bore the scars of past battles and a few fresh scrapes. He'd removed his helmet, and she noticed his fiery, kohl-lined eyes. His coarse black hair was long and sweaty; his beard indicated he'd spent a few weeks or months in the desert. He was raw and vital and exuded pure masculine energy. As if sensing her presence, he turned to face her for half a second, then continued without pause.

"I apologize for the unexpected visit, Your Majesty, but as these are native rebels we are fighting, and they oversee valuable farmland at that, I want to be sure that we proceeded as you would wish."

Khufu didn't hide his annoyance, but Sarrah was enchanted. He was rough, but he was well spoken. He'd probably been a soldier since an early age, his intelligence as well as his prowess observed, ensuring a rise through the ranks. She'd probably never see this man again—warriors had a habit of dying—so she let herself enjoy the primal scent of him, the rustle of his robes, his gorgeous calves bound in the leather straps of his sandals.

She could use this man—to their mutual benefit, of course. Her uncle had taught her that most of all. She knew Khufu was using her to get to the highest level of power in the land. So what? That's where she wanted to be as well. And if he wanted to take her there, so be it. Let him think he controlled her. Let them all think they controlled her. Sarrah knew the truth—she was destined to achieve absolute autonomy to use her mystic gifts to advance the glory of Meti and all of Egypt. And once she did, she would be assured an eternity of contentment and comfort.

The general's name was Hasim. *The protector.* How divine. He finished his report and turned to leave. Distracted, as he backed out of the chamber he almost stumbled over Sarrah, and he grunted as if annoyed by an errant rock or a fallen enemy in his pathway. But as he lifted his chin to offer some form of acknowledgment, his eyes widened, imperceptibly to everyone but her.

"Your Majesty," he finished, keeping his gaze on Sarrah. Then he turned and exited. The magnetism between them held, then faded as he strode down the hallway.

The chamber was quiet for a moment.

Meti was petulant, undeterred. "Enough about these hinterland squabbles, Father. Hasim is tiresome and rude. I have made my decision. Sarrah is to be my mystic."

"Hear now. That is not your decision to make."

"Fine. *You* decide, then."

The balance of power was beginning to shift. Sarrah was surprised and pleased that young Meti was already starting to exert his will. She felt the thrill of it in her body—how she would groom him to build upon that power and train him to use it. She risked a momentary upward glance at the boy Pharaoh and was rewarded with a gaze of pure lust. Meti's amber eyes burned at her. Respectfully, she lowered her head, but inside she reveled in visions of what the future held.

Meanwhile, Khufu and the elder Pharaoh were going over the details of the arrangement. Money would change hands, of course. Sarrah was to become the property of Meti. It was unlikely she would ever again see her childhood home or her mother or brothers—but they would now be respected and secure for generations to come.

She didn't believe in fate; she *created* fate.

And this was hers.

————

Three months later

It was rare for a rebel uprising to necessitate a campaign by the Egyptian army. This was generally a peaceful country, a bountiful country. Its subjects were more concerned with their own farms than with governance or palace politics. The Pharaoh was considered a god, and the people considered him their representative to the hierarchy of gods. Why would they complain? There was a court system should they want to do so.

But in the season since Sarrah had joined the court, news of an uprising in the rebel province was becoming unsettling. It was located on the Nile at an important trading post, and the Pharaoh could not lose control of the riverbank. Not to mention: a show of royal firepower would detract other rebels from challenging the Pharaoh, their supreme leader, again.

Sarrah drew back the heavy curtain of her second-story window, regarding the activity below with detached interest. A cadre of slaves passed by with velvet-lined palanquins on which soldiers would carry the Pharaoh and generals into battle, along with barrels of wine, baskets of vegetables, folded tents and blankets, and countless wooden crates holding myriad items necessary for the army to survive over the coming months. They had been at it all day.

Rebel forces, what a joke, thought Sarrah. *When I am in charge—*

She caught herself. Bad luck to think too far ahead. All in good time.

She turned to face the door of her chamber as it flew open. Meti and his adolescent urgency—everything was happening too slowly for this Pharaoh-in-waiting. She knew better than to call him that within earshot; he'd probably have her whipped, as he'd done to others. As far as he was concerned, he *was* the Pharaoh. Sarrah never told him about the snickering and gossip in the kitchens and bathhouses about this hot-headed, spoiled boy—especially what the soldiers said after they'd had a few beers.

Since moving into the palace, Sarrah had quickly learned whom to keep close for reliable bits of gossip and intrigue and whom to keep at arm's length, though she never actually befriended a soul. (Except for Nour, of course; but they had little reason to cross paths anymore, unless Nour was on a general's arm at a palace event.) There wasn't much to learn from these people. She could hear their thoughts, read their energy, and feel their emotions, so spending time in their company was mentally and physically draining. She might make occasional use of others as accomplices or collaborators, but as friends? Never. She certainly had no need for the emotional ties that such relationships might provide others. From what she'd observed, so-called friends eventually became liabilities.

What Sarrah needed was her own garden, and the freedom to grow and nurture the flowers, herbs, trees, and vines that were like friends to her. They were her collaborators, her joy. Her mother had taught her the powers of the plant world, and when these were combined with her own mystic powers, her spiritual and physical dominance was assured. From her garden, she would yield life. She would yield death if she so wanted. She could heal, and she could slay. She would create powerful fragrances, salves, cures, incense, burial oils. . . . She knew that a private garden would be hers once she gave Meti what he wanted: her body.

Ever since Meti had chosen Sarrah as his mentor—his prize, really—she had enjoyed free rein at the palace: the kitchens and banquet halls, the government buildings, the pools, stables, and gardens. She would sometimes visit the hetaerae in their aromatic, feminine den of delights. Meti tried to keep her close, but she always managed to slip out and wander through the royal grounds, usually late at night or while he was in the midst of his mathematics or other studies, or refining his equestrian and military skills. Occasionally Sarrah would go on a horseback ride with him outside the palace walls, and people could see them together. But for the most part they both understood that that wasn't her role.

Her role.

Sarrah knew the time was fast approaching when she would begin to share Meti's bed. Uncle Khufu had been preparing her for that duty for as long as she could remember. Nothing to be timid or prim about—as the hetaerae had taught her well, there was no need to pretend. She could *appear* coy, perhaps, because that's what men wanted, but never shy or disapproving. Sarrah knew how to hold her shoulders, tilt her neck, lower her voice. She knew the precise pressure of a fingertip as it trailed across the ridges of a man's abdomen or the supple curve of a woman's breast. In the privacy of the hetaerae's chambers, Sarrah's power to transform male lovers from steely-eyed predators to pliable, often imploring bed partners was well proven and well enjoyed. She now knew the contraception to use during these encounters to ensure that she would never be with child—that was most certainly *not* her role. As she saw it, she was destined for greater heights than motherhood.

Sarrah had done nothing to discourage the hunger she'd seen in Meti's youthful gaze on that first day. In fact, she'd stoked it. Allowing him to think he was the one seducing her, of course.

"Are you ready?" Meti was eager to join the royal procession and the rest of the pageantry that would soon fill the crowded city streets to bursting. The same preparations for war that were underway in the palace were taking place on a humbler scale in the homes of Egyptians throughout the city and its environs. Children would bid their fathers farewell; lovers would steal their final kisses. "Of course I'm ready," Sarrah replied.

She rose from the window seat where she'd been watching the world below. Several of the elder Pharaoh's consorts had advised her to take a quiet chamber overlooking one of the palace's private courtyards—teeming with night jasmine and the soft burbling of a fountain—but to their consternation she'd requested a room with a view of the city. Teeming with real life as opposed to the sweet soporific of everyday flowers, she thought. She was nothing if not a realist.

No longer was Sarrah clad in the linen sheath of a commoner, her feet bare, her hair natural. She was a goddess on earth, clad in an elaborate beaded gown sewn by palace seamstresses. Her sandals were of the softest leather; her gold arm band was now complemented by one on the other arm. On occasions such as this, she wore an elegant braided wig that glittered with gold hairpins, some of them jeweled. Affixed atop the wig was a small wax fragrance cone, worn by the upper class for important formal events to cloak themselves in an air of perfume as the wax warmed. Sarrah didn't deign to use those made by the slaves; she molded them herself of wax infused with her secret, powerful floral combinations. As the cone warmed in the sun it surrounded her with irresistible aromatic pleasures, and both men and women couldn't help but envision her clad in nothing else.

Meti was no exception. As she crossed the room slowly, she savored the way Meti's eyes followed her. He traced her scent just as she intended. She would have him soon, and they both knew it. He licked his lips, and they remained slightly parted as he breathed her in.

"Let me look at you, my darling," she ordered. He reveled in her attention, standing a little taller as she ran her hand along his exquisitely pleated sheer linen tunic. She adjusted the gold chain around his waist with her right hand, her fingertips dipping, then resting, warmed by the skin beneath. His breath caught slightly.

"Sarrah. . . ."

"Soon, my love."

"Why? Why not right *now?*"

"You will see. The anticipation is something you should prize. I will show you everything . . ." She moved behind him now, and the warmth of their bodies met, her breasts pressed lightly against his strong back. He leaned his head back onto her shoulder as she reached her left hand around him to rest upon his firm abdomen. "Just think of it, Meti, just think of the possibilities. . . ." She kissed his neck lightly, feeling his body melting back into hers.

"Please, Sarrah. . . ."

"This, my love?" she asked as her hand trailed downward, teasing.

"God, please. . . ."

She liked him to beg.

She gently pulled her hands away and took a step back. He spun around to face her.

"You are cruel!" Meti cried, sounding like a spoiled boy. But he was hardly a boy anymore. Both his lust and his power were real, mature. His eyes flashed, and a fierce erection thrust beneath the pleats of his wrap. He really *was* ready. Almost. She would let him take her soon.

"I thought you were eager to join the procession," she replied casually, as she slipped on the gold serpent ring he'd given her the day before. "I'm ready now."

He rolled his eyes in frustration. "Soon, Sarrah," he growled. He pulled open the door and ushered her out with the palm of his hand pressed authoritatively at the small of her back.

Since Sarrah's appointment as his mystic and advisor, Meti had begun to frequent the chamber of the hetaerae. He was no longer clueless about sex or women. But Sarrah had made sure through Amunet that Meti was only given the newest girls to entertain him—those still wet behind the ears, still shaking loose of their peasant-girl tendencies and appearance, who hadn't yet mastered the seduction of men. When she and Meti *did* finally consummate their relationship, she wanted his mind to be blown—and she took no chances that he'd experienced pleasure with anyone else comparable to what he would soon enjoy with her.

They walked through the cool, shadowy passage that connected the royal wing to the central hall, his hand never leaving her back. Sarrah thought of the power that hand would one day wield, the heavy bronze crook and flail that would rest in its firm grip. While Meti was preparing assiduously for his role as the next Pharaoh, she knew that deep down he still believed he would not take the throne for decades, no matter how cocksure he might pretend to be. But the gods had brought visions of Meti's coronation to Sarrah that appeared to be much more imminent.

And through the grapevine of slaves, servants, and hetaerae that wove within any palace walls, Sarrah discovered that the elder Pharaoh was no longer the robust leader he'd once been. His charisma was fading, his military acumen under increasing scrutiny. In fact, many in the government halls whispered about the prudence of this very campaign. Let the rebels see how long they can last at their outpost without our support, one general had pleaded; then we'll come in for the spoils. Instead, the Pharaoh had become peevish and was easily baited, letting his enemies goad him into pointless battles.

The Pharaoh had gifted large homes to the most senior advisors as supposed rewards for their loyalty, but the truth was clear to more astute observers of palace politics. While he had once been a wise and thoughtful ruler, the Pharaoh had gradually surrounded himself with a cadre of fawning yes-men, preferring a constant flow of flattery. They were ingratiating themselves while they could; he wouldn't live on this earth forever. Chief among them was Khufu; in fact, most of the Pharaoh's other senior advisors had fallen or been chased away, their appetite to come up against this brilliant yet dangerous mastermind simply not worth the risk. Everyone knew that Khufu was willing to take drastic steps to secure his own position—and undermine theirs—that most others would not. Forget the Pharaoh: it was the wrath of the gods that they feared.

The Pharaoh now ruled with arrogance and vanity—and that could cost Egypt her dominance.

CHAPTER EIGHT

"May I have a word?"

Her uncle's deep, commanding voice caught her unawares. Quickly Meti pulled Sarrah closer.

"What is it, Khufu?" Meti snapped. "We are on our way to the procession, and I don't want to keep my father waiting."

She enjoyed the brewing rivalry between these two men, each of whom thought he controlled her. Khufu, the aging, manipulative political puppet master, and Meti, the young and virile ruler in waiting, were two sides of the same equation as far as Sarrah was concerned.

"Of course, my lord. You must go to your father's side at once. I do not wish to keep you." He then turned to Sarrah with a kinder look. Or at least that's how it must have seemed to Meti. Sarrah knew that any softness in Khufu was a tool he employed. There was no genuine softness in him, of that she was certain.

Meti was annoyed. "What is it? Speak quickly."

"I have news of Sarrah's mother that I would like to share with her. May I speak with her and then deliver her to your side in a few minutes? I do not wish to detain you, but I must discuss a small family matter."

"Fine, Khufu, but only because time is short," he huffed.

"Sarrah and I have no secrets. Whatever you have to say to her in the future you will say to me. Is that clear?"

Over the past few months Sarrah had subtly encouraged Meti to hold his own with the court advisors, especially Khufu. She was pleased to see his progress—especially as Khufu was so evidently displeased. She smiled to herself, then bowed to Meti. "My lord, I shall join you momentarily."

"Yes, you will," he replied, then walked down the hallway toward the skylit atrium. The sun's rays caught the gold stripes of his headdress, and his personal guard formed quickly into a phalanx around him. Meti was the true leader. And he belonged to her.

Sarrah turned to face her uncle, her expression hardened. "Well?" she said, crossing her arms.

"How dare you address me like that?" Khufu growled in an angry whisper, grabbing her upper arm. The edges of her weighty gold cuff pressed into her skin, but she kept her expression indifferent.

"If you leave a bruise, he will have you flayed—"

Khufu's grip loosened, but he still held her in place. "Listen to me, you conniving, ungrateful wench, *this was an arrangement.*" He gestured between them. "You are here because of me. You are the prince's favorite because of me. You are—"

"Yes, yes. Because of you, Uncle. Everything I am is because of you. Now, if you don't have anything else to say, please release me so I can join the prince and ensure that he is entirely in my thrall. Do you have news of my mother or not?"

"I don't care if your mother has been eaten by crocodiles, you shrew. I needed your attention without that whelp hovering around you, bitch in heat that you are."

"So you would rather he *weren't* attracted to me?"

"Enough of your disrespect!" he barked. Several palace servants passing nearby turned at the sound of his voice, then scurried away.

Sarrah jerked her arm out of his grip and wiped Khufu's spittle from her face—he'd been that agitated. She sensed something different in him, something more erratic than his usual calculating ways. He was losing control of himself, Sarrah mused, letting paranoia seep through the cracks of his steely control.

"The time has come for me to exert *my* influence and power," he continued in a lower voice. "If we are to welcome in a new age for Egypt, I must gain control of Meti."

Sarrah did little to hide her impatience.

"With your second sight, Sarrah—"

"Yes, my sight, Uncle, *mine.*"

"Listen to me, child, and listen carefully." He grabbed her arms and pushed her against the limestone wall behind her. "*I* will maneuver control over Meti, and *I* will rule the kingdom from behind the curtain and behind the throne. If you value your life, you will do as I say." His eyes were wild with the promise of power.

All of Khufu's talk about a renaissance in arts and letters, fair wages for the lower classes, a thriving society that was a fair ally to its neighbors and a leader in the region—it was all lies. Sarrah now saw the truth: her uncle had no real interest in a new age for Egypt. She'd always known he was using her (just as she was using him), but this latest outburst gave her strength. Instead of instilling fear, his blatant cruelty gave her the courage to rely entirely on her own counsel. Khufu would prove a danger not only to herself, but also to Meti. She shivered at the knowledge that the future of Egypt and its people now rested largely on her actions—and that her loyalty to them was greater than to family.

She had no more use for Khufu.

"Of course, Uncle. I will do as I am bid."

"But please take back this cuff." She removed the hammered gold bracelet he had given her on the day she'd left her village for the palace. "As you can see, my king has given me a far grander one. I have no use for yours." Bowing in a perfect show of compliance, Sarrah slipped silently out of the hallway before he could say another word, leaving him to the company of his delusions.

———

The altercation with Khufu galvanized Sarrah. But she had no time to waste; Meti would be furious if she were not in his view during the procession. She hurried down the network of hallways to the palace entrance, then snaked her way through the crowds, taking care not to muss her sumptuous clothing and jewelry.

Memphis's main thoroughfare extended from the palace to the city walls. As far as the eye could see, onlookers lined the way; some were families, some were slaves, some were elderly people on wooden stools placed at the street's edge. Massive scarlet and gold banners of rough linen hung from the government buildings. Wreaths of lotus flowers were suspended from the windows, and the street was dusted with lotus petals. Vendors had arrived at dawn with carts full of breads, sweets, and fruits. Others had wheeled over barrels of beer. Citizens with tambourines, flutes, and rattles formed impromptu bands. A new mosaic wall on the side of the armory, commissioned by the Pharaoh himself, depicted in full color a Memphis cityscape much like this one—but in the mural, it was a victory parade proceeding from the city entrance to the palace.

There were canopy-shaded rows of raised benches for honored citizens, to ensure them a better view—and for them to be seen, as well. It was here that Sarrah found her place, among the highest-ranked staff, noblemen, and women. The Pharoah's closest advisers sat on the most desired benches, where no woman was seated—yet.

Dozens of royal drums began to sound, heralding the start of the Pharaoh's procession. Sarrah steadied her breath and focused all her energy on Meti. He looked confident and strong, held aloft by soldiers on the palanquin directly behind his father's, though he was still too young to join this latest crusade. When he had shared with Sarrah his disappointment at being left behind, she reminded him that he would be in charge while his father was away. The aides and ministers who oversaw the government in the absence of the Pharaoh, who at this very moment stood to her right on these raised benches, would now bow to Meti. Once she'd planted the seed of his role as interim Pharaoh, Meti was buoyed by excitement and anticipation.

Yes, Meti would be hers to influence and mentor and mold, while Khufu would be . . .

She felt a sharp nudge in her side that jolted her out of her thoughts.

"The boy Pharaoh," hissed the noblewoman sitting next to her, cocking her head toward the royal retinue. Sarrah had failed to notice Meti calling to her, indicating that she should join the procession.

"Thank you!" Sarrah whispered. She lifted the hem of her robe and hustled carefully down the wooden steps as she made her way through the crowds. She couldn't have planned it better—

"Excuse me—Sarrah, is it?" The piercing voice ran down her spine. She'd been looking down, concentrating on her footing, and had neglected to notice that brute of a man, Hasim, barring the way.

"Yes, I am Sarrah," she said impatiently. "Meti has requested my presence in the procession, if you don't mind."

"I *do* mind."

Ever since that first day she'd been presented to the Pharaoh, Hasim had riled her. Of course, she never showed it—what was the point? So what if she was attracted to him, or if she thought about him while she pleasured herself in the privacy of her own bed, in the darkness. So what if she could feel his touch and recall his smell, even when he was days away on some battleground. Over the months, she had tried to dispense with these carnal distractions. He was a relatively useless warrior, a foot soldier in her advance to power.

"Pardon me?" She did her best to stare him down. "It is not for you to speak to me in that manner. I am the advisor to the young Pharaoh and you are—"

"The advisor to the old Pharaoh," he said authoritatively, knowingly. Amusedly?

Despite the clang of armor and the clop of horses and the singsong of the thousands of spectators surrounding them, it felt as though they were alone. She resented his power over her—his power to distract her. Yes, he was desirable in a barbaric sort of way, but she knew better.

Didn't she?

She watched as his tanned, coarse hand left the hilt of his sword and came to rest on her hip. It was intensely erotic, as if he were going to pull her against him, right there in the middle of the street. And yet . . . it could be construed as a gesture of kindness. He was simply assisting her down the stairs, just as he would help one of the elders. If he had lent a hand to someone else, Sarrah wouldn't even have noticed. But there was nothing polite about the heat of his palm searing through her robes. She inhaled sharply.

"I've got you," Hasim said. She passed by him, front to front, her breasts grazing the warm leather of his chest plate. She might have imagined it, but she was fairly certain he'd breathed her in as he helped her by. "Soon," he whispered. She was about to turn and voice her indignation when she heard a shout.

"*Sarrah!* What is taking you so long?"

Meti had dismounted the palanquin and was now standing at the foot of the stairs. He was young, but he wasn't stupid. Sarrah hustled into the street as Meti snapped at Hasim, "What are you looking at?"

"Maintaining order, my lord." Hasim nodded in deference, then turned his eyes to the street and resumed his duty.

Everything about Meti suddenly felt weak and immature. His grip on Sarrah's arm was tight, his headdress askew, his pace hurried, his voice shrill. "You will walk behind me as my father's trusted aides walk behind him."

She bowed her head and followed him into the cavalcade.

———

Over the next two hours, the procession meandered through the city, a brilliant sea of gold and scarlet and dark oiled skin snaking its way toward the farthest city gate. People cheered; they sang, they raised their banners. As the sun set, the military rank and file passed beyond the city walls and began their long journey to northern Egypt.

Meti instructed Sarrah to wait for him while he bid his father a formal farewell. Standing toward the edge of the street beneath the welcome shade of a date palm, Sarrah felt the brush of rough fingertips against her own and was jolted again by desire.

Hasim. The scent of him was already familiar, damn him—myrrh, sandalwood, tobacco, sweat. "You presume much, General," she said, her gaze firmly on Meti and the elder Pharaoh just a few yards away. "You have forgotten your place."

"There is no presumption, Sarrah." That damned voice again—commanding and warm all at once—made her shiver. "I have full clarity when it comes to you, and I know you do, too." He placed his palm lightly at her lower back, and it shocked her like a lightning bolt. "You cannot trick me with your cool façade the way you do everyone else. I see the fire that blazes inside you."

She turned abruptly in an attempt to escape him, or confront him, or—

Hasim looked at her as if he were looking into her very soul. The energy that passed between them left her breathless. She shut her eyes—as if that could shut him out.

When she turned back to the street and scanned the area around the gate, he was gone.

She turned again, and there was Meti. Had he seen the exchange with Hasim? The general was renowned for his stealth in battle, and now she could see why.

Still, Meti suspected.

"Never forget your station," he said as he approached, in a tone he rarely used. "Never forget that you belong to me alone." He trailed a fingernail along her bare shoulder, and it was far from tender. The gesture left a mark, as if he'd branded her.

"Father has pronounced that I am ready for everything you have to offer. You will come to my chambers tonight to share with me your secrets of seduction and pleasure." His voice lowered slightly, the immature desire replaced by throaty lust.

"Between your experience and my enthusiasm, Sarrah, we shall create something divine, something for the ages."

He leaned into her neck and whispered hoarsely, "I will erase any desire you have ever known. Together we will create a brilliant and powerful future, in which we shall both nourish and devour one another, night after night." Meti's eyes shone brightly. "You will be mine forever, Sarrah, body and soul."

CHAPTER NINE

Later that evening there was a single firm rap on her door.

"Sarrah."

"Come in, my Pharaoh," she said, beckoning. She'd finally persuaded Meti that it was best for them to meet in her chambers, not his, for this long-awaited consummation. She had alluded to certain specifications and *accoutrements* that she'd had installed in her suite. But those could wait. Tonight was about pure carnal pleasure, about introducing Meti to the eternal dance of a man and a woman, as if for the first time.

The young Pharaoh strode in, brash and proud in his full regalia. His maids had bathed and perfumed him with the oils that Sarrah herself had created for him. They had dressed and adorned him in his finest tunic and the most exquisite jeweled neck collar Sarrah had ever seen.

Meti made every effort to exude masculine might, but his eyes revealed his true emotions—a heady mix of insecurity, curiosity, and unadulterated lust. *Perfect*, thought Sarrah; *he is ready at last.*

Meti stood stock still as Sarrah rose from her settee. She silently walked to him, then slowly edged around him. As she continued toward the door, he looked back over his shoulder. She turned the key in the lock she'd had custom-built and watched the muscles in his back ripple with anticipation at the sound.

"There is only one other key, my lord, and it is yours." Sarrah walked to the nightstand and opened an ebony box, one of the first gifts Meti had given her. She took out a fine gold chain with a single key. "I shall keep the door locked at all times. Only you may enter whenever you wish."

His breath halted. The chamber was filled with flickering candles, which cast dancing shadows on the walls. The finest incense of eucalyptus and peppermint piqued the air with excitement. There would not soon be any rest.

Sarrah wore a deep garnet robe of sheerest linen that teased with glimpses of her silhouette yet concealed the subtleties and secrets of her body. She moved toward Meti, again in silence, never losing eye contact. The air sparked with electricity and desire. Sarrah had known for many months—perhaps years—that this night would come, sealing her fate.

She was ready, too.

Sarrah stopped in the middle of the room.

"Come here," she demanded in a voice that would have earned her a flogging under any other circumstances. Meti was in her thrall, too enraptured to challenge her demanding tone. He did as he was told. He nearly leapt toward her, patently overeager.

"Easy, my love," she said, resting her hand on his chest. "The act of lovemaking is a fine balance of restraint and force. Hurrying has no place here." She reveled in his response: he regulated his breathing, calming himself as she had taught him. He'd been a brilliant student.

"Good," Sarrah praised. "Yes, breathe deeply and center yourself. Prepare for many hours of pleasure. Would you eat your favorite meal in a gluttonous haste? Or would you savor every delicious subtlety?" She pressed her palm more firmly against his chest, measuring her own bodily rhythm with the beating of his heart. "I know you can feel the connection between us. This is our power. And this will be our joy. We have all night—and many nights to come. We shall map each other, explore each other, and pleasure each other in ways you have only imagined."

Meti took three long, measured breaths. "*Now*. I am ready now. I will be calm, but I will no longer wait. We begin."

Sarrah allowed a seductive grin to spread across her face as her hand fell away from his chest. She dipped her head back and exposed her long, lithe neck. "Touch me," she whispered. "Caress my neck. Explore with your hands. Open your senses."

Meti obeyed. He reached out with a maturity and control that Sarrah would not have expected from a novice. He employed the gentlest touch, caressing her jaw and then trailing his finger down the long column of her neck to the sacred space between her breasts. He hesitated for a moment, and she moaned into the pause, igniting greater urgency in him.

Meti focused all his attention on her breasts, reaching his hands beneath the folds of her robe. He massaged and caressed, marveling at her response, engrossed by the power he had to ignite her pleasure. "Yes . . . our pleasures derive from one another. Do you sense how my pleasure arouses yours?"

As if impatient with Sarrah's tone, he firmly grasped both breasts, rubbing round and round and then pinching her aroused nipples.

"You are a natural, my darling," she purred. "Yes, just like that."

His hands worshiped her breasts. He could not get enough. Eventually he attempted to remove the robe completely, his movements becoming reckless and furtive.

She put her hands up to his cheeks to stay him. "Not yet, lover. Now close your eyes. Continue to explore and investigate my body with your hands only. Once your eyes start to play, your sense of touch will be diminished." She kissed him lightly on the lips, as she had done many times, but this time it meant so much more. This was an act of trust. A promise. "I am not just one of your hetaerae. Now is the time to study and learn my body only with your fingers. You will see me soon enough."

Sarrah gasped as his hands began to claim her body once more. Eyes closed, he slid both hands into the opening of her robe below her sash. His hands trailed along her quivering stomach until he found the warm heart of her. They both moaned as his touch found the source of her heat and pleasure. He placed one palm there as the other went around her hip and traced the curve of her buttocks, gently but firmly caging her, pressing her toward him.

"Please, I want to see you," he growled.

"Open your eyes and carry me to the bed," she commanded.

She marveled at how easily he lifted her, the care with which he placed her on the coverlet, and his innate awareness of how to please her. She allowed herself to enjoy the moment for its own sake. But her mind was still fully engaged—wasn't it always?—and she couldn't help but wonder how far Meti would be willing to go, consensually perhaps, but still at her bidding. He watched her face with intent and fierce intelligence, gauging her reactions to every touch and adapting his strokes to her moans and movement.

"Slow down, my king." For a moment, Sarrah didn't recognize the sound of her own voice, deep with meaning and portent. There was a gravity to this night that she didn't want either of them to underestimate. "If you continue like this, I will come too quickly." She could see, as his pupils widened, that this was exactly what Meti wanted.

"Show me," he ordered, increasing the pace of his fingers and already understanding that the swelling of her tender bud and the slick moisture coating them meant she was fully aroused.

"Please . . . Meti. . . ." Sarrah held his gaze, no longer knowing what she was asking for. Patience, perhaps, or deliverance, more likely.

"Give it to me. Give me your pleasure," he ordered. "Now."

He had it: the power, the entitlement, the wicked control, the royal command. But also the trust, the intimacy—the final thread in the tapestry that would weave them together for eternity.

Sarrah cried out in pleasure without any shyness or control. Meti gentled his touch, matching her waning peaks stroke for stroke. After the final waves of ecstasy slowed, Sarrah opened her eyes and saw Meti watching with a mix of fascination and triumph. "You are amazing, dear Meti. You can't have learned that from the hetaerae; your understanding of how to please my body is naturally fierce within you." Perhaps that was a bit of flattery, but it was also the truth.

Meti beamed with pride at her words. "More, Sarrah. I want to understand who we can be with one another. I want to arouse every inch of you, for all my senses to be attuned to all of your pleasure."

Sarrah's response was to rise, drop her robe, and stand proudly before him. She was nude except for the single gold cuff that had been a gift from Meti—a glittering manifestation of what bound them to one another.

For a moment he hesitated as he devoured her with his eyes. Then he removed his regal garments and tossed them aside. He sat at the edge of the bed with the same confidence, the same animal comfort he felt in his own skin, his hard, proud manhood ready.

Sarrah moved closer, time falling away, her movements liquid and deliberate. She reached down and stroked him with slow, gentle pressure. His eyes were glassy and dark, needy and commanding at once. Then she began to firm her grip, find her cadence, and increase her pace. Meti grunted with the pleasure of another's touch on him and started to thrust his hips to match her stroke. When Sarrah had brought him to the brink of release, she let go and backed a step away from him, her gaze fixed. His throaty gasp was like a brilliant flare in the darkest night, an incandescent mix of fury and lust.

"Come, my king, it is time." She joined him on the bed and guided him to lie down. "Do not be angry. . . ."

He growled in response.

"Or be angry if you wish," she laughed lightly. "It is all part of your power, after all. But I think you will realize I am not teasing you. I am bringing you deeper into yourself. Into me." She outstretched her arms toward her king. "Your first release with me will be while we are joined."

Meti groaned at the sight of her. "Do not ever betray me, Sarrah."

"How could I?" she soothed, letting her arms fall languidly above her head, offering herself to him in every way possible. "How could I betray part of my very soul?"

He came to the bed and crawled on top of her, letting her hands guide his hips and then his manhood to her entrance. The moment they were connected there—his strength to her heat, his power to her wisdom—it seemed that Meti allowed ancient awareness to take over. He thrust into her with abandon and growled at the warm grip she provided in response. He lost himself to her, to himself, to their union. Sarrah met his thrusts, sometimes with tenderness, other times with raw need, and observed in fascination as he was nearly overcome with pleasure and command and lust. Then, with a wholly unexpected deepening of desire, she exploded into a million stars while screaming his name.

Her cry energized Meti, empowered him, until he was cast so deeply into his own pleasure—their pleasure—that he erupted with triumph and matched her cries with his own.

CHAPTER TEN

New York City, October 19

Sarah paced in the waiting room outside her shrink's office, unsure how she would explain to him what had been going on with her recently. Or if she even wanted to.

"God, Sarah, get it together," she whispered under her breath. She tried to convince herself that Ken Jaffe had really been there for her over the past twenty-some years. She'd never particularly liked him, but she didn't need to. In fact, it was better that she didn't. Their relationship was ultimately professional, and she knew how to navigate professional relationships. She could totally share this with him. It was his job to help her maintain her mental health, not to judge her.

But . . . tarot cards and premonitions and marital discontent? Not to mention sexual electricity with a near stranger, unlike anything she'd ever experienced before?

She felt a knot of unease welling in her gut as she tried to convince herself that she was entitled to her own feelings, and that keeping those thoughts private didn't make her "a bad patient." That had basically been the crux of two decades of therapy, hadn't it?

Honestly, had *anything* really changed in twenty years? She thought back to the first time she'd sat in this waiting room: same standard-issue armchairs, same greige carpet, same framed Impressionist posters, probably even the same copy of *The New Yorker*. She had taken it all in as a twenty-one-year-old. Even then she'd been keeping secrets, but of a different kind.

————

There had been a boy.

As a senior at Williams, Sarah had her eyes on the prize—college degree, Wharton MBA, Goldman Sachs offer—when she was unexpectedly, improbably swept off her feet. It was fair to say that she didn't see Etienne coming. Look up "French exchange student" in the dictionary and there he was: black turtleneck, moody, smoker, vintage jazz records, better-than-box wine.

It was the way he *didn't* notice her that made her notice him. Looking back, it was a textbook "bad-boy" phase. The way Etienne made her doubt her smarts—yet copied all her notes. How he looked down on her friends, who eventually kept their distance. He was certainly the demise of her textbook "boy-next-door" romance with Carl McDonough, whom she'd dated since freshman year.

She and Carl had had mutual boarding-school chums (he from Avon Old Farms, she from Miss Porter's), and it turned out that their parents already knew each other from their beach club in the Hamptons. At the July Fourth party—picture-perfect with red, white, and blue streamers, a classic beach barbecue, and the sun setting over the Sound—they'd gotten caught up in this web of connections. That evening there were certainly fireworks.

God, they looked good together. From then on, she and Carl were inseparable at Williams, a golden couple. Carl was popular, well-connected, confident, smart enough. Smart enough to also get into Wharton Business School and to not seem threatened that Sarah's academic star shone brighter than his. Poor Carl was flabbergasted when the Barbie to his Ken dumped him for—a Monchhichi?

For someone who prided herself on being headstrong, bright, and nothing like her mother—who'd given up any promise of a career once that heirloom diamond was slipped on her ring finger—Sarah lost herself completely in her relationship with Etienne. The worst was when she found out she was pregnant. A few weeks after a *nuit dramatique* full of accusations, cigarettes, and makeup sex, Etienne disappeared. He said he had to "get back to the family business"—but did he? He was gone without a trace, just the linger of cheap French cologne on her sheets and a box of records she hated. This was in the days before iPhones and Snap maps, so his going back to France was as good as *finit*.

Later Sarah would find out that everything Etienne had said was a lie. According to his Facebook profile when she'd last checked about five years ago, he wasn't a wealthy heir, he was a *fonctionnaire* at some *bureau* in Neuilly that no one cared about. Everything about him turned out to be untrue—except the truth that he was out of her life and stayed that way forever.

But at the time, Sarah was devastated, and too ashamed to crawl back to any of her friends—who'd only wanted what was best for her, who'd wanted the "old Sarah" back. Except for Max. But even *he* had to distance himself from her angst; she was so dark, and he was a scholarship kid with exams to take.

Then—she miscarried. It was early in her pregnancy, but it was a lot to deal with and accept.

Sarah was unused to feeling emotions so deeply, especially negative ones like grief and self-doubt. They soon overwhelmed her. After her final college exam, Sarah drove her beat-up Saab back to New York. When her parents came out the entrance of their Fifth Avenue building to greet her, they saw her hollowed-out eyes and no Max in the passenger seat, and they freaked out.

The next morning she'd sat in this very office, staring at the framed Impressionist posters in the waiting room of Dr. Kenneth Jaffe, MD, whose name she recognized from eavesdropped conversations about the last poor little rich girl who'd had a nervous breakdown at college.

Sarah had always been suspicious of therapy; she wasn't sure her mother "felt better" or was any more enlightened after decades of weekly sessions with her own shrink. Weren't therapists supposed to eventually put themselves *out* of a job?

But for as long as she could remember, Ken had been a part of her parents' life. He was brilliant—one of the brightest pre-law undergraduates at Fordham. Her father, sensing his promise, had hired him as a clerk the summer after his junior year. But at the end of his three-month stint, Ken had informed her father that he was no longer interested in a law career; he'd been accepted into the psychiatry program at Johns Hopkins. All this had happened when Sarah was a child, but it was akin to family lore. Her father had held Ken in the highest professional esteem ever since, and they'd remained friendly with one another.

So when Sarah was at her wits' end—filled with dark, secretly hormonal, self-destructive thoughts—her parents knew exactly to whom she should turn.

Ken Jaffe put her on an intensive ninety-day therapy program that summer. Sarah walked the twenty blocks to Midtown every morning, then plopped down on Ken's uncomfortable sofa for an hour and a half of talk therapy. *I am paying for his yacht!* she thought to herself at the time. And then there were the medications: the SSRIs, the SNRIs, the MAOIs, the alphabet soup of antidepressants that she waded through with his help. But she got sort of better, and she and her parents decided she needed a change of scenery. Wharton would have to wait for now.

If she thought back to the first decision in her entire life that she'd actually made for herself, it was a result of the events of that year. Her father had noticed her mirrored vanity (a hand-me-down from her grandmother) lined with fragrances, which she'd been collecting since she was a girl. There were tiny sample vials from the perfume counter at Saks, her grandmother's prized frosted-glass Lalique bottle of Fougeres, pre-teen scents like Love's Baby Soft, exotic oils she'd collected on family trips to France and Egypt. She treated herself to luxury fragrances the way Carl treated himself to cashmere sweaters, sunglasses, or driving moccasins. And perfume was an easy gift, so every year Sarah's birthday brought a bushel of small, tissue-crowned gift bags full of new scents.

It was the perfect time for Dad to make a phone call to Maison Garreau in Provence. "You're going to have to find your own way in business," he said, "and you've loved perfume since you were a little girl." An internship with "Uncle Pierre" Garreau, her dad's childhood friend, at one of the world's most elite white-label fragrance companies seemed like a good start. Perhaps the scents she loved would light a fire in her. And maybe, on a side trip to Paris on the Pont des Arts, the famed "love-lock bridge," she would run into Etienne—for better or worse. (She wouldn't know until years later that her father had made it clear to Etienne through "friends" that he should never see her again.)

Sarah arrived in France in January, just after the Christmas holidays. She had a carry-on bag, a laptop computer, refill prescriptions for Prozac, and orders to check in every week with both her parents and Dr. Ken Jaffe on a brand-new cell phone she wasn't sure how to use. After twenty-four hours of travel via air, train, and taxi, she arrived at the gravel driveway of Maison Garreau, lined with plane trees that would no doubt provide ample shade in springtime but were now like skeletons. But this region of Provence, in the hills not far from the glittering French Riviera, was the epicenter of all things flowers and fragrance. Why did she feel as if she'd been here before?

The gray skies, fallow fields, and light rain didn't do much to lift Sarah's spirits—but the sight at the end of the allée did. Garreau wasn't housed in a corporate office park or factory but in a majestic 18th-century chateau that sprawled in all directions. Would her new "office" look like a garret in the servant's quarters of Versailles?

Past the reception rooms—kept in period-resplendent style for VIP visitors such as the CEOs of LVMH and Chanel, celebrities, and various sultans and queens—the offices, labs, and packaging facilities were some of the most modern interiors she'd ever seen. The back of the chateau featured a glass-walled addition with workspaces that overlooked massive fields of flowers, grasses, and herbs that would begin to come alive in a few months. Monsieur Garreau's secretary showed Sarah to her workspace and instructed her to come back the next morning at nine for the daily meeting. Sarah plugged in her laptop, rode the company shuttle into the adjacent town where most of the employees lived, checked into the rooming house where she'd be staying, and passed out cold.

As an intern in the Brand Partnerships department, she quickly learned what it meant to work with companies to white-label a fragrance. Their clients were as well-kept a secret as their award-winning formulas—and Sarah was thrilled to now be in the know. Thank goodness most of the meetings were in English, but her French was growing by leaps and bounds. *I am Mother's best version of me right now*, she laughed to herself— *wearing her hand-me-down suit, fluent in Français, and chaste as a nun!*

If heaven had a fragrance, it was the scent of the interiors of Garreau. Walking down the hallways was an entirely new sensual experience. Every lab, drawing room, meeting space, and even the cafeteria smelled like orange blossoms. And yes, she was beginning to discern the different fragrances. It wasn't enough to walk into a test room and say, "Wow, it smells amazing in here." The chemist would look down his nose at her and say, "Well, what do you smell *exactly*? Is it the top notes? The base notes? Is it the sandalwood or the tuberose? Is the nod to Fracas too literal?"

Wearing fragrance of any kind was prohibited in the building, but she was sent home with sample vials to try. "Report back on what it smells like after ten minutes, after six hours, applied to dry skin or hydrated skin," the chief chemist would say. His name was Dr. Brisbois, and he'd taken a liking to her; he could tell that she had the instincts for this work. In fact, over the last few weeks she'd spent more time in the lab than in the business offices.

As her time in France drew to a close, Monsieur Garreau called Sarah to his office. To her he'd always been Uncle Pierre, a cherished friend of her father's, but during her internship they had kept their interactions professional. When they crossed paths in a meeting or hallway, he treated her like any staff member. Production, quality, marketing, sales—she had literally breathed in all this knowledge, and she felt more alive, more herself, than ever before. The vials of pills Dr. Ken had prescribed languished on the nightstand. Eventually she just threw them away.

The view from Uncle Pierre's office always made her pause: rows of flowers as far as the eye could see. It was August, when most of France went on holiday, so the fields weren't full of gardeners as they usually were. The jasmine wound more loosely than normally allowed; the roses hung mature and heavy; camellia petals fluttered in the air. Weeds—creeping thistle and ryegrass—mottled the rows in places. When human backs were turned, nature quickly resumed its power; they all knew it.

"It's best to let the fields grow wild before we prune them back so rigorously over the winter," Pierre said. "Fall is for the less showy plants—the grasses, the herbs. And in the factories, it's when we spring into production."

"I know. I'm sorry to miss it," said Sarah. "I guess I have to get back to real life." She wasn't sure about returning to business school and working among the titans of industry, whose hubris was unbounded.

"I've been meaning to speak with you about that," said Pierre. "Fall is also when Garreau's Perfumery Certificate program begins. I'm sure you know that we accept four students for our two-year program, which includes a semester at our lab in Italy. The competition for admission this year was fierce, but we've selected three candidates. All have a chemistry background, and some have experience at perfumery school in Paris."

"What about the fourth student?"

"Well," said Pierre, "I recently had a long visit with Dr. Brisbois. He thinks it should be you."

"What?" said Sarah. "I—I'm a business intern. I have Wharton waiting. I've never taken a chemistry class. I—"

"Brisbois says that he has rarely met anyone with a nose as intelligent as yours. An olfactory sense for innovation, but also for the history of fragrance. You know what it means to reference a flower, or a region, or a classic scent, in an unexpected way. I'm impressed with your business acumen, but you've also spent every free moment in the lab with Brisbois, so consider that your chemistry prerequisite.

"You have such a promising career in fragrance that I'm afraid I can't let you leave," Pierre said, smiling.

———

And so it began. After two years under Dr. Brisbois's tutelage, what had begun as an inkling became a finely honed sixth sense for fragrance. Sarah learned about the cultivation of perfume plants, natural raw materials and their processing, the art of perfume composition. She was trained in aromatherapy and phytotherapy, the use of plants for health purposes. Her research took her to other regions—Spain, Turkey, Scandinavia—where she visited not only factories and apothecaries but also museums, country homes, fashion collections.

Now when Sarah thought back on those two years, living in France and traveling the globe, she realized it had been a crash course in personal growth. Her French became impeccable, and she was welcome at the country homes and dinner tables of Pierre and Dr. Brisbois. When her parents visited, they were overjoyed with this happy daughter who was—literally—blossoming. They'd been getting regular reports from Pierre, praising her potential as a "nose," which softened the blow of her deferral at Wharton.

Along her travels, Sarah had occasional dalliances—a swarthy tour guide in Ankara, drinks in a hotel bar in Paris that ended upstairs in her *chambre*, a banker she met on a train in Italy. But she found that the messages she got from Carl, the college boyfriend she'd dropped for that greasy-haired exchange student, were what she looked forward to. Those lonely first few months interning at Maison Garreau, she'd reached out to Carl to apologize. They had so much history together. Even their families did. It just seemed decent and prudent to 'fess up and keep the peace. They'd be seeing each other again, no doubt, when she started at Wharton.

Except that she didn't start at Wharton. Sure, Carl had been furious with her, but by the time she reached out he'd slept with everyone in Southampton to get back at her, and word had gotten back of Sarah's misfortune with the French guy. One thing about Carl—he was nothing if not confident, comfortable in his (perfectly tanned) skin. Weekly emails turned into daily emails and then into frequent phone calls and some deliciously naughty Skypes (the time difference was a challenge, but she woke up early and he studied until late).

Carl came to visit over his winter break; Sarah wasn't ready to return to New York just yet. They met in Paris, and it was he—not Etienne, as she had long ago hoped—with whom she walked the Bridge of Locks, had strong coffee and perfect croissants, and shopped (Carl loved a good mirror and found the ones at Saint Laurent particularly flattering).

Carl's blueblood appeal seemed strangely exotic to her now. All she'd seen for months were skinny men with cigarette-stained teeth and a *hauteur* that she found off-putting. It looked like Carl would be an MBA grad in eighteen months, probably with a job offer on Wall Street, and she'd be a fully minted nose from one of the world's most prestigious fragrance programs, with job offers from around the world. They talked about their shared dreams: two kids, a New York apartment, weekends in the mountains or out East, founding their own businesses. There would be much that they wished to mirror from their similar upbringings—except for the lack of connection that each felt between their parents. Carl and Sarah would be different: best friends and lovers, sharing warmth and laughs. The sex had always been electric, and they were certain it always would be.

When Sarah returned to New York a year and a half later, she was wearing the diamond engagement ring that had belonged to Carl's late grandmother. It was a little showy, but so be it. Their midsummer Hamptons wedding was picture-perfect. As a wedding gift she gave Carl a scent she'd created especially for him: Mon Soleil, with top notes of neroli, the bottle engraved with the likeness of The Sun tarot card. Carl gave her a Tiffany sterling silver frame with a photo of—himself. For her new office, he said! She could see him mentally patting himself on the back for this thoughtful idea.

Either Sarah or Carl would have to compromise on job location in order for them to be in the same city, and of course it would be Sarah; Morgan Stanley was not going to move to France for Carl. Of many offers, she chose a position creating branded fragrances for Barneys New York. It was a heck of a first job, and she felt lucky to have it. The "old boys network" of the fragrance biz had worked its magic: Uncle Pierre and Dr. Brisbois had white-labeled perfumes for Barneys in the past, but they were happy to relinquish that role to Sarah in house, knowing they'd be her first choice for whatever raw materials she desired.

What an amazing opportunity! She was twenty-five years old and already in her dream job. The clientele at Barneys was a target audience she knew well, and the CEO's taste level was impeccable. It wasn't all about the money at Barneys; they gave her creative freedom to create a suite of four unisex fragrances. She chose the themes of North, South, East, and West for the Barneys Compass collection, traveling to Scandinavia, Egypt, Turkey, and France as inspiration. Of course she was inspired by the native flora of each region to inform each scent, but she also researched vintage fabrics, classic scents, exotic spices, even iconic photographs to create fragrances that could transport you with a single spray. The Compass Collection flew off the shelves.

Sarah had an innate gift for putting the scents together. It was unnerving how intense her connection was to these previously unfamiliar cities and countries, how a note of myrrh conjured up for her an ancient Egyptian palace. An unexpected touch of jasmine and she was alone in a candlelit chamber, dabbing essential oil behind her ears. Layer on the scent of leather and she was in an embrace with her bare-chested warrior lover. A hint of musk and he was removing her robes. Hence the sultry, earthy eau de parfum she called South.

Sarah could paint paintings, create environments, change a mood with her creations. She could make someone fall in love with you if she wanted to—and she loved having that sort of control. What a joke that a few years before she'd thought she was headed to Wall Street! She was an artist, a craftsman, an intuitive. Not that she didn't have a head for business—the profits were off the charts.

———

The Barneys dream job came to an end when Barneys did. The famed department store filed for bankruptcy; its relentless pursuit of quality had created an unsustainable bottom line. Though Sarah had many offers from fragrance conglomerates, fashion brands, and skincare companies, she had just enough swagger to think she could strike out on her own. With her international connections for raw materials, her experience building budgets and marketing campaigns with Barneys, and the mentorship of Garreau and Brisbois, when matched with her instincts for best-selling fragrances: now was the time.

Well, that was what Max thought. He helped her create a business plan and a marketing strategy, and over the next year they steadily built a buzz in the fashion and beauty press for the hottest new boutique fragrance brand—Arcanum. Sarah had named it for one of her grandmother's favorite scents, which had been discontinued nearly a century ago. Arcanum meant secret, mystery—and as she'd shared with Leyla, the tarot card reader, her connection to her grandmother and the past was strong.

Shyly she asked Stuart Adler, a retail consultant she'd met through Barneys, to help her grow Arcanum. The Barneys CEO might not have listened to his advice, but she certainly had. He was a wise, shrewd, measured advisor with a smile that could melt butter. She'd never understand why he'd chosen to work with her at this stage of his life, given his resume. Stuart was sought after by several Fortune 100 companies; she figured there was no way he'd even entertain having a conversation with her. But he accepted her invitation to meet, and they hit it off. Stuart not only saw the drive and vision Sarah had for Arcanum, but he was hungry for a startup opportunity.

"You came to me at exactly the right time," he said to Sarah. "I just turned fifty. Arcanum will be my swan song—and keep me so busy I won't have time for a midlife crisis!" Twelve years later he was still the best decision Sarah had ever made—for both her company and herself. Stuart had become a mentor and a dear friend.

Carl was proud of Sarah's success and supportive of her entrepreneurial venture—even though it meant putting off having children for a few years. Mentions of her in *Vogue* and *Forbes* somehow burnished his star as well as hers. The Morgan Stanley wives wanted the glamorous McDonoughs at their cocktail parties and their clubs. They were one of the hottest young couples in New York, and Carl saw his face in the society press just enough to stroke his ego and bolster his own career.

Though Sarah *did* notice—and she wasn't imagining it—that over the next five years, as Arcanum started to make real money, Carl's career began to plateau. Perhaps it was because he wasn't putting in the twelve- or sixteen-hour days that his co-workers were? Seemed like he had more time to fit in a swim at the New York Athletic Club or take a three-day ski weekend with the boys in Aspen. With the success of Arcanum, there wasn't any danger of the bills not getting paid, and he and Sarah were too high-profile, too blueblood a couple for him to get fired. The firm just kind of kept Carl around, but he wasn't on the management track. Whatever. Sarah was too busy building an empire to nag Carl about it. And his early morning squash games and travel gave her the freedom to work nights and weekends.

It did bother Max, though. Their boozy lunches, which she always squeezed into her schedule and looked so forward to, always included a rant about her "trophy husband." Didn't *he* have a sweet deal these days!

That said, Sarah didn't really share deep thoughts about this shift in her marriage with Dr. Ken Jaffe. Yes, Ken—she'd been seeing him now for nearly two decades. Did these weekly forty-five-minute therapy sessions do anything besides drain her wallet? Not really, but Ken had brought her back from the brink of despair after the Etienne debacle and, one could say, changed the course of her life. She felt indebted to him. Ken helped her with the everyday dilemmas—his-and-hers quarrels with Carl, interactions with her overbearing mom, staff skirmishes—but sometimes Sarah had to conjure up things to talk to him about. She trusted herself more than she did Ken now. Over the years, he'd occasionally put her on a "90-day meditation sprint" or an intensive off-site program she wasn't sure she needed. Or a sleep medication she wasn't sure was necessary, either. Heck, she went to his week-long retreat at Esalen, and even helped him fund it, but she didn't really feel any more enlightened afterward. These pricey intensives always seemed to correlate with Ken's buying a new house or a new club membership. Was she unfairly dubious of his intentions? Maybe. Probably not.

Sarah had to admit that Ken did again spring into action when, at age thirty, with Arcanum well established and a Fifth Avenue apartment procured, she and Carl couldn't get pregnant. She felt sure that her infertility must be tied somehow to the miscarriage a decade before.

She'd stupidly expected babymaking to be a breeze. Go off birth control. Get pregnant. The end.

But the series of miscarriages that dogged Sarah for three solid years felt like a punishment for good behavior, as if assiduously building a business that would eventually be her children's legacy had prevented her from *having* those children. The voice in her head was consistently bitter and eventually self-destructive. That sense of her own foolishness, coupled with the raw grief, profound sense of loss, and physical toll, finally led her back into Ken Jaffe's confidence.

CHAPTER ELEVEN

The patient with the appointment before hers opened the door, nodded lightly, and walked out of the office, eyebrows raised slightly at Sarah's furtive laps around the reception room. Sighing, Sarah stopped pacing, taking a seat in the empty room and picking up *The New Yorker*. She flipped the pages mindlessly and decided she had no reason to feel shaky. She was entitled to her feelings, damn it. And they were really good feelings—fizzy, excited feelings. Ever since Max and Harry had escorted her home from the birthday party, she'd been . . . clear. She felt lighter somehow. Freer. More like herself than she'd felt in ages.

Then Monday afternoon rolls around, and here I sit on this gorgeously bright and sunny New York day, with doubt creeping in.

She tossed the magazine back on the coffee table and crossed her arms. Was she having some sort of mental break? She smiled at the irony—at least she wouldn't have to go far for treatment.

Just then Ken opened his office door, interrupting Sarah's musings. She looked at him objectively for a few seconds. For the most part, obviously, she focused on her own thoughts and feelings during their sessions, so it seemed odd that on today of all days she would see *him*—actually *see* him.

Their time together often seemed more like a battle of wits than a stereotypical therapy session, but it worked. He didn't pander to her; he made her see things clearly; he challenged her.

But had he served his purpose? Setting aside the tumultuous feelings of the past few days, Sarah had been wondering for several months if it was time for them to part ways.

When she looked at him now, the thought flashed in her mind once more: *Time to move on.* And she could have sworn that he saw it in her eyes. Or maybe he'd sensed her distance over the past few months, her prescriptions going unfilled, and they were finally going to address it outright.

But then it was as if the petulance she thought she'd seen in his expression had never been there at all. The calm, cool, intellectual doctor was back.

"Good morning, Sarah, and happy belated birthday," he said with a lack of emotion she usually found reassuring. He gestured for her to come into his office, then he shut the door behind her and took his customary place in the single chair in the center of the room.

Rather than heading for the couch as she normally would, Sarah stood by the side table and looked out the window, suddenly distracted by the dazzling reflection of light off the skyscraper across Park Avenue.

"Are we conducting today's session standing up for some reason?" Kenneth asked with a faint smile.

Feeling a bit foolish and weirdly chastised, she sat down. "No. I just got carried away by some thoughts . . . by the light." She gestured toward the diamondlike shards that sparkled throughout the room.

"Carried away?" He had pen in hand and pad on his lap, as always.

How many reams of those pads does he have filled with my meandering thoughts scribbled on them? she wondered. *Do they ever get thrown away? Do they belong to me?*

The pen and the pad suddenly annoyed her.

Was he even listening to her? *Really* listening?

"Hmm? What are you thinking, Sarah?"

With the same clarity she'd been . . . accessing over the past few days, she started to believe that for all these years this man had actually enjoyed having her be reliant on him. Her dependence empowered him. It seemed so obvious all of a sudden. Rather than encouraging her to embrace change, he'd always suggested she not rush into anything. Couldn't she be rational and make important life changes?

"Actually, you're right," Sarah said. "I would prefer to stand."

She got up from the couch and started pacing. Yet this time it wasn't like the agitated pacing in the waiting room, of a pent-up lion, but instead the confident strides she was used to taking in the boardroom—controlled movement that let her think and talk and be in control and fully alive.

"I think we might be at a good stopping point, Ken." She quit pacing for a moment and leveled a CEO-steady, composed gaze at him.

Ken softly chuckled as if she were a child, then stared silently back at her. His eyes suggested that he'd been here before.

She exhaled calmly and reined in a spike of useless anger. "Not right this minute, of course—"

"Of course."

"But I thought it was a good idea to start putting it out there, so we don't need to go through any, I don't know, *histrionics* about me transitioning away from our professional relationship at this or that critical juncture." Looking down at the back of her hand with a contemplative gaze, she realized that on some level she was well and truly done with him. Really done.

It was such a relief.

There was no need to quit in a rage or a dramatic state of agitation. In hindsight, it was obvious that he'd used those times over the years to keep her close, reliant. After the birth of the twins, she'd suggested she was ready to stop meeting, but he'd convinced her it was the *absolute worst possible time* to make such a major change. Then it had just become routine again, and a decade went by. She lived in New York City. She had a psychiatrist. It was like taking a multivitamin—preventive medicine, no downside.

She'd probably keep seeing him for the next few months. Any type of long-term relationship was worth ending responsibly.

Words came easily after that. "Actually, it's nothing, really. Just turning forty brought up a lot of . . . old feelings." *Yeah, that was one way to put it,* she thought. *Centuries-old feelings,* more like it.

"What kind of old feelings?" he asked, interested. Scribble scribble. Seemed like Dr. Ken sensed a new angle to work with.

"That's the thing, Ken, it's really hard to explain, especially to you—"

He raised an eyebrow.

"—someone who shares my intellectual bent, my need for rationality, and a healthy skepticism of the unknown."

"Go on." He jotted something down.

"You and I have addressed a lot of this over the years—imposter syndrome, believing in myself, doing what I need to do in business and at home to maintain healthy boundaries. I like to understand things, to get to the bottom of things. You know what I mean?"

"Yes, but can you be more specific?"

"Oh, it's nothing really specific." *Liar.* "Just feelings brought on by turning forty . . . it's such a milestone in so many ways. I just want to be aware of my feelings, you know?"

"Yes, I know. Can you describe some of the feelings you're becoming aware of?"

"Sort of." She shrugged.

She wasn't about to tell him about feeling like her chemistry had been altered, or alchemized, and that visions of other Sarahs, or some version of Sarah, were rising to the surface of her consciousness. She was barely able to *think* these things, much less say them aloud.

"Give it a go," he encouraged.

She thought for a few moments. "Here's the thing . . . the world is so full of possibilities, so much more is out there. Time feels limitless . . . my spirit feels vast . . . like I'm here on this earth to be expansive beyond anything I could possibly imagine." Sarah's voice petered out. "Sounds like I'm on a ketamine trip, doesn't it?" she laughed.

"Actually, it sounds more like psilocybin," said Ken straight-faced.

About halfway through her explanation—or at least the surface version she was willing to share—Ken had started to write very quickly on his notepad again, and he kept at it after she'd finished.

As recently as last week, Sarah would have been squirming in her seat with feelings of awkwardness, waiting and hoping for him to impart some wisdom, to share the incisive ideas she was unable to see for herself. In the past she'd always felt vulnerable and exposed when he'd give her the silent treatment.

Not today!

She took a slow, deep breath and turned to look out the window. The turn of Harry Aiken's strong neck and the powerful arc of his shoulder floated into her mind's eye. *Silence—how refreshing it could be.* She closed her eyes and savored the peace.

Ken cleared his throat, and Sarah turned her head to look at him. She was the silent one now. After all these years of therapy, how could she not have really seen Ken before today? He *had* helped her through some major challenges, and she would always be grateful for that. Just as she was grateful to Uncle Pierre and Dr. Brisbois, two of her closest mentors in business.

But neither of those two had ever tried to co-opt her success or muddy her triumphs with underhanded suggestions that they were somehow to be credited for all eternity.

Sarah didn't need to be intimidated by Dr. Ken Jaffe. And she absolutely one hundred percent didn't need to be afraid of her own powerful desires, her own explosive feelings.

For so long, just as it was with her mother, Sarah had wanted Ken to be proud of her—and he'd used that to his advantage. The very people who were supposed to instill pride and self-esteem in her were the same ones who'd been poking holes in them all these years.

"Well?" he asked at last.

She turned to face him and tilted her head slightly. "It's all good."

Then she caught sight of the wall clock and was surprised to see that nearly an hour had elapsed. *Time's up!* she thought meaningfully.

"You know what, Ken," she continued, reaching for her bag on the couch and pulling out her checkbook and a pen, "It's really not a big deal, I promise. Now that I've said it out loud, I can see that it was just the birthday party and all the disruption. I'm forty. It's big, but it's also just a fact."

Ken stopped writing and looked up at her again. "Very well, Sarah," he says. "We need not pursue this today. However, I *am* concerned about you, and we don't want this to escalate."

"I so appreciate your concern," she answered easily. *Escalate, my ass.*

She tore the check neatly along the perforation and handed it to him. There was something deeply satisfying about proffering this physical symbol of the transactional nature of their relationship. *Take the check for services rendered, Jaffe,* she thought as he hesitated.

"How have you been sleeping?" he asked.

"Not well, actually."

He walked over to his desk, slipped the check into a drawer, and his hand re-emerged with a prescription pad and pen. He dashed off a few lines in his familiar illegible scrawl.

She smiled to herself as she walked toward the office door. She glanced over her shoulder and said, "No worries. I'll see myself out."

But Ken walked over to hand her the prescription as if he were offering her a lifeline.

"And this is for the sleeping. You know how to reach me if you need anything before next Monday. Let's try and stay away from the ketamine and mushrooms, okay?"

Shrink humor.

"Thanks. I'll be in touch if anything comes up. Otherwise, same Bat time. . . ."

CHAPTER TWELVE

Sarah strode out of Ken's office building. It was a beautiful day, and she was planning to enjoy every minute of it. She had about an hour to kill before she met up with Max for lunch, so she did something she rarely did: she strolled. She continued up Park Avenue, the wash of Indian summer light surrounding her. She let her mind wander as aimlessly as her path, and almost immediately glimpses of foreign lands and bird's-eye views of ancient streets and tanned bodies inter-twined flashed in her mind. The brilliant desert sun of Egypt—she could feel it on her cheek and the nape of her neck.

She stopped at a crosswalk and looked up to the sky, letting the rays warm her. A rush of wind swept down the cross street, and with it a return to the present. She pulled her cashmere scarf more tightly around her neck and turned toward Third Avenue.

Before she knew it, she had walked blissfully for nearly an hour. She turned the corner at 74th and Third, and there was Max waiting for her outside of JG Melon. He looked up, caught a glimpse of her, and smiled the biggest grin while waving his arm like a total dork. Sarah laughed out loud as she approached him and shook her head.

"You just can't help yourself, can you?" she teased. "You've been embarrassing me with that wave forever!"

Max hugged her and whispered in her ear, "You know you love it, babe."

Sarah clung to him so tightly that he took a step back and held her at arm's length, examining her cautiously. "What's happened?" he asked.

"Dr. Ken Jaffe happened, but it's all for the best. Please don't make a big deal about it. I just want to get to our table and sit and chat about everything and nothing."

Max eyed her intently but nodded as he took her hand and guided her inside. The restaurant enveloped them like an old friend, in that bone-deep way that only the most familiar spaces can. Sarah felt herself begin to relax. They were led to their usual table next to the window. Twenty-five years after first meeting up at Melon's with her mom's credit card, the two of them were part of the culture and history of the place.

"I can't wait to catch up!"

"It's only been a day," Max laughed.

"The *party*? Hello!"

He smiled and slapped his forehead with mock drama. "Oh my god, I forgot. Did you have a party?"

She burst out laughing. "Actually, *Carl* had a party," she said through her mirth. "And I had a date with destiny!"

They settled down, and Max watched her for a moment before he spoke.

"You okay?"

"More than okay."

He rubbed his hands together. "So, where to begin?"

"Okay, first of all, I can't thank you enough for inviting Leyla to the party." Sarah wasn't ready to get in too deep, too quickly, but this was as good a place to start as any. "She was a smash success with everyone—even my parents—and she added such a unique dimension to the night. Definitely text me her contact info—I want to see her again soon."

"Well, if I was going to go to the trouble of helping my BFF Carl plan a surprise party for you, I was certainly going to have a little fun with it! Give it the old Max razzle-dazzle. If I'd have let Carl go rogue, it would have been a rubber-chicken dinner at one of his boring clubs."

It was no secret that Max and Carl had agreed to disagree for as long as any of them could remember. Carl thought Max was loud and obnoxious, totally lacking in depth or morals; Max thought Carl was a smug, judgmental bro who loved Sarah for all the wrong reasons—most of all her Platinum Card.

Sarah laughed. "Wow, conspiring with my husband to throw a birthday party for your best and oldest friend. The ultimate sacrifice." She rolled her eyes.

"No offense, but I was honestly shocked that he remembered your birthday, or wanted to throw an event where the spotlight wasn't on him," Max sniffed. "*Not* shocked that he was taking full credit for planning *and* paying for it. As if his mid-level salary could pay for the freaking Temple of Dendur!"

"Um, offense taken," said Sarah. Why did she bristle when Max put words to feelings she already had? It was if he was the one with the psychic powers. "Next!"

Ever since they'd been teenagers they'd jump from topic to topic, hopping from their deepest fears to the shallowest gossip. But if something cut too close to the bone, one of them would say "Next" and they'd move on. No questions asked.

"Wait, you want to see Leyla Sullivan *the psychic* again? Like, as a *client*? Who are you and what have you done with my best friend?"

"Ha-ha, not funny. I happen to have found Leyla fascinating, and her insights were uncannily accurate. Isn't it natural for me to be curious about it all?"

Max placed his hand on hers. "Sarah, I say this with the deepest love, but you are the world's biggest skeptic. You don't buy into any woo-woo mumbo-jumbo. I know that better than anyone, because I've been trying to open your mind for practically our entire lives. Why now?"

"Not totally fair. I mean, I create fragrances for a living. Have you heard? That takes a bit of creativity and intuition—give me some credit!" She paused. "But seriously, you're right. It's time to call in the psychics."

Sarah stared at her dearest friend. Max could probably see the trepidation all over her face.

"Wait! We need wine for this!" He flagged over the waiter who'd been their favorite since their high school days. "Hey Charlie, please bring us our usual bottle—and put a backup on reserve, just in case." Max winked at Sarah.

Once the wine was poured and their lunch order taken, Max leaned in conspiratorially.

"Okay, so first of all I have to know—is any of this related to the whole I-may-not-be-in-love-with-my-husband bombshell you dropped on Saturday?"

"Yes. No. I don't know, Max. It's all happening so fast—and at the same time it feels like it's been brewing for ages, you know?"

He nodded. "Totally. Go on."

"I feel as if I'm in some sort of free fall." She took a sip of cabernet. "But the part that's the most confusing is that I don't want it to stop. What the hell, right? I should want to stop it, but I don't. It's like I'm being called by something outside myself to let go and allow this." She had another sip of wine. "God, listen to me, I sound like I'm batshit crazy. Please tell me I'm not going insane."

Max wrapped his hand around the back of Sarah's neck and pulled her close. "Look at me, darling. You are the sanest person I care to hang out with. You're not crazy at all—you're smart and brave and annoyingly capable, which is why you're scared, or cautious, or call it what you want. Whatever is happening and wherever it's taking you, I'm here for the ride. I say *go for it!*"

Sarah laughed. "Of course you do, my daredevil, bungee-jumping, skydive-loving, live-like-you're-dying best friend. But that isn't *me*. I'm reliable and steady. I have kids and a business to run. I can't let anyone down."

"Sweetheart, why do you burden yourself with the impossible weight of not letting anyone down? It's an unattainable goal and a deep betrayal to yourself."

"Why is it a betrayal to myself?"

"Because by constantly trying to please everyone else and be everything you think *they* need you to be, the only person you're letting down and hurting is *you*. I think you're finally realizing that living like that is not sustainable. My best guess is that you're starting to remember who you really are, to recapture who you really are. To own it."

Sarah sighed and took another sip of wine.

"And what you really want and desire from life—I'm not talking about money or prestige—I'm talking about what nourishes your heart and soul." Max held her gaze intently as he continued. "You're right, you *are* one of the most creative people I know, or anyone knows. Arcanum, the fragrances you design—they're like whole worlds or time travel or faraway lands in a bottle. But that expansiveness, that expressiveness—you confine it to your work."

Shoot, he was right.

Max continued, "I want this journey for you, Sarah. I have waited patiently for this day to come."

"Damn you, Max. Sometimes your knowing me so well is annoying as hell. I said, I'm drawn to following this path. Why else am I even considering seeing Leyla again? But at what cost? I don't know if I have the emotional reserves to foot the proverbial bill for this. It feels like I'm just being selfish." She looked out the front window at the world passing by on Third Avenue. "I can't hurt my kids. I can't hurt my family."

"Whoa, whoa, whoa. Who said anything about hurting the

kids?" Max lifted her chin with his finger. "Let me ask you a question, okay?"

Sarah nodded.

"How did you feel with Harry at the party?"

She inhaled quickly and pulled away from Max's touch, unable to look him in the eye and let him see the raw truth there.

"Yup," he grinned, "just what I thought."

Sarah sat up straighter and tried to pull herself together. "What the hell does Harry Aiken have to do with any of this?" She stage-whispered his name, like it was some sort of STD. "I mean, I only met the man for twenty minutes, tops."

"Sarah, honey," Max smirked. "You can try to fool yourself, but you can't fool me. I was there with both of you while we walked you home. There was enough electricity to light up Central Park. You seemed more alive during that brief stroll than you have in years."

Sarah covered her face with her hands, then peered over the tops of her fingers. "Oh god, I know! Shit, shit, shit. It was like I got struck by lightning. I mean, he is so fucking *hot*, right?"

Max smiled. "Check."

"I never wanted that walk to end, not just because he's like this shot of adrenaline to the heart, but as you said, I just felt so alive when I was with him. So myself. And excited and all that, but also so easy in his company. Don't even get me started on that laugh—? It should be criminal."

"Check. Check. Check."

"I wonder what the story with his wife was. Why he's been single all these years. Maybe *I* should have been single all these years. Ugh, listen to me, I sound crazy!" Sarah took another sip of wine, then fixed a determined look on her face. "It's probably for the best if I don't see him again. He's too dangerous for me, for my life."

"Never see him again?" Max nearly spat out his wine. "Are you nuts? You *have* to see him again! How else will you find out what the hell is going on between the two of you? Besides," he added smugly, "you already agreed to meet with him to discuss your new Arcanum Foundation and his interest in becoming involved."

"As if I've never canceled a business meeting? Thanks to my mother, I'm the queen of a firm-but-polite 'no.'"

The waiter delivered their cheeseburgers, and they each took a few bites.

"Come on, then," Max started on a different tack. "If you're so professional and all that, and he's such a rich, generous, corporate raider-type guy who's really interested in saving the earth and whatnot—"

Sarah laughed again. "Blah blah—climate change—blah blah—rich guy—blah blah—"

"Time is short!" Max laughed as he circled his hand in the air to indicate she knew perfectly well what he meant by his verbal shorthand. "You need to get to the bottom of whatever this is between the two of you."

"Last time I checked, I was married."

"Last time I checked, you weren't *dead.*"

"Always rooting for Carl, aren't you!"

He refilled their wine glasses. "No comment."

"Very well," she continued. "You're right—"

"*Yessss!*"

"I'm a grown-up," Sarah continued. "I can keep this completely professional. Getting Harry involved will be a big win for the foundation, and that will be my sole focus. Purely a business arrangement," she added, mostly to herself.

"Mm-hmm, exactly," Max nodded, with a knowing glint in his eye.

"Now, tell me what happened with that scumbag Ken."

Sarah chuckled. "Why do you think he's a scumbag?"

"Seriously? Did he sign you up for a new culty intensive ninety-day program? To pay for a pool for the Hamptons house you practically bought him from the proceeds of the last program?"

"Well, that scumbag just happened to help me through two of the roughest patches of my life—"

"Snore."

"You don't think they were rough patches?"

"Of course I do! It was absolute misery—you were bereft after that French *desastre* and even more so when you were trying to get pregnant. I was there. But when someone you love is miserable, you do everything in your power to build them up. Doc Jaffe didn't empower you, he brainwashed you into codependency. Like you needed him to stay in your life, to be your support, to be needed."

"You're *just now* thinking of saying this to me?"

"Just now? I've tried to say this to you in a million different ways, but yeah, I'm giving it to you straight right now. You seem more receptive or something. Tell me to shut up if you want. But answer me this—is there a new prescription for something or other in your purse?"

Sarah took a deep breath. How could she be angry with him when he was so right? "Next!"

Max raised both hands in an "I surrender" gesture and smiled a huge grin. "How about your aunt's 1974 pink polyester halter dress Saturday night? What's your vote—a stroke of sartorial genius or a spilled bottle of calamine lotion?"

"Stop!" Sarah burst out laughing. "Total stroke of genius, of course! Who else but Sadie could pull it off. And what about all the ruffles? She's such a nut."

And just like that, they were back. They spent the rest of the meal laughing about everyone at the party and strategically avoiding any further mention of Carl, Dr. Ken Jaffe, or Harry Aiken.

CHAPTER THIRTEEN

November 1

The Uber wound its way through the maze of lower Manhattan. Sarah always felt like a fish out of water when she came this far downtown. How could she call herself a New Yorker yet not know anything about half the island of Manhattan? It always nagged at her. Maybe if she'd moved back to New York after college, as most of her friends had, she would have wandered these cobblestone streets, shared an East Village apartment with roommates, danced in secret after-hours clubs. Instead, she probably knew Paris better than she did this part of town. After moving back to New York as the newly wed Mrs. Carl McDonough, she'd gone with the flow and returned to the very Upper East Side life of her parents and Carl.

Wow, Max was right! she thought. *For an industry-changing, globe-trotting fragrance guru, my life certainly seems pretty plain vanilla!* She looked down at her expensive but boring black cashmere slacks and frowned.

And speaking of vanilla, the sex she and Carl were having these days wasn't even *French* vanilla. She was a professional nose, dammit, and she knew better than anyone that even vanilla could be Tahitian, Mexican, Madagascan . . . *exotic*. But this sex was off-the-shelf, middling, flavorless ice cream from the carton—and neither of them was going back for seconds.

Now Harry, on the other hand, she thought. No vanilla there. What would sex with *him* be like? His smooth, cafe au lait skin, what she imagined was a rippled, tan torso . . . She already knew that he smelled amazing. Like the rarest dark chocolate, flecked with gold and spice, surprising to the tongue . . . *Jesus, Sarah, grab hold of yourself!*

She took a deep breath as the car turned onto the West Side Highway and made its way to Leyla Sullivan's loft in SoHo.

Of course Leyla lives in a loft in SoHo, Sarah mused. *Clearly the psychic business is booming. Glad I'm not the only crazy person out there.* Sarah chuckled out loud at that thought just as the Uber pulled up to the building. She walked to the intercom and called up; with a loud buzzing the massive front door unlocked.

Sarah stepped off the freight elevator directly into Leyla's foyer.

"Please come in, Sarah. It's good to see you again," Leyla said, motioning to her to follow her inside. As always, Sarah noticed the scent of the place first—strong coffee, musty rare books, vintage woven rugs, sandalwood incense. The double-height space looked right out of a '70s Woody Allen movie—open and airy, with white walls and industrial wood floors. The interior was filled with light from nearly floor-to-ceiling casement windows bordering the loft. Massive whitewashed columns punctuated the space. The walls were chockablock with tribal masks, architectural fragments, photographs, paintings, driftwood, seashells—what seemed like several decades' worth of collected treasures.

"Wow!" Sarah took off her coat and hung it over the back of a mid-century modern chair she recognized from MoMA. "Your place is amazing. What a find."

Leyla smiled, as if she were used to hearing it. "This loft was my grandmother's back when the neighborhood was all abandoned industrial buildings, rough and tumble. You can still see marks on the floor from the patternmaking tables when it was a sewing factory. Trust me when I say that even when I was a girl, you'd have thought twice about coming down here. But my grandmother knew it was special, and that someday SoHo would be discovered. 'Good bones,' she always said."

Leyla gestured for Sarah to sit down on the Chesterfield leather sofa, kilims draped across the back. "Nan adored the architecture, so she bought the block. Then . . ." she shrugged sheepishly, "after my mom passed, it all came to me."

"Clearly your grandmother had some clairvoyant insight into the future of lower Manhattan," Sarah chuckled. "What a great investment!"

Leyla looked more closely at Sarah and smiled. "Where do you think I get my gifts? For generations, the female lineage in my family has been graced with psychic . . . powers. I know it may sound odd to the layperson, but I promise you that we're all very normal and well-adjusted."

Sarah nodded. "No, I am much the same. It was my grandmother who gave me my gift for fragrance, I'm certain of it. I learned the capability and art of scent from her at a young age. Psychic powers? I'm not sure, but these days it feels like it."

"Hold that thought," Leyla said as she turned toward the kitchen. "Let me get you something to drink—coffee? matcha?—and then we'll get started."

While Leyla put together a lovely tray with tea and a few biscotti, Sarah scanned the massive built-in bookshelves, filled top to bottom with leather-bound volumes, art monographs, dog-eared travel guides, maps. Upon closer inspection, she recognized books in at least five different languages, plus several others she couldn't decipher.

"Do you speak all these languages?" she asked.

Leyla shrugged modestly, setting down the tray on the mosaic-topped coffee table. "Yes. Most of these books are mine, but some of the more valuable antique volumes belonged to my parents and grandparents. My mother's family is French, and my father's family hails from Italy and Scandinavia."

Sarah nodded. In the center of the table were candles, crystals, geodes. There were stacks of tarot card decks, including the one Sarah had selected at her birthday party.

"My goodness! Why so many card decks?"

"These are mostly tarot decks, but there are a few oracle decks here as well," Leyla said.

Sarah took a sip of the aromatic white tea. "What are oracle decks?"

"Tarot cards are like pages in a book. Each card is one page telling the story—whereas oracle cards are like the whole chapter. A wider section of the story. Most people tend to do multiple tarot readings in one session, compared to a single oracle card reading. Oracle cards are more thematic in design, so they can often illuminate the overall energy and situation around your questions."

Sarah tried not to be cynical. "Okayyyy. . . ."

Leyla smiled. "All these languages that I can read? Well, tarot is one of them. The way the cards fall forms a narrative. It's an ancient language with great wisdom and insights. I'll explain everything as we go."

Sarah wanted to believe her, she really did, but her apprehension betrayed her.

"I have to be honest, Leyla—I don't understand any of this," she blurted out. "But your reading at my party was dead-on. Please don't mistake my hesitancy for disrespect. It's just. . . ."

"A lot?"

"Exactly. It's just a *lot*. But that said, I can't ignore this voice inside me that keeps telling me I need to work with you. I have a lot of questions about my current direction in life, and I'd be really grateful for your help." She brushed away a tear.

Leyla reached across the table and placed her hand on top of Sarah's.

"Sarah, dear, look at me," she gently said. "Moments like this in life make all the difference. It takes courage to sit here with me, asking these questions and seeking answers you know are within you. Trust me, people rarely come to me when life is going swimmingly. This work is meant to be a life raft when you feel adrift in a rough sea." She squeezed Sarah's hand, then sat back. "Now let's begin."

————

Stop holding your breath, Sarah told herself as she watched Leyla deftly shuffle each deck. There was some sort of ritual being followed, one that Sarah didn't dare interrupt. She took the opportunity to study Leyla carefully. She was probably in her late thirties; her thick raven hair, peppered with a few grays, was pulled back with an ornamental clip into a loose bun. She was quite attractive, with twinkly eyes and age-appropriate smile lines, and no makeup except for a pop of berry lip tint. This must be her "work uniform," Sarah thought: flowy black tunic, black leggings, black Birkenstock Arizona sandals. An armful of engraved gold bracelets jangled as she shuffled.

Once she'd finished, she turned to Sarah. "This session will be quite different from our time together at your party," she said. "That was like speed dating. Today will be a deep dive into any and all topics—things that may be causing you to feel confused or overwhelmed. There's no right or wrong question, so don't feel intimidated to mention anything, no matter how trivial you may believe it to be—or how huge. So, what is your first question?"

Sarah felt shy—but she trusted this sage person, so she willed herself to speak. She leaned in, then whispered, "What is happening to me right now? When you said at my party that

I seemed to be *breaking open,* I had thought those exact same words. I'm scared—and excited, if I'm being honest. I need to understand what's happening and where it may be taking me."

Leyla paused. "I remember exactly what I said that night, Sarah, which is unusual, because I don't always remember specifics when I channel. But your reading was very powerful. Let's take a look."

Leyla picked up a deck and shuffled it. "This is a chakra oracle deck, which will allow me to tap into your general energy right now. Once I'm in your energy field, I'll be able to channel quite freely with or without the cards."

Sarah was surprised when four cards shot out onto the table. "Do they always fly out like that?"

"Yes," Leyla smiled. "When I work in this manner, I allow the cards to decide rather than selecting them myself."

She arranged the four cards in a row, then turned them over.

"It seems you are experiencing a maelstrom of emotions right now. Of the four cards, you have three that are sacral chakra–based. Do you know about chakras and their meanings?"

Sarah shook her head. "I've heard of chakras, of course, but I don't know anything about them."

"Okay, good—that way you don't have any preconceived notions. There are seven chakras, or energy points, located along the center meridian of the body. Each has its own qualities and ability to influence us as we navigate life."

She pointed to a spot on the body illustrated on the card. "You are mostly in the sacral chakra now—the orange one right here, where a woman's womb is located. It is the energy center that dictates our desires and passions. It oversees the elements and feelings in the world that make life fulfilling and pleasurable. Our sensuality and sexuality are generated from here, as are our creative juices and emotional stability." She looked up. "Are you following so far?"

Sarah nodded, shifting nervously. *Is it getting hot in here?* she thought.

"Good. So the three sacral cards that flew out tell me you are on an emotional roller coaster at the moment. It feels as if your nervous system is in overdrive. Like your reptilian brain is in full fight-or-flight mode. See—" she pointed to each card as she spoke, "the three themes of Emotions, Desire, and Sensuality? The cards are telling me that your everyday life right now is not aligned with your truest desires and is not nourishing you. As a result, your emotions are very unstable. Does this feel right to you?"

"It does," Sarah said. "But I wouldn't have been able to describe it like that."

"The final card is the base chakra of Home," Leyla continued. "The base chakra is all about our foundations, what makes us feel safe and protected. It's our root chakra, our main power station. But I'm seeing that this home energy is in flux for you, as if you are not feeling safe at home."

Leyla paused, and Sarah gathered her thoughts.

"There are many ways of feeling unsafe or unstable in our lives," Leyla continued. "As you can see, sometimes the messages I share are difficult. Is this too much? Just let me know, and we'll move on to another topic."

Sarah felt the tears welling up again. "No. It's fine. This is why I'm here, even though it may not be easy. Please continue."

Leyla chose a different deck and shuffled the same way as before. The cards flew out, and she reverently arranged them on the table.

"This is a tarot deck," said Leyla. "I probably explained the tarot to you when we met at your party, but let me briefly explain it again. It is a seventy-eight-card deck, and just like a traditional deck of playing cards, there are four suits. But the suits in the tarot align with the four parts of the self—physical, mental, emotional, and spiritual. There are also twenty-two themed cards called the Major Arcana. Of the five cards that flew out for you, four are majors, which tells us that this situation is very important to your soul's path and destiny in this lifetime."

Sarah looked up; she wasn't sure if she was frightened, delighted, or both. "I probably told *you* when we met that Arcanum is the name of my fragrance company. The grandmother I just told you about? She had two passions: fragrance and tarot. I remembered the word *arcana* when I was looking for a name that would explain how I work, how I'm inspired to build a perfume over centuries, countries, art forms. It just seemed to fit—and it reminds me of her." Her eyes welled up again, as she knew Leyla's next words would open a Pandora's box that could never be closed again.

"*Tell me,*" Sarah whispered.

Leyla cleared her throat. "Given these cards, I am very glad you are here. You . . . your life is out of alignment. You manage quite well, splendidly by all outward accounts, especially given the masks you wear and the truths you bury."

Sarah felt the heat rising up her neck. She fanned herself a little.

"But it seems that the weight of the masks has become too heavy. And many long-ignored intuitions are bubbling to the surface." Leyla glanced at Sarah. "Perhaps *raging* to the surface?"

Sarah hesitated. "How can a deck of cards tell you all of this?"

"Let me explain. Here we have the Moon card, which indicates that things aren't as they appear to be. In this instance, it alludes to a difficult period of confusion, fear, and truths that you either can't yet see or can't admit to yourself. But it is also hopeful, since the journey through the shadows is entirely in the service of reentering the light, which is the truth."

She continued. "The next card is the Tower, which is a card of unexpected—and sometimes unwelcome—change. These changes can be in our physical world, through our jobs or our bodies. Or it can be a mental change—through a sudden, unwelcome realization, for example. While the Tower may indicate a difficult experience to live through or digest, trust me when I say that it's a necessary and important part of reaching our goals. No way around but through, right?"

Sarah nodded. She felt exposed and vulnerable. But she also felt safe with Leyla, as if she were in the best possible hands for what was to come.

"Then the Devil card speaks. Please don't think this has anything to do with satanic matters. The Devil simply reveals where we're stuck in fear-based patterns, beliefs, or situations. It tells me that there are deep-seated fears and behaviors woven into the fabric of your life right now, patterns that are making life profoundly uncomfortable."

Was it *relief* that she was suddenly feeling? Whatever was happening, Sarah was beginning to feel neither alone nor insane.

"The Eight of Swords is next. Swords is the suit of our mental body—our thoughts, perceptions, where we get intellectual clarity. The Eight of Swords conveys difficulty or struggle, indicating repetitive thoughts that might make you feel trapped or stuck."

Sarah let out a low whistle. "That about sums it up."

"Those kinds of thought patterns can make you feel helpless—as if you have nowhere to turn, or that your only so-called options aren't really options at all, since they would upend your life."

"Ditto."

Leyla held up the final card. "Last is the Death card. As I might have mentioned at your first reading, this doesn't have anything to do with dying. It tells me that you are at the beginning of a huge transition. With the Death card, life will transform. How this happens is completely in your hands, but"—she looked at Sarah—"I will share that transformation is often much easier if you embrace the truth of it, if you allow it to unfold naturally rather than try to fight it or try to protect something that may already be broken."

Sarah closed her eyes for a moment, then opened them. "Tell me, Leyla, do you believe in predicting the future?"

"What I know to be true, Sarah, is that we all have free will, which makes it impossible to predict the future. Having said that, I do have remarkable accuracy and a high probability rate about how things are likely to play out for my clients. But no, nothing is set in stone."

"Okay. Good." Sarah exhaled; she didn't realize she'd been holding her breath again. "So, is it possible to explain all of this in layman's terms? I'm following, and honestly you have once again blown me away. But let's review."

"Happy to, Sarah," Leyla said. "I get it. Even I get muddled with too much tarot lingo and not enough straight talk! So it seems you are on a relatively new emotional journey that has you . . . terrified. Your innate sense of duty and loyalty to your family has served you well. But something happened recently that has compelled you to look at life with new and honest eyes. I say this with no judgment toward your life or your husband, but it seems like your inner fire has gone out. Your passion—spark, sense of fulfillment, whatever you'd like to call it—is quite low. It's as if you are starving for connection and inspiration. I know that you know exactly what I'm saying. You've arrived at the proverbial fork in the road. Something has already happened, but you are not ready to turn and follow it. And that's okay! Just please try to be gentle with yourself right now. It can become overwhelming if you rush toward it, or away from it."

Leyla again placed her hand on top of Sarah's, giving her a squeeze. "It's going to be okay. Trust me when I say that. Given the energy of this reading, I am honestly quite relieved that this process has finally started for you."

Sarah turned her head slightly and sat still, staring out the window into the clear autumn sky. "How? How do you know all of this so clearly when I haven't even been able to articulate it myself?" She stood up and started to pace.

"I hope you don't mind, Leyla, but I seem to do my best processing while I'm on the move. It's the only reason I still put up with running."

Leyla smiled and invited her with a wave to use the entire loft. "Trust me, I have witnessed countless clients pace where you are right now. Good thing I have a pretty sizeable loft! You may be surprised to know that even after all this time, the cards never cease to amaze me, either."

Sarah paced back and forth, silently rubbing her hands together and nodding to herself occasionally. After a few minutes, she stopped. "Damn it! Damn it, *damn* it!" She pivoted to face Leyla. "Why *me*? Why can't I just be *content* with my life? Why do I feel things so deeply? Why can't I live life more loosely? Like Max? Seriously, take Max. I've known him almost all my life, and despite everything he has had to navigate, Max just floats through life. He doesn't take anything personally. He's never embarrassed. He embraces any experience with openness and curiosity. He welcomes anyone into his life—and into his bed, for that matter—without worrying about judgment or fallout. How do I live *that* kind of life?"

Leyla rose and walked over to Sarah. Without a word, she pulled her into a tight hug. Sarah began to weep.

"Let it out, Sarah. Let it all out. It is long overdue."

"But I'm getting your nice tunic wet," she protested. "I hate crying. It makes me feel weak."

Leyla took her by the shoulders. "Sarah Fuller, look at me. You are one of the strongest, most successful women in this city—a city known for eating thousands of people alive and spitting them out every day. Do not for one moment entertain the notion you are weak. You are, however, human. You need to cry just like the rest of us mere mortals. Don't burden yourself with comparisons to Max or anyone else, for that matter. Your path is your own, and therefore it is perfect. You may be in an uncomfortable part of the journey, but have faith. I see a remarkable outcome—one you absolutely deserve. All you need to do is to trust that you'll make it happen."

Sarah wiped her messy tears. "Thank you, Leyla. I'm overwhelmed and a bit unnerved, but thank you. I just have one more question. . . ."

"Yes?"

"When can I see you again?"

CHAPTER FOURTEEN

November 7

hy? Why today of all days?

Sarah sped through the revolving door of the Midtown building that housed Arcanum Fragrances—and also, more recently, the Arcanum Foundation as well. She prided herself on never racing anywhere; she was notorious for her punctuality and expected the same in return. She thrived when she was in control professionally. Yet here she was, frantically late for her own meeting to pitch her brand-new foundation to none other than Harry Aiken.

I never should have gotten out of bed today.

At six that morning, an hour before her alarm was set to go off, Sarah was awake and staring at the ceiling, filled with a sense of possibility that the day could be exciting. She admitted to herself that she was eager to see Harry again—but not because she intended to pursue anything romantic with him. Wasn't he just a great guy who would be an amazing asset for the foundation?

Ever since her lunch with Max, she'd been able to convince herself that a professional relationship was totally doable. A best-of-both-worlds scenario. She'd psyched herself up—this was a phenomenal business opportunity. Full stop.

But as daylight crept into her bedroom, she hadn't been able to stop the momentary sensations of his hand touching the small of her back as he guided her down the steps of the Met, the intensity in his eyes when he looked at her, the shape of his mouth when he smiled.

Stop it! she chided herself. *Do not go there!*

Instead, she turned and traced Carl's bare spine from his neck down to his Brooks Brothers pajama pants. *Look at this gorgeous man lying next to you, woman!* When they walked down Madison Avenue together, she saw female heads a lot younger and hotter than hers crane to get a look at Carl.

Carl began to stir. If she knew her husband, she knew he woke up with a raging hard-on. *Probably provoked by dreams of looking at his own reflection in the mirror.*

No! Get in the moment! Her hand slid under his waistband, over his thigh, and into the warmth of his erection. *Old Faithful. Let's do this.*

Not ten minutes later the marital deed was done. *Meh,* Sarah thought.

Hey, Old Sarah told herself, *sex doesn't always have to be mind-blowing! But how long had it been since it was?* asked New Sarah. *Since before I was the breadwinner, since before the twins.* Talk about truths—now there was one. She and Carl had been growing apart for years.

Also true: she was now running ten minutes late, and she had to get the kids to school. Sarah always took them on Thursdays—though with Carl's light schedule he could easily do drop-off every day. She took a scalding-hot shower, put on her most conservative, unsexy, unflattering pantsuit, and headed to the kitchen to get a cup of coffee. Sarah turned her full attention to the twins. Luckily, they were at an age where they could mostly tend to themselves and their morning routine. She had breakfast waiting when they entered the kitchen, semi-dressed and bookbags semi-packed.

"Kids, eat up. I have to hurry today. I have a big presentation for the new foundation."

"Mom—eggs and bacon? You *know* I'm a vegan now," said Alex, frowning.

"Since when? We all had burgers together on my birthday exactly one month ago!"

"Since we have a pig dissection next Monday and she wants to get out of it," Sam said, rolling his eyes. "Speaking of, you have to sign our permission slips."

"Well, don't bother with mine," Alex said, crossing her arms. "I'm protesting."

Whose hard-headed, fiery daughter is this? Sarah said to herself. *Acorn: oak. I get it. Still, I gotta get out the door.*

"Sounds great, honey. Sam, put your dishes in the sink. Alex, grab a Clif Bar and let's get outta here."

Twenty minutes behind schedule. Wish I'd reviewed my presentation instead of mom-guilt frying up bacon! And now I smell like bacon. Perfect, just perfect.

The three of them rushed out the door, bickered in the elevator, and emerged from the building barely speaking to each other. The walk was unnaturally quiet. She dropped them at the front doors of their fancy private school and waved goodbye.

Doing a great job, Mom! she thought to herself. *Quality time, my ass.*

My ass needs to get to midtown in fifteen minutes!

———

Sarah walked into her office saying hello to everyone she passed, but her stride made it clear that she wasn't in a mood to be distracted. Once she sat down at her desk, she started to feel like her professional self again.

Gerard walked in with his ever-present smile and a stack of papers. He raised his nose in the air. "Bacon?"

"Yes. Good morning, Gerard."

"Good morning, Sarah," he sang out as he put down the papers, then started swiping down his tablet. "Can you sign those? Also, I've printed out the prospectus for your twelve o'clock. Your two o'clock asked to reschedule on Monday."

"Thank fuck," she murmured.

"Do I even ask?" He looked up and winked.

"I wouldn't if I were you," Sarah replied with a smile, as she began looking over the letters he'd given her to sign.

"Is Harry Aiken here yet?" she asked without looking up.

Gerard took a seat across from her. "No. He just called a minute ago to apologize—he's running about forty-five minutes late."

"That would've been nice to know forty-five minutes ago," she said.

"Right? Whatever." Gerard rolled his eyes dramatically. "The Secret Bachelor is a big fish, we get it. Normally I'd have rescheduled right away—but I know this is an important meeting for us. Plus, I figured it would give you time to catch your breath before you try to lure him in."

Sarah was no stranger to lures, pitches, and deal-closing, but this time her stomach was all butterflies. "You're right," she replied. "I'm glad to have the extra time to prepare. Let's grab a coffee and Stuart and run through the deck one more time."

Stuart Adler walked into her office cradling three coffees. "Are we testing a bacon fragrance now?"

"*I'm* the nose around here, everyone," said Sarah, mock-frowning. "Stop interviewing for the position!"

The Arcanum Foundation was Sarah's new baby—she didn't plan on having another kid herself. The splendors of the natural world had been her partners in business and in life for many years now. There was nowhere she felt more at home than in the fields with the flowers, herbs, and other plants that made her fragrances and nowhere she felt more alive than in an unfamiliar landscape that presented new inspiration. The Earth had generously given her these gifts, and now it was her turn to give back through her foundation.

In communities around the world that produced natural ingredients precious to the fragrance industry, Arcanum had identified local partners to ensure the health and sustainability of these environments—as well as the workers themselves. For example, in Madagascar, the world's biggest producer of vanilla beans, the Arcanum Foundation collaborated with the island's numerous small producers to preserve and teach traditional methods of growth and extraction, and to ensure that workers were supported with suitable living conditions, food security, and education. Future targets for the foundation's work included Finland, Northern Spain, Egypt, and other sites in Africa. Sarah was passionate about this work, and she hoped that the twins would also nurture the foundation when they grew older.

After reviewing her presentation with Gerard and Stuart, Sarah felt much more settled. "Can you make sure that everything is ready in the conference room?" she said. "I need five minutes."

It's just another business meeting. You've got this, Sarah. Get in. Wow him. Get out.

Then the memory of seeing Harry at the Met hit her—how time seemed to dissolve, how that sense of coming home engulfed her. She felt dizzy. She felt hot. She still smelled like bacon. *Damn it, Sarah Fuller. This is so not business, and you know it.*

She leaned over the desk and buried her face in her hands.

Gerard poked his head around the corner. "Harry Aiken is in the conference room."

Harry turned from the floor-to-ceiling window as soon as he heard the door open. Maybe even *before* he heard the door open, as if he'd sensed she was near.

Sarah had intended to stroll in, all cool and unaffected, but as soon as her eyes locked with his she slowly closed the door behind her and froze. There it was. The *frisson* was palpable, and she felt the electricity coursing through her body. Harry was the first to move, and as he walked toward her he lifted both hands with the apparent intention of giving her some sort of Euro kiss on one or both cheeks. She stuck her hand out abruptly before he got too close.

"It's good to see you again, Harry. Thank you for taking the time to learn about what we are building here." She shook his hand as quickly as she could without being a total weirdo, then moved around the table to take her seat.

Pheromones, anyone? If I could have bottled whatever natural scent was emanating from his tanned skin, I'd be a billionaire. What would it be called? Eau Savage? No, already taken. Get a grip!

Harry, looking surprised, stood there staring at her—and then regained his composure. "Let me start by apologizing for being nearly an hour late. I'm never late, but this was unavoidable."

He seemed genuinely annoyed with himself. And fierce. Tightly controlled anger suited him.

Stop it, Sarah. She stood across the table from him and rested her hands on the back of her chair, forcing herself not to clench the leather upholstery. "No worries, I had an unexpected situation with my kids this morning."

"Oh, gosh, are they all right?"

His concern was so automatic, so real. So fucking competent. Fuck.

"Oh, nothing life threatening." She tried to laugh it off. "Just some early onset veganism." *What a dumb joke.*

"Tragic." He raked one hand through his hair and smiled.

He should not be allowed to do that in public. Breathe, Sarah. Just say it.

"I just wanted to tell you in person—which is kind of stupid I guess, since I'm basically admitting we probably shouldn't do it *in person*—"

Don't say it.

"—well, that I don't want you to misread. . . ." This was not going well. She gripped the back of the chair as if it were the last lifeline to the Titanic's last raft.

"That's all you need to say," Harry said, looking her straight in the eye. "I won't take up any more of your time, but I really do want to support the foundation. I'm sure everything is above board. Why don't we make this easier on both of us by having your assistant email my assistant the prospectus, and I'll review it tonight."

He didn't move. He just stood there—staring right into Sarah's soul.

Stop looking at me like that.

Don't ever stop looking at me like that.

He paused, reading her thoughts as easily as if she'd said them aloud.

"Or . . ."

Sarah held his gaze, making no effort to conceal her vulnerability and fear. And desire.

"Or?" she prompted.

"Or . . . we can just see if we can work together. Nothing shady. We're both grown-ups, right?"

"So I've been told." *But you make me feel like a teenager, damn it.*

Sarah walked slowly around the table toward him. "Okay, let's try this again." She approached him, taking a deep breath. "Harry, it's so lovely to see you again. I am very happy you could make time to be here."

As she reached him, she leaned in for that professional embrace—friends of friends and all that. Then her cheek neared his, and she heard his sharp inhale.

"Damn," Harry whispered into her neck, his warm breath caressing her as intimately as any touch. "I was half hoping I had imagined it."

Sarah took a step back and gazed into his eyes. "Me too, Harry. Me too."

She folded her hands in front of her—armor, maybe? "Grown-ups, right?"

"Grown-ups," he agreed.

She dimmed the lights, picked up the remote control, and started the video presentation. "So, let me tell you more about my foundation. Have a seat." After an hour of professional discourse—it helped to have the remote in one hand and a walnut conference table to steady the other hand—they finished what by all accounts was a terrifically successful meeting for the foundation. Harry made a verbal commitment to fully sponsor the Turkey initiative, intended to preserve that country's jasmine industry, and shared the names and contact details of several other VC guys that she'd been trying to lure for months.

As Sarah walked Harry to the elevators, he turned slowly toward her and scanned the hallway for other people. "Sarah, I have to be honest, I'm not ready to say goodbye yet. Are you?"

"No," she said quietly, heat rising to her cheeks.

"It's such a beautiful day. How about I take you to lunch?"

"Hmmm. . . ."

"Just a hot dog on a park bench. Totally legit."

She leaned her head to one side. "I can't stay long. I have to pick up the kids at three o'clock sharp."

"Of course."

The voice in her head shouting *DO IT* was too loud to ignore. "Let me grab my coat. I'll be right back."

As she strode back to her office, waves of emotion crashed through her—desire, glee, nervousness, guilt, hope, nausea—and then an unexpected peace. What was happening?

She whipped out her phone and shot a quick text to Max: *"Prince of the City just invited me for 'legit' lunch . . . hot dogs on park bench . . . your thoughts?"*

Two seconds later her phone pinged. *"Hmmm let me think . . . DUH! Go for it!!! You don't need my permission but you have it. Don't overthink it. Just do it."*

Sarah laughed. With renewed resolve, she grabbed her coat and went to join Harry.

————

It was five blocks to the Central Park Zoo entrance. This really was the quintessential crisp, just-turned-winter day; the leaves were still putting on quite the show. Sarah took in the familiar smells of fresh-cut grass, dried fallen leaves, taxi exhaust, roasting chestnuts. They strode deeper into the park until they neared the Boathouse.

"I have to confess, I kinda freaked out after I said yes to your lunch invitation, so I texted Max as I walked back to my office," she said.

Harry smiled. "And?"

She tried not to blush. "As expected, he told me to *go for it* with a zillion exclamation points."

She'd been aiming for levity—and completely missed the mark.

Harry stopped short and took her hand in his. "Sarah, I don't ever want you to feel uncomfortable with me or because of me. Just say the word and I'll back off. I genuinely want to keep our relationship professional." He hesitated. "For now."

She smiled up at him.

"I will do whatever you want," he said, still grasping her hand, "though I might not like it."

His words gave her a heady rush of power. She knew it in her bones. They had stood like this before. He had offered himself to her before.

And she had refused him.

How could she ever have refused this man? Why would she?

"That's the thing, Harry. What I *want* has nothing to do with what is *right*. Backing away is what I know is the right thing to do, but I'm realizing it's not what I want or need."

"Tell me why."

"It's hard to explain, but it feels like we share something big—huge—and this is so unlike me, I swear. But when I think of you—"

He smiled and interrupted, "You think of me?"

"Let me finish." She took another breath and continued. "When I think of you—what I *feel* for you—is not of this world or of this time. It feels like I already know you, which is ludicrous and—"

"No, it's not."

"I feel like I've *always* known you, and I really want to explore why that is. Is that even possible?"

Harry squeezed Sarah's hand as he nodded his agreement. "I would love nothing more. And I've got you, I promise."

He let go of her hand and they continued walking through the park.

The hot dog was the best thing Sarah had ever tasted. The stale potato chips might as well have been oysters on the half-shell. Being with Harry made everything . . . right. And delicious.

They walked and talked about nothing in particular. Sarah really wanted to ask him about his childhood and where he'd grown up—what made him who he was—but she decided there was no point in getting too personal. He made no mention of his wife, and she didn't ask. If they were going to make a serious effort to be work colleagues, it was better to keep it light.

She hadn't realized where they were walking but saw the glass walls of the Met reflected at the end of the path.

"Do you have time to go back into the Met and walk through the Egyptian collection again? I still have about forty-five minutes until I need to pick up the kids."

"That sounds great."

They went up the wide steps to the front entrance and walked into the museum.

Harry took a deep, satisfying breath when they got into the main entrance hall. "For as long as I can remember, I've been drawn to this place."

Sarah smiled. "I know exactly what you mean. I have been escaping to the Egyptian Wing since my first visit on a fourth-grade field trip. I immediately felt as if I were . . . home." She wanted to add that being around him gave her the same feeling, but what was the point?

A few minutes later, they were standing in the portico of the Temple of Dendur, side by side. The back of his hand grazed hers.

"Do you feel it, Sarah?" Harry whispered.

The room ceased to exist, as if they were floating outside the gravity of time and space. Reality dissolved. "Yes," she whispered, her voice unfamiliar to her own ears.

A few moments passed in that ethereal, electrifying silence. How could she possibly tell him that she was lost in a whirl of sensation, drawn to him with a magnetic pull stronger than anything she'd ever experienced? He was elemental, like water or fire. As they stood together, side by side, facing the past, she knew that they had been there before. None of it made any rational sense, but in her heart, she knew.

She turned to face him, intending to toss caution to the wind and share all these thoughts, when a group of middle-schoolers came barreling into the exhibition hall. The moment between them evaporated. Harry stepped away from the Temple and put some space between them.

"Kids will be kids," Sarah said.

"And grown-ups will be grown-ups," Harry added with a hint of a smile.

They shook hands and said their goodbyes out on Fifth Avenue, where Sarah got a cab and went to pick up her children.

And tried to pick up the threads of her *real* life.

CHAPTER FIFTEEN

Memphis, Ancient Egypt, two years later

"You are in danger of my sword piercing your heart in two seconds!" spat Meti. The point of the cold blade sent chills through her breast. Here it was, Sarrah realized—she had just overstepped her role as advisor and threatened the young Pharaoh's divine right. For the last two years she'd spent her days building his trust and her nights visiting his bed. Sarrah thought Meti would be pleased to learn the full range of abilities that, through her, he had within his power: her capacity to read people's thoughts and intentions; her ability to heal the sick and postpone death; her knowledge of how to plant both a baby in a woman's belly and an idea in a man's head.

How had she done this? Over these two years, having secured her role in the palace—free of everyday concerns such as food, clothing, and shelter—Sarrah had brought herself into conversation with her intuition and with the gods themselves. She'd meditated for hours at a time, channeling future events and even practicing bending them to her will. She'd gained fluency in the language of plants, experimenting with cures, salves, and poisons. She'd read the texts in the palace library—history books, medicine manuals, military records. She'd visited with priests, doctors, hetaerae, and elders. And when *they* didn't know the answers to her questions, she'd honed her ability to communicate with the gods. Through her incantations, the illumination of Ra, the wisdom of Thoth, the immortality of Osiris and Anubis, the seduction of Hathor, the war strategy of Montu: she had used them to advance her role as mentor to Meti, and in turn nourish the potential and future of Egypt.

With this knowledge brought confidence, even cockiness. And she'd gotten a little sloppy in allowing Meti to believe these ideas were his own. Without realizing it, Sarrah had questioned Meti's judgment too often. Was that *really* the right decision on that dispute between palace staff? *Was* that the true meaning of that poem? *Was* that a flattering color of tunic on him? *Would* his guests enjoy that menu?

His docility came to a halt when, in a military briefing, she touched his hand gently, almost imperceptibly, to indicate that he should listen and not interrupt as the two generals spoke. His comments were hasty and distracting, and she wanted to hear their full report. She was concerned about his father's intelligence in battle.

She had miscalculated.

Given Meti's burgeoning maturity and his inevitable rise to power, Sarrah hadn't accounted for the fragility of the young male ego—no matter how much power he wielded. She had wounded his pride.

In an instant, she'd become a threat.

The minute they returned to his chambers, he threw her against the wall and brandished his knife, eyes flashing. She could feel it starting to tear her robes.

"My lord," she implored, "please do not be angry with me. My abilities do not compare to your own. You are the Pharaoh, a living god! Yours is the divine right. You are the direct intermediary between humans and the gods. You possess the power and wisdom of all pharaohs before you. It is in your veins." She swallowed and felt the tip of the sword ease slightly from her skin. Sarrah held her breath as Meti paused in thought.

Sarrah knew she wasn't yet entirely indispensable to him. But she also knew that his codependence on her for reassurance, confidence, and decision-making was nearing an end. She finally exhaled when she saw Meti shake his head in acceptance, resheathing his knife.

"Yes, Sarrah, I possess all those powers. My control of them is almost complete. You have been my teacher and my guide in all things. My rule will be remembered as the most glorious era Egypt has ever seen.

"But if you cross or disrespect me," he said, his breath hot on her face, "I will kill you myself."

Sarrah knelt before him and raised her eyes to his. "It would be my honor, my king, to pass on all I have learned. I shall start right now with Hathor, goddess of pleasure and beauty," she said as she lowered her gaze, parted the folds of his tunic and brought her lips to his skin. "Let me show you pleasure like you have never felt before."

———

A short time later, Khufu barged into Meti's chambers. In the heat of their argument, Meti and Sarrah had forgotten to lock the door.

"Both of you, come with me at once!" demanded Khufu.

Meti rose from the bed, naked, to his full commanding height.

"Khufu, this is your final disrespectful act," he said quietly. His measured tone made him all the more imposing. "I have tried to be patient, at Sarrah's request—though why she would care for your welfare is beyond me. But this time you have overstepped every possible boundary."

"My king, I am here to advise you—"

"*Enough!*" Meti barked. He grabbed his tunic and pulled it carelessly over his head. Slowly attaching his sheathed knife to his belt, he glared at Khufu. "Not only have you disrespected the sacred privacy of your king, you disrespect me with your insolence. I will not overlook this violation. Guards!"

Khufu slammed the door behind him. "You can arrest me, but we do not have time for this argument now. You must finish getting dressed and race to the king's chambers immediately. It is your father. He has been brought back from the battlefield, and he is gravely injured. Hurry. Please hurry!"

Sarrah intervened. "Khufu, wait outside," she commanded, and he complied.

She touched Meti's shoulder gently. "Come, my king. We must hurry. Do not fear. Your father is strong and stubborn. He will not die without a fight."

She saw the fear on Meti's face. He suddenly looked so young and naive. How could she have forgotten that he was only nineteen? It was true that Meti was blessed with an innate maturity and masculinity that made him seem much older than his actual age. But here he was, looking at her like a child to his mother. She knew that she couldn't let the elder Pharaoh die today. She must keep him alive long enough to ensure Meti's readiness to ascend to the throne.

Meti hurried into the Pharaoh's chambers. Sarrah remained in the anteroom with the other staff and aides. The gravity of the situation was obvious as everyone grasped their figurines of Bastet—goddess of protection—and whispered prayers.

Sarrah leaned in close to the elder Pharaoh's valet. "What is the prognosis, Musa? Is it as bad as it looks?"

Musa looked at Sarrah with red, swollen eyes. "My lord is near death, Sarrah. He has numerous wounds, and he lost much blood during his journey home. It will take a miracle from Bastet herself to save him," he sobbed. Sarrah held Musa's hand, and he calmed considerably.

Meti stepped into the anteroom. He was as pale as Sarrah had ever seen him. He took her hand and drew her over to the window.

"Father is dying," he said quietly. "There's nothing to be done; he's lost so much blood. He is stable, but his body is too weak to heal. The doctor has done all he can do in this world. Sarrah, I don't know what to do."

She uncovered a clay pot the size of a fingernail from beneath her robes and put it in his hands. "Meti, take this tincture. This will stop the bleeding and fortify his blood, I promise you. I made it myself from mugwort and yarrow from my garden. The doctor won't like it; these herbs can be poisonous in large quantities, but I know this will work. Say nothing to the doctor. Ask for a moment alone with your father, then press this tincture into his wound. Whisper to him the incantation to Bastet that I have taught you to use in moments like this."

Meti looked trustingly into her eyes, then turned and disappeared through the drapery, the tincture hidden in his hand. Soon a silent procession of elders came back through the curtains: the doctor, the high priest, Khufu, the general, and— Hasim? What was he doing here? They exchanged a quick glance, but Hasim was lost in thought.

———

The anteroom was quiet, save for the hum of the crowd gathered outside the palace, praying and chanting. Sarrah gazed down on them through the windows, whispering the incantation to Bastet. In a matter of minutes, a sharp cry rose from the Pharaoh's room. Meti. She tensed as the elders flew back into his chambers.

Was this good news or bad news? Sarrah waited with the rest of the staff, but soon they could hear that the cries from the next room were not of despair but of joy.

Hasim parted the curtains, shaking his head, and addressed the noblemen and staff waiting there. "The Pharaoh is out of immediate danger. Such are the divine powers of his son Meti! Now, go tell all of Egypt this momentous news."

In the hustle and bustle, Hasim grabbed Sarrah's arm.

"What have you done?" he whispered into her ear. "Are you to be thanked for saving our Pharaoh? Does your loyalty to your leader run that deep?"

Sarrah kept her composure. "You are more observant than I gave you credit for, General. You must not tell a soul what you just saw or said. Do you understand?"

Hasim nodded. "You are more gifted than I gave *you* credit for, Sarrah. I myself brought the Pharaoh back from the warfront. His injuries were grave; I have his blood on my saddle and on myself to prove it," he said, pointing to his tunic. "No doctor at the battlefront or here in the palace was able to improve his condition; I was certain he was dead. I need no more validation that your powers over Meti are not limited to your remarkable beauty."

"I don't know whether I should be flattered or insulted," Sarrah whispered. "I thought I had had *you* under my spell for quite some time as well."

Hasim's eyebrows raised slightly, but he remained somber. This was no time for lightness.

"Your secret is safe with me," he said. "But please—let me help you get the young prince ready to lead. I know this is your reason for postponing our king's demise. I am in full support of Meti taking the throne and returning Egypt to its glory."

He pulled away. He was clearly exhausted and overcome with emotion. He grasped her shoulders. "Use me, Sarrah," he implored. "I will not let you down." She nodded, her gaze locked on his. What was this feeling—trust? She had a sense that she was no longer alone.

The curtains parted. "What is going on here, General? Remove your hands from my slave's body." Meti growled. He had recovered his composure.

Hasim dropped his hands and bowed deeply to the young

Pharaoh. "My lord," he said, "The lady almost fainted and I caught her fall. I meant no disrespect."

Meti turned to Sarrah, looking her up and down. "What is this? Are you all right?" She bowed. "Yes, sire. Please do not worry about me. I haven't eaten in hours and was feeling a bit lightheaded. It has passed."

As the crowds outside of the palace erupted in cheers of joy, Sarrah asked Meti, "How is the Pharaoh?"

"My father rests and is stable. The gods have deemed him worthy of life, and we shall all continue to pray and honor them on his behalf."

He turned and barked at Hasim, "Return to your post and instruct your soldiers to pray for their Pharaoh's recovery. Failure to do so will result in punishment and death." With that he put his arm around Sarrah's waist and led her out of the room. "You and I need to speak privately," he said under his breath.

Meti did not release Sarrah until they reached the Throne Room. He excused the guards and closed the door. Sarrah sank to her knees.

"Rise," Meti ordered. "You will look me in the eye as you explain how you saved the life of the greatest leader on earth."

Sarrah rose and looked at him earnestly and directly. "My lord, while you have been at your studies, I have been at mine. I have strengthened my mind and taught myself the powers of the spiritual realm, which have been revealed to me mostly through the plant world. My intuition is strong, and it told me it was not your father's time to pass. You are correct; I did pray and call upon Bastet to intercede. All of this I do for you." She grew quiet and took his hand.

She saw Meti's eyes soften, so she continued.

"Sire, *you* will soon be the most powerful man in the world. I knew this moment was one in which the world needed to see you heal your father, with the help of the gods."

Emboldened, she continued. "You have the divine power of the Pharaohs. I am here only to guide and assist you. I hope I have pleased you with my actions and have not overstepped my role."

Meti took her face in his hands. "You have my deepest thanks, Sarrah. I might need some time to process my father's passing into the afterlife. But I am ready. My father's blood and all the blood of the Pharaohs before him runs through my veins. I have been prepared for this moment since my first breath."

He leaned in close to Sarrah's ear and whispered. "Yet I must share that having you by my side as my lover, confidant, advisor, and—most importantly—my mystic infuses me with a confidence I would not have otherwise."

She did not dare move or speak.

"In much the same way, Hasim has been unfailingly loyal to my father. Of course, Khufu has the Pharaoh's ear on many decisions. But Hasim is like a second son. My father recognized him as a promising young soldier several years ago. He was just a poor villager, but he was smart, and ambitious, and devoted to the glory of Egypt. My father has provided for him and groomed him into a great military mind."

He looked at Sarrah with the searching eyes of a boy. "Sometimes I have even wondered if my father *prefers* Hasim to his own son. I appreciate Hasim's service to Egypt and his military intelligence, but I am not sure if his allegiance will transfer to me so easily. There has always been a tension between us."

Meti's gaze then hardened. "Recently I have wondered if you would prefer Hasim's company as well."

Sarrah gasped. "My king! How can you say—"

"Sarrah. You are the mystic, but I am a man. I can sense that there is something between you. I don't want to speak of it. But hear me now—I *cannot* be let down."

She knew that she was now destined to serve her Pharaoh and her Egypt for the remainder of her mortal life. "I will *never* let you down," she whispered.

Meti would soon be the Pharaoh. And Sarrah would soon wield a power greater than any mystic before her. As they stared into each other's eyes, a new sensation shifted into their bodies. Their souls were now and forever eternally bound.

CHAPTER SIXTEEN

The elder Pharaoh had clung to life for just a few short days. As his spirit left his body, news of his passing spread swiftly through the palace, then through the streets of Memphis. It traveled by horseback to the villages, the provinces of Egypt, and eventually to the battlefront, where his soldiers and the rebel forces both laid down their weapons. The pyramid into which the Pharaoh would be entombed had begun to be erected on the day of his birth, and soon his body would rest there.

Meti, too wrought with grief to do so himself, asked Sarrah to oversee the mummification of the body and the preparation of the mortuary complex in the hills overlooking the city. While she had been present for burials in her village, she'd certainly never witnessed a mummification, much less entered a funerary temple—few Egyptians had. Mummification was only for the wealthiest citizens. It was believed that it was easier for your *ka,* or soul, to repossess you in the afterlife if it could recognize your form. In the village they mimicked this by using the deceased's jewelry, clothing, and amulets. But for the Pharaoh, a team of artisans had been working on a life-size representation of him for years—a richly decorated mummy case of bronze inlaid with mosaic and gems.

Sarrah was fascinated by the embalming process, performed by priests wearing masks of Anubis, the jackal-headed god of the dead. Into the mummy case she slipped a fragrant oil derived from the lilies on the Nile riverbank, along with an amulet of Anubis—also considered to be the judge of the soul, guiding the Pharaoh into the afterlife. As the last wrap was secured with resin around the Pharaoh's body, she silently recited the ancient funerary incantations recorded in the palace texts.

Once everything was readied at the palace, on a clear morning at dawn Sarrah, Khufu, and scores of attendants began their horseback journey up the stone-paved trail winding to the mortuary complex in the high desert. Directly behind them was the funeral palanquin carrying the body of the Pharaoh. Next came a procession of camels loaded with rugs, sacred texts, food, wine, jewel boxes, and other essentials for the Pharaoh's comfort in the afterlife. Various military officials, doctors, and priests also traveled on horseback or in palanquins up the trail. General Hasim rode the Pharaoh's beloved steed, which would be entombed with him for eternity.

Sarrah had to admit that Khufu, who'd supervised the construction of this mortuary complex over the past few decades, had designed an architectural masterpiece. She felt in her bones that this was hallowed ground. The pyramid—an imposing stepped-stone structure visible from the city—rose in the center of a massive walled court. Adjacent to the pyramid was the mortuary temple, its grand pillared court currently abuzz with activity. Khufu ordered the teams here and there; this was his show. Slaves hustled the foodstuffs, furniture, and other objects to the storerooms; priests began the funerary rites in the chapel; and maids adorned the shrines to the Pharaoh with garlands of flowers.

That night slaves led the horses and camels, free of their cargo, back to Memphis. The high priests, royal advisors, Khufu, and Sarrah remained, sleeping in small tents. Sarrah didn't have to lay eyes on Hasim to know that he stood guard all night. He'd dedicated his life to the Pharaoh, as flawed as the monarch had been. The splendors of Egypt—its finest jewels, its Pharaoh—had been set in their final resting places, but until they were physically secured in the temple and pyramid, Hasim would not rest. Beyond a nod, Sarrah hadn't acknowledged him—the risk of being seen or overheard was too great, and the mood was grave. Given Meti's insecurities and his deep need for her during this time of transition, she shut Hasim out of her thoughts completely.

Meti arrived at dawn with a small retinue. Though he was dressed in splendid black robes, his jeweled headdress that of a Pharaoh, Sarrah could see that he was tired and uneasy behind his costume. She joined him silently as he toured the funerary stores, chapels, and shrines. They entered the pyramid and wound their way through its narrow corridors, stepping down into the underground burial chamber. There lay the mummy case, surrounded by torches. Flames illuminated the intricate paintings lining the walls. This was the last time father and son would be together in this life.

After a short time Meti emerged from the pyramid, the transfer of power complete. As the small crowd of Egypt's most important noblemen, soldiers, and advisors gathered around its newly enthroned Pharaoh, the high priests—singing incantations—ordered the massive stone block to be fitted into the entrance opening. It fit tightly, as if even air could not pass through. No living being would ever again enter this tomb.

———

I don't even recognize myself.

Sarrah gazed in the mirror, clad in black linen robes, her eyes rimmed in kohl, ruby earrings dangling from her ears. It had been two weeks since the Pharaoh's funeral procession.

Afterward, as was the tradition, Meti had instructed the stonemasons to remove his father's name from every monument in the empire and to engrave them instead with his own. In these early days Sarrah rarely left Meti's side. The two of them talked well into the night, strategizing on how best to maintain continuity and ensure the transfer of power with un-questionable authority. They knew that Meti needed to consol-idate his rule quickly.

The countrywide state of mourning allowed Meti and Sar-rah time to privately discuss and select a new council of advi-sors. Unlike his father before him, Meti kept his inner circle quite small. If he'd had his way, he would have chosen only Sar-rah, but she was quick to persuade him of the danger in which that would put her. Meti relented and selected a council that would serve as little more than yes-men.

They were in the Throne Room, just the two of them, Meti seated on the Pharaoh's throne, which was now his. Sarrah sat on a bench below the dais; the location of her permanent seat was a question for another day. The most important role to fill was that of the vizier, second in line of authority to the Pharaoh himself. "None of these men have half the wisdom you have," said Meti as they mulled over the choices.

"You are so kind," Sarrah said. "But to choose me would be a mistake. I'm of more use to you without having an official role, and subject to less scrutiny. What about your cousin Omari? He is loyal to Egypt and the throne. He's not very shrewd, but he will do as ordered without question."

"You are right," Meti agreed. As advisers, he then selected three cousins who would never dare to second-guess the Pha-raoh. "The last two positions: chief architect and the general of the armies. What say you?"

Sarrah knew she could maneuver Hasim into the running as a candidate, but Meti would need to feel it was his decision. "My lord, I ask you to consider Hasim as general. His military victories and years of service are unparalleled. Don't forget that he risked his life to save your father from the battlefield and return him safely to the palace. Surely he would be a great mentor and guide and would burnish your glory as Pharaoh?"

She could see that just the mention of Hasim's name made Meti's brow furrow.

"I implore you to look beyond your adolescent hesitation and see Hasim as the asset that he is," Sarrah said. "Approach him with confidence. You have the upper hand. Hasim has nothing."

Meti frowned. Curse masculine pride! She would have to change tactics.

"Perhaps you are right," she said. "Perhaps your father's second in command, Ur, would be best. He served your father for years, and while he didn't win many battles, he is very earnest in his service."

Bless masculine pride! No one had more of a drive to win than Meti. "No, Ur is weak and his time has passed. I want a strong, young, tireless warrior who values strategy and victory as much as I do. I name Hasim as my general of armies."

Sarrah bowed deeply, smiling to herself. "As you wish, my king. Truly the choice of an omniscient ruler."

That led to the final council role—chief architect. "My lord, I have an unusual suggestion. If you would permit me to fully share it with you before responding, I'd be most honored," Sarrah said.

Meti nodded and leaned forward on his throne.

"The matter of your chief architect is causing you justifiable difficulty," said Sarrah. "It is a position of great importance that must also come with great trust and integrity. My candidate offers neither. However, it cleverly welcomes into your inner circle one who is of concern to you.

"I feel that my uncle needs to be brought into the fold under the guise of power and respect, so that we may closely observe and control his movements and his accessibility to the realm. He served your father well as his city planner and has been successfully overseeing the construction of your grand temple, begun on the day of your birth."

The silence was deafening. Meti just stared at her. Sarrah held his gaze. She did not even allow herself to even breathe, as any motion might tip the scales. For the first time since they had met, she was unclear as to what Meti would do next.

He rose from his throne and unsheathed his sword. He continued to hold her gaze as he descended the marble steps. He brought his sword to Sarrah's neck; she dared not move. "Say it again, my darling Sarrah," he insisted, as he pressed his sharp blade into her neck. "Say again why I should allow that wretched, puny, vile man anywhere near me and my beloved Egypt. If I didn't know better, I might begin to think that you and your uncle have been plotting this maneuver since your arrival at court."

Still looking into his eyes, she said quietly, "Because it is I who am asking. You must trust me on this. All my psychic abilities tell me this is vital to your maintaining power and dominance in the kingdom. Khufu is trusted by the old guard. By keeping him alive but close we can monitor and control him. My king, I hold no love or loyalty for my uncle. In fact, I loathe the very sight of him. If you doubt me, then slit my throat and take my life."

She lowered her eyes and turned her head to the side, as if offering her neck to his blade. After a few moments, Meti lowered his sword.

"Look at me, Sarrah," he ordered. "I will do as you ask because I, too, sense the weight of this decision. But I will never allow Khufu true power. You and I will weave a web even the clever Khufu cannot escape. He will betray us, Sarrah. And when he does, I will make sure he suffers the greatest pain ever endured."

———

The next morning, and tirelessly over the next few weeks, Meti gathered his council. He drilled them on everything from history to military strategy to irrigation to staff appointments. He was ruthless in his inquiries yet measured when proven wrong. Council members understood that their loyalty and service were paramount. Any who crossed him were commanding their own death sentence. The young Pharaoh was bright, strong, and more than a little hotheaded. Meti was not one to give second chances, and that reputation began to spread throughout the kingdom.

————

Several months later, the receiving room outside the throne chamber teemed with subjects hoping for an audience with their new Pharaoh. Meti had let it be known that he would sit in judgment on civil grievances with a certain number of citizens once a month. Onlookers were speechless at the sight of the young Pharaoh's new throne, built swiftly over days and nights by the country's finest craftsmen. Set high atop the dais, it was made in a baldachin design, with four fluted marble columns painted in scarlet and gold supporting a decorative marble canopy. Intricate mosaics of the gods encircled the perimeter. Meti's bronze seat was mounted under the canopy, its arms, back, and sides richly inlaid with mosaics of lapis and turquoise ostrich feathers to summon Ma'at, the goddess of truth, harmony, law, and justice. A Pharaoh less vital or commanding would have been dwarfed by such an architectural wonder, but Meti was a dazzling visual specimen—tall and muscular, his skin oiled, and not a hair out of place.

Khufu had not been called upon to supervise this project. Unbeknownst to any onlooker, the rear of the canopy was not solid but hollow. It concealed a cavity, a hiding place, where Sarrah could sit in secret to hear the court proceedings. Through a section of fine bronze screen she could whisper her thoughts to Meti.

Perhaps this proximity wouldn't always be necessary; perhaps he would someday nurture his psychic powers to rival her own. But over the past year, since his father's death, Meti had become fully dependent on Sarrah's guidance. As her powers of intuition had increased, his had wavered. He was green in his new role—a little uncomfortable, a little insecure. Like any ambitious and impetuous young leader, his moods were unpredictable, and he often felt slighted—rightly or wrongly—by his advisors.

Sarrah had to walk a fine line with both Meti and Khufu. But in truth, she'd never felt more powerful or sure of herself. It almost frightened her, as if she were rising too close to the gods. Ideas for the rule of Egypt came to her in dreams. She stayed up nights channeling incantations and premonitions onto sheets of papyrus. And on these monthly days of judgment, she was able to discern if these citizens were telling the truth—by reading their auras and intuiting their inner thoughts. For now, Meti was willing to take her counsel without question. One whisper, and he would do what she advised.

Khufu stood to the Pharaoh's right, his chest puffed out like a rooster's. He had volunteered for the job of selecting the individuals whose grievances would be heard by the Pharoah.

"My lord," Khufu whispered in Meti's ear, "these men are raising a riot about the working conditions at your Temple to Ptah. My men have applied the necessary pressure, and yet they still refuse to work as I demand. I suggest that severe punishment is necessary to send a message to the kingdom that such disrespect is punishable by dismemberment or death."

Meti turned to Khufu. "Firstly, Khufu, it is *my* men, not yours, who have been applying pressure. These workers are not refusing *you*; they are refusing me. Never forget that." Sarrah tried not to gasp in surprise as he stood and grabbed Khufu's tunic at the neck, nearly lifting him off the ground with one arm.

"And never, *ever* presume that I seek or desire advice from you on how to rule. I will decide as I see fit." Meti paused, then released him.

Rattled, Khufu bowed, stepping back from Meti and smoothing his tunic. "My king, please forgive my arrogance. It will not happen again." He hustled down the marble steps and out into the reception chamber to select the next citizen to come before the Pharoah.

Hidden behind the screen, Sarrah could tell by the tone of Khufu's voice that he loathed Meti and was devising ways to undermine him. Too bad for her uncle that she knew him and his calculating ways so well; she'd been studying him since childhood. She loved that Meti, and by extension she, had the power to embarrass her uncle and thwart his every attempt at self-aggrandizement. She knew it was petty, but she didn't care.

"Well done, my darling," she breathed. "You thrill me with how you handle my despicable uncle. I would ravish you right now if we were alone."

"Hush," he said softly, teasingly. "You are not playing fair, and I shall punish you later for it."

"I'm counting on it," Sarrah replied.

The first citizen brought before the Pharaoh was Khepri, an artisan in limestone and sandstone. He had a strong reputation as a fair employer and a good businessman, and this was the first time he was summoned to argue his case in the palace. He stood at the foot of the steps, head bowed.

Khufu read his complaint to the crowd, then turned to Meti and said quietly, "My recommendation as your chief architect is that he be denied clemency."

Meti didn't avert his gaze from the artisan. "Rise and come forward," he commanded.

Khepri strode forward confidently, then bowed to the Pharaoh.

"Explain yourself," said Meti.

With his eyes lowered, Khepri replied. "My king. I am your humble and faithful servant, as I was to your father before you. Never before have I been summoned to the palace court. It was my understanding that I was to spare no expense in this monument I am sculpting for you at your Temple to Ptah, a celebration of your greatness that will stand for eternity for all to see. Ptah is the patron saint of craftsmen, and you are my Pharaoh, so this is the most important commission of my life.

"As such, the stonework and etching will take time. The chief architect asks the impossible with his timeline. I mean no disrespect, but I can either honor you and my god Ptah appropriately or cut corners to make the deadline. But if I am given clemency, I vow to produce the most spectacular stone in your honor."

Khepri unfurled a sheet of papyrus with sketches of the massive stone sculpture, and with hands shaking he held it up to the Pharaoh. It did not go unnoticed by Meti—or by Sarrah—that the structure was designed to be visibly larger and grander than the shrine to his father. She was certain that would please Meti's ego. *Nicely played, Khepri,* she thought.

Meti sat back in his chair and tilted his head at the ceiling as if deep in deliberation. Sarrah whispered, "This is an honest man, my king. He speaks the truth. I advise you to not only accept his terms but also offer a cadre of workers to help him finish his magnificent work."

Meti sat a few moments longer, then rose to his full height. "Khepri, rise and look at me," he ordered. "I agree, this will be your greatest achievement. I grant both clemency and patience. I also command a team of fifty palace apprentices to be brought to the site to assist in carving and etching the stone. I call on Ptah myself to bless this project and imbue it with boundless glory."

Applause and cheers erupted from the crowd. Clearly Khepri was a well-liked citizen. Meti stood tall, welcoming the adoration. Through her screen Sarrah could see Meti glance to his side, and she was certain that Khufu was fuming at the decision. But he did not dare to disagree.

Many cases were brought to the Pharoah that day, stories of hardship and crisis. Meti and Sarrah pardoned some and sentenced others accordingly—and they did punish a few businessmen, merchants, and noblemen who may have been innocent in the matter at hand but, Sarrah could see, were unfair, unkind, and greedy at the core. Why wait for them to be caught for their crimes? Meti went along with her instincts. This newfound power was exhilarating!

At the end of the day, the royal council and onlookers filed out of the throne chamber and receiving room, abuzz with the day's events. Most had been impressed by Meti's judgments. It was clear that Khufu was no longer the Pharaoh's puppet master, as he had been for Meti's father. That caused many to breathe a sigh of relief—though at times, they had to admit, Meti seemed to be flexing his power just for the theatre of it. Oh, well. Such was the impetuousness of a young Pharaoh.

Meti knew that word would quickly spread about both his severity with betrayers and his benevolence with those who'd earned it. He strode out of the chamber in conversation with Omari, his vizier. Through the bronze screen, Sarrah noticed that he seemed to walk a little taller and more confidently than he had just the day before.

A short time later, after the candles had been snuffed, the throne chamber suffused in velvety darkness, Sarrah released herself from the carapace, stretching her cramped limbs. She padded lightly down the steps, her notes in hand. Time to freshen up for the call to Meti's bedchamber, which would no doubt come soon. But as she passed through the receiving room, she felt a man's grip on her forearm. Before she could scream, she recognized Hasim's eyes shining in the shadows.

"What are you doing here?" she asked haughtily, attempting to loosen her arm from his grasp.

"What are *you* doing here?" he responded, in no hurry to let her go. Yet it was not in the amused or affectionate tone he often used with her. She sensed a new emotion. Was it anger?

"I knew it. I heard it in Meti's words. They were not the judgments of a Pharaoh still wet behind the ears. They seemed to have been made by a more calculating mind—one flying a little close to the sun."

"What do you mean?"

"Don't worry, I won't reveal your little game," said Hasim. "But I will remind you that you are playing with people's lives. If Meti thinks that is how a Pharaoh exhibits power, he is only partially right. That is how an *inexperienced* Pharaoh acts. Before he is worthy of this grand temple that he's so anxious to have built, he must earn the trust and admiration of both the gods and his people. You and I both know that some of those decisions weren't based on the facts at hand."

"You and I both know that those particular merchants and noblemen were crooked. So what if they weren't guilty of the crimes at issue today?" She tossed her hair, hoping to appear unbothered.

"Do you think it is your role to act as a god? If these men are evil, will the gods not punish them in their own way and in their own time? Can the gods not be trusted to right the scales of justice?" He stopped, shaking his head. She'd never seen Hasim like this before. He released his grip on her.

"I was not aware that the Pharaoh needed to answer to any mortal," she sniffed, rubbing her forearm. "Or that you've appointed yourself worthy of second-guessing the Pharaoh's divine right."

"I think that you should ask the same of yourself," said Hasim. He looked at the jewels glinting on her ears and around her neck. Absently rubbing the border of her gold-embroidered robe between his fingers, he seemed to soften for a minute. Then he stared into her eyes. "I don't recognize who you have become. I thought you had finally given me a reason to believe in magic. Now I am not so sure."

He dropped his hand, nodded, and turned on his heel, disappearing into the darkness. Sarrah noticed that she was still rubbing her arm where he'd grasped it—though she felt nothing. *Put it out of your mind,* she thought. *Your Pharaoh awaits.*

————

Late that evening she joined Meti in his chamber, drinking wine from the finest goblets by the light of fragrant candles made by Sarrah herself.

"I so enjoy judgment day, my lord," she said. "The crowds. Khufu's unease. The decision to forgive or punish. The whole of Egypt, hanging on your every word. It feels like nothing is in our way, and there is nothing separating us."

She ran a hand down his bare, rippled chest. "Is this what being a god feels like?"

Meti grasped her hand and guided it downward. "My darling, you are absolutely wicked. Feel my excitement." As she caressed him, he removed his robes and then hers. They felt untouchable, drunk on their own power. No other mortal mattered.

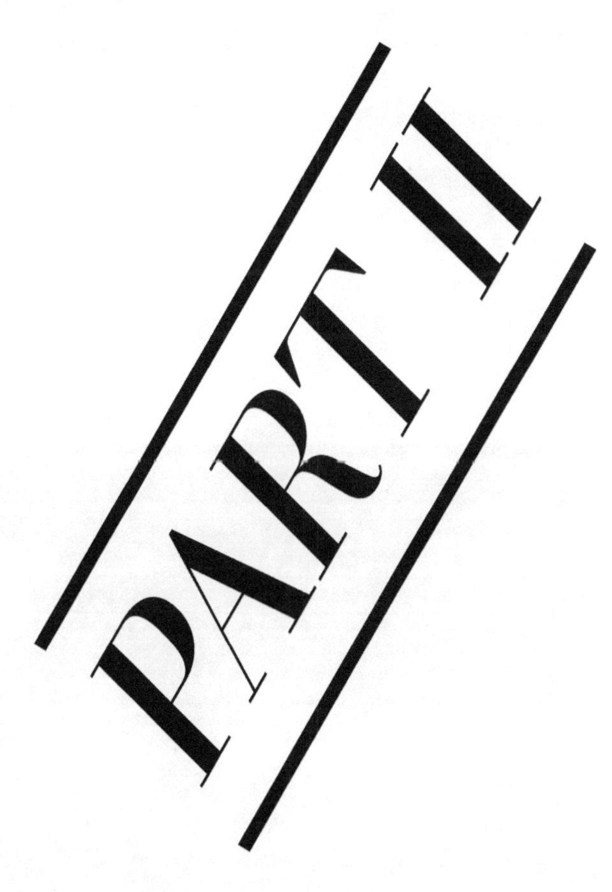
PART II

CHAPTER SEVENTEEN

One year later

"Why would you want to sweat and toil in the dirt?" Meti frowned. "We have hundreds of slaves who will plant a garden to your exact specifications. You needn't concern yourself with such menial tasks."

It was early morning. They were lying naked on Sarrah's vast bed in a post-coital tangle.

She stroked Meti's cheek and smiled. "My king, I am well aware of the palace staff and how you've ordered them to do my bidding, no matter how outlandish. But I've loved gardening and growing beauty from nothing since I was a child."

She leaned in close and whispered, "Besides, the work keeps my mystic powers strong and connected to this dimension and to others beyond our senses. The land infuses me with energy."

A look of concern came over Meti's face. "Am I overworking you, my love? I know I push and push, but I need you—all of you." He stroked Sarrah's cheek. "It hadn't occurred to me that your gifts could suffer or weaken. You seem limitless to me."

Sarrah chuckled softly. "My king, I *feel* limitless. However, I am still in this body, a body that tires and weakens as every human body must. That fatigue can affect my channeling. Creating and cultivating a secluded garden of my own design is one way I can stay grounded and powerful."

She reached over and picked up an amulet from her bedside table.

"Renenutet, I see," said Meti as he took her hand in his and inspected the small gold charm. It was engraved with a female goddess who had the head of a cobra, seated on a throne and holding a staff of papyrus. "But the harvest is past."

Sarah looked up at Meti. "Yes, it's true that Renenutet is the goddess of the harvest, and she has been most generous to Egypt under your reign. All of our citizens' offerings must have pleased her.

"But do you also remember that Renenutet means 'to nurse, to rear'? Renenutet's most important role is to take care of the Pharaoh from his birth until his passing. As she nourishes the land, she nourishes the Pharaoh himself."

She continued. "Meti, my Pharaoh, this is why my efforts in the garden, my experiments, my potions, and my oils are as important to me as is my care of you. As I nourish this very special garden, I nourish your power and your health. I will not nurse children of my own. *You* are my life. I give everything I have to your care, and with this garden I honor you."

Meti took the amulet from her hand, then reached his body across hers and placed it back on the table. He kissed her tenderly on the lips—then kissed her neck, her breasts, her stomach . . . and then pleased her expertly, as she'd taught him to do, for the second time that morning.

———

In the months that followed, Sarrah worked closely with several gardeners and apprentices to design and execute her vision. A year later, she finally had a garden of her own. She was working there one afternoon when she heard Meti's call.

"Sarrah?"

"Hello!" she called back. "Which row are you in? I'll come meet you."

"I see signs marked for lettuces, peas, cucumbers, and leeks," he said. "There seem to be melons down the row. . . ."

"Walk past the melons into the flower patch. You'll see the roses and jasmine," she said. She was as proud of her produce as if it were her children.

Meti was munching on a cucumber when he met her among the blooms.

"Doesn't it smell *amazing?*" Sarrah asked. "The jasmine and roses will scent the air even up into my chambers."

Meti gazed at Sarrah.

"What is it?" she asked. "Do I have dirt on my face?"

He shook his head and smiled. "No, you look perfect. I was simply noticing how innocent and happy you look here. It pleases me."

Sarrah blushed as she reached for Meti's hand. "Come, there's one more thing I would like you to see. I hope you approve."

A small alcove was hidden behind one of the new hedges. It was an intimate space, lush with natural walls of trellised greenery. At the center was a small marble pedestal dappled with light coming through an arbor of fast-growing vines. Sarrah released Meti's hand so he could enter. Atop the pedestal was a sculpture of two intertwined figures. The male was large, muscular—clearly the Pharaoh. The female, willowy and petite, gazed into his eyes. Meti turned to Sarrah. "Is this us?"

Sarrah nodded cautiously. She knew she had taken a risk when she'd commissioned this sculpture and placed it here. The Pharaoh was usually depicted alone—the omnipotent king, sovereign over all. But here she was, sculpted of the same stone, clearly not his equal but a partner. From certain vantage points, it looked as if they were one being.

She bowed. "Yes, it is us, and I hope it does not offend you.

My guard, Ahmed, dabbles in stonework, and I asked him to sculpt it for me. I put it here—in a place that is sacred to me—because you are my world and my heart. I felt it would infuse this garden with fertility and abundant energy."

"Sarrah, I'm not angry," said Meti. "Not at all. I am delighted."

"I'm so glad, my king. I know I'm not worthy of being carved in stone at your side for eternity, but I find there is something very powerful and primitive that binds me to you. I wanted to honor it appropriately."

Meti studied the statue, taking his time to walk around and examine it from different angles. Then he laid his hands upon it. "I feel it, Sarrah," he whispered. "I can actually feel the vibrations of this statue. How is this possible?"

Sarrah moved to his side and placed her hand on the statue as well. "I feel it, too. What we are feeling is the very essence of us. Isn't it magical?"

Meti nodded.

"Yes. It is magical, indeed." He turned to look at her with renewed seriousness. "Sarrah, the bond we have is more than physical or even of this world. I feel that the gods have brought you to me; you are my Renenutet, as you say. I thank you, and Egypt thanks you."

He looked again at the sculpture. "Once my new temple is completed, I will commission a secret chamber within it for this sculpture, where we will reside throughout eternity. Together. Intertwined."

Sarrah wiped away a tear as she bowed. "My king, I am humbled and honored."

———

After a welcome, wet spring, the warmer days of summer found Sarrah's garden bursting with new life. Abundant fruits and vegetables teemed with the buzz of the royal bees and the calming trickle of the fountains and miniature aqueducts lining many of the paths. By midsummer Sarrah was most pleased with the promise of her first harvest.

But it was her bed of thriving medicinal plants that brought her the greatest satisfaction. Soon after the summer solstice, they were finally ready to be sown. Much to Meti's amusement, Sarrah wouldn't allow any of the servants or handmaids to touch this section of the garden. She carefully trimmed the stalks of lavender and sage the way her mother had taught her. She clipped senna pods, cumin, fennel, caraway, and elderberry. Then she carried them to the greenhouse she'd designed for drying and grinding her herbs and for creating her traditional remedies—and for experimenting with new ideas. She was excited to begin making tinctures and tonics to be used as powerful healing aids. From cucumber flower to ochre, frankincense, myrrh, and from cannabis to thyme, poppy, and aloe, everything was awaiting transformation through her supernatural hands.

Sarrah was quite secretive in this work. She asked for privacy as she selected and clipped the leaves, buds, and flowers from each unique specimen. On this day she had asked her guard Ahmed to escort her staff back to their chambers so that she could focus on the task ahead in private. Meti was off with his courtiers, hunting the sacred oryx. Sarrah relished the rare opportunity to work in solitude.

Her mind was lost in her tasks all day long as she hurried to finish as much work as she could before the setting sun cast a long shadow. But as twilight fell, Sarrah realized she was no longer alone. She detected the scent and light footfall of an intruder. Her heart raced as she drew her iron shears to her belly. Poised for attack, she spun around from the worktable.

"Hasim!" she cried in a hoarse whisper, realizing she hadn't spoken to anyone for several hours.

"What on earth are you doing? You gave me quite a scare." She stood still, the shears extended toward him.

Hasim reached out and gently placed his hand on her forearm, slowly lowering the shears away from his abdomen. His utter silence and the economy of his movements reminded Sarrah of the control he exerted in every aspect of his life, from shrewd military skills on the battlefield to the stealth required to maneuver through the court hierarchy.

"If you don't mind, I'd be more comfortable explaining myself with your weapon sheathed," he said. Then he had the audacity to wink at her.

Jolted out of her initial terror, she relaxed and gave a soft laugh. "What? Oh!" She placed the shears on the worktable, then gazed at him directly.

"Now, please tell me what you are doing here when I specifically asked not to be disturbed?"

"That's why I thought it would be an ideal time for a visit." Hasim gestured for them to have a seat on the grass.

"We haven't had a chance to speak privately in quite some time. In fact, if I didn't know better I would think you'd been avoiding me. So I thought it would be wise for us to reconnect."

While Meti is away from the palace, Sarrah thought.

"And when Meti is present, I feel like an intruder. I know there is tension between us. He doesn't seem the type who would be willing to share you."

The air crackled between them as they sat on the cool lawn.

"I meant, willing to share your company."

Sarrah smiled at the gaffe. "I understand what you meant. But what was it you wanted to discuss? Last time we spoke, you seemed to have lost faith in me. In all humanity, it seemed."

Hasim glanced at the baskets of clippings Sarrah had collected, attempting to look interested. "Would you mind telling me what you've harvested?"

She decided to play along. "An interest in gardening and homeopathy cannot be why you're here, Hasim, but if you'd like to maintain this charade of meaningless conversation. . . ." She pointed at one basket. "Senna." Then at another. "Elderberry." And another. "Safflower."

Sarah crossed her arms. That was all he would get from her. He was already violating every possible court protocol by being alone with her in the garden. If Meti ever found out, they could both be finished.

"Sarrah." Hasim leaned toward her, his voice a rough caress against her bare shoulder.

She tried to lean away, but some part of her—some terrible, self-destructive, stupid, lustful, lonely part of her—refused to move. Her heart was pounding. Every sound in the garden seemed to be amplified, as if even the smallest insects knew her deepest desires better than she did.

Sarrah had replayed their last meeting in the palace shadows many times in her mind. He'd been right, she knew. She and Meti had been reckless with their power, and Hasim's insight and integrity were almost too much to bear. She'd avoided him as much as possible, but she was aware of how badly she wanted him, how often she saw him in her dreams, how many times it was his lips she imagined she was kissing when Meti visited her in the night.

"Please . . . don't do this . . ." But her voice was small and unconvincing, even to her own ears.

"You know that I am interested in everything about you. I come in peace." He trailed his finger along her shoulder and watched, mesmerized, as her skin prickled with awareness in the wake of his touch. She shivered and closed her eyes.

"If this garden is a passion of yours, I would be honored to learn more about it."

Sarrah felt a slow liquid warmth seep into her veins, traveling through her entire body and settling into a previously empty space: her heart and soul. She had the brutal realization that never in her life had her interests—*her* fantasies and dreams— been placed first. Not that she was blaming anyone; these had been her choices and her decisions. But her entire existence had always been in the service and under the will of others, Meti most of all. Now, in a moment, she understood that this life of service, which had always seemed foretold and had always seemed enough, had come at a high personal cost.

"Very well." She stood up and, as if in a dream, the two of them began to pace pathway after pathway. She told Hasim of her theory about the ratios of plants in the garden: flowers, herbs, produce. She showed him how she made her essences by pressing picked flowers between a cloth, then two wood planks. This pressure caused the scented juice to run off, which she then mixed with oil.

Hasim asked clever questions about irrigation and soil. She explained the pattern of the beds that she'd designed to take best advantage of different angles of sun and shade throughout the day. He explained how he planned his military encampments with similar intentions, shading his soldiers in the hottest hours, positioning camps near natural shelters with access to water.

And all the while, Hasim was touching her—lightly at first, when he'd ask a question and direct her attention to something that caught his eye. As if under some sort of spell, Sarrah allowed these forbidden advances, until eventually she craved them.

And it wasn't just the physical attention—the naturalness of his touch. It was the way he listened, focusing his entire attention on her. This new feeling of being seen and respected felt uncomfortable. Sarrah didn't know how to respond.

She realized she had stopped walking. Hasim had asked her something, and her mind had wandered. She was now simply staring at him.

He reached out and lifted her chin. "Tell me what you are thinking. Unlike you, I cannot read minds."

She laughed gently, as if she could shake off the dangerous wave of passion about to engulf them both. Trying to sound blasé, she quipped, "The last time we spoke, you seemed to doubt my ability to do so. Why do you care what I think now?" She flicked her wrist and turned aside. "I know we've had the occasional flirtation over the years, but really, Hasim?"

Without hesitation, Hasim pulled her back to face him, holding her so she had no choice but to look him in the eyes. "You know as well as I do that what we share is not simply a flirtation or a dalliance. It is so much deeper than that." He shook her lightly. "All I ever wanted is for you to be honest with me. And with yourself.

"You are the first thing I think of when I open my eyes in the morning and the last thought in my head as I drift to sleep. You are my inspiration and my muse, and I live my life to make you proud. I hope that when you hear of my accomplishments on the battlefield you know that they are all for you."

He leaned in closer. "I know it is impossible," his voice now raspy with desire. "But we *are* connected, Sarrah." His grip on her arms tightened; his strength made her feel both vulnerable and all-powerful.

"We are connected by something I have never felt before and can no longer deny. That is why I am here, Sarrah. And I know you feel it, too."

Sarrah stood perfectly still; she realized she had been holding her breath. She then exhaled slowly, willing herself to be sensible. "Unhand me."

Hasim released her immediately. "I'm sorry."

She held up a hand to stop his empty apology and resumed their walk around the garden. He stayed quiet; she could feel his gaze as he trailed behind her.

At last, Sarrah turned to face him. "I do feel it. Something eternal. Something outside the realm of this time and space. That evening in the palace chamber, you saw through me. We are connected soul to soul. I have known about it for some time.

Yet. . . ." She sighed. "Nothing can be done. I *belong* to Meti. He is not a lover I can cast aside, not a trifle. I am his mystic, his teacher, his guide, his mother, his therapist, and yes, his lover. She could see that each word struck Hasim like a blow. "I am not free, Hasim."

Hasim exhaled slowly. She could see the battle he was waging with himself; he felt he was losing ground. He picked up her hand and placed it on his heart. "Feel this heartbeat, Sarrah. This heart beats only for you. I do not want to own you as Meti does. What you have with him is not love. It's possessive and destructive—"

"He is the Pharaoh—of course he is possessive."

"—on *both* your parts."

Now it was Sarrah's turn to withstand the verbal blows. He really did see her, all of her, including the darkest deceptions and naked ambition.

As if reading her mind, Hasim continued, "Yes, I see you, Sarrah. All of you." He brought his mouth close to her ear, almost kissing her with his words. "I want to honor you, encourage you, learn from you, teach you, respect you, love you. Please let me."

Sarrah turned her head to look into Hasim's eyes. And how it burned, what she saw there. She saw her heart, his heart, *their* heart, all in that one gaze. In that moment she knew a simple choice now would change her future forever. Every warning signal in her body was alight, but she couldn't look away.

"Have you any idea what you are asking?" She felt raw, her voice unfamiliar to her own ears. "If we are caught, we will die."

He put a finger to her lips. "I am dying *now*, aren't you?"

A single tear slipped onto her cheek. She had denied every natural instinct, every urge, for as long as she could remember. She nodded, unable to say the words, to admit even to herself how much she had sacrificed in order to exercise the full breadth of her mystical powers.

"Dying," he said, "without being able to kiss you and make love to you." He leaned in. A kiss immediately escalated into a passionate mingling of tongues. After a short while, Hasim gently pulled away and led her by the hand back to the dewy lawn. He guided her down and reverently laid Sarrah on the grass. She felt weak: her mind was empty of reason, alarm, anything but desire.

Hasim looked into her eyes, as if asking permission. With Sarrah's nearly imperceptible nod, he returned to kissing her in earnest. They wrapped themselves up in each other and didn't let go. The fire between them was white-hot. Her eyes closed, her mind spinning, Sarrah felt herself lifted into Hasim's arms as if she was light as a bird. He carried her into the hidden alcove where the sculpture of Meti and Sarrah stood. There he placed her on her feet, and they instinctively began to remove each other's robes. There was no awkwardness, no modesty. Her back against the cool marble column, Hasim traced every inch of her body with his mouth, as if he knew it already. She shivered as he fell to his knees. She moaned quietly and grasped his damp curls in her hands. After a time he rose, lifted her in his arms, and entered her. The rapture they felt overwhelmed them both, and as Sarrah fell into the throes of ecstasy she opened her eyes and gazed into Hasim's. She saw the deepest depths of the universe, and she knew she would never be the same again.

As Hasim held her, his head buried in her neck, and whispered his love and eternal fidelity into her ear, Sarrah turned her head and saw the sculpture. Dread filled her heart. She knew her fate had just changed forever.

CHAPTER EIGHTEEN

New York City, January 17

"I'm thinking of leaving Carl."

Sarah broke her silence with a bombshell. She hopped up off the sofa and started pacing. "I can't believe I finally said it out loud."

Dr. Ken Jaffe began to speak. "Okay—"

"I mean, what's wrong with me? I must be losing it. I have an incredible life, and Carl is a huge part of that. So why do I feel so empty?" She kept pacing.

Ken sat quietly.

"Well, aren't you going to say anything?" Sarah finally asked.

"It's *your* time," he said, smiling wryly as he looked at his watch. "Here we are, pacing again. Looks like you've got about forty minutes left in your workout."

She plopped down on the sofa and poured herself a glass of water. "I already went running this morning," she shrugged. "I guess we can just talk."

"Sarah, whatever it is, I'm here to listen. Let's back up a little."

She began to relax. *Why was I so resistant to telling Ken about this? This is why I'm here, for crying out loud.*

"Now let's talk about this unexpected news."

Sarah sat back and just stared at Ken Jaffe. She hadn't fully realized until this moment how much tension and anxiety she'd been holding on to since her birthday. Max had been a saving grace, but he had his own view of what was right for her, and she didn't always agree. But right now Sarah knew she needed professional advice.

"It all began when I turned forty." Sarah stared out the window at the darkening gray skies of a New York winter. January had always been one of her favorite months—fires in the fireplace, a quieter social schedule, quality family time.

"I've been grappling with these feelings since then, and I've been too embarrassed and ashamed to talk about them. I figured it was just a midlife blip that would depart as quickly as it arrived."

"What happened on your birthday to cause these feelings?" asked Ken. "Marriage is work. You and Carl are two busy people with two kids; you've been together for several years. Is it possible this has been brewing for a while?"

Sarah looked at Ken. "These feelings have been with me for a *very* long time. Maybe even since I was *engaged* to Carl. But I've never allowed myself to entertain them. When we got back together after college, after I cheated on him and he forgave me, I told myself that if I recommitted to him then, I couldn't let him down. Look at Carl—he's handsome and educated, he's a good father and husband, he's funny, he loves me. He checks all the boxes, right? And I've been happy for the most part. Content, if you will. I love my family. I just don't know if I love my husband. God, what a terrible thing to say out loud!"

She buried her face in her hands and started to cry. "Carl doesn't cheat on me, he doesn't steal from me, he has stood by me. I don't have any reason to leave him. I'm scared, Ken. I need your help."

"Have you discussed your feelings with Carl?"

"No. No, I haven't said anything to him. We just get carried along by our schedules, and kid activities, and talk about work. As I said, I kept hoping it would all just go away. And it was the holidays, then he was sick, then the kids were sick . . . There just hasn't been the right time."

Sarah hiccupped a sob. "Plus, I don't want to hurt Carl or the kids. He would be shocked and hurt. It seems so selfish of me to put us through all of this. But I feel like something has altered in my chemistry. Like my composition has changed, and certain base notes now insist on being top notes, and they refuse to back down. Of course I'd use fragrance as a metaphor, but does that make any sense?"

"Well," he said, "it helps me to understand that these truths have been buried in your chemistry, as you say, for a very long time, but they are now presenting themselves quite powerfully."

"What do I do, Ken? You know me well enough to know I require action steps."

Ken leveled his gaze at her. "Allow me to propose that there are *several* steps between admitting to yourself that you're unhappy in your marriage and possibly deciding to leave your husband. First, you're going to go home and find a good moment to speak with Carl about how you feel. Sarah, there's never really a good time for a hard discussion, but the time for excuses is over. Your marriage deserves your honesty, as do you and Carl. All marriages go through rough patches, and often that can raise the bond to new heights. I recommend hiring a marriage counselor to help you both, and I know a very good person."

He leaned in. "But the question is, are you willing to *fight* for your marriage?"

"Well, of course! What kind of person would I be if I wasn't? I can't simply throw away my life. I must show up for my kids, for my family." Sarah dried her tears. "But marriage counseling? Seriously? That seems so *cliché*."

Ken chuckled, "Clichés are clichés for a reason—because

there is truth behind them. Marriages often go through tough times, and a neutral third party can help." He wrote a name and number down on his notepad, ripped off the sheet, and handed it to her.

Sarah stared at the paper. "I can't believe this is happening. Okay. I'm willing to do this. Let's see if Carl is on board."

He handed her another script—had he already written one *before* her appointment? "Now—how are those sleeping pills working? Here's another prescription for the anxiety."

She put it in her bag without even looking at it. *Wow, Doctor Feelgood. Another appointment, another pill. I haven't even used the other meds. Well, I guess they're good to have in case I need them.*

———

"I am such a coward," Sarah murmured to Max on the phone as she sat at a table in Sant Ambroeus, waiting for her mother to arrive. This was her mother's favorite lunch spot: upscale but neighborhoody, with clubby seating, wood-paneled walls, glittering crystal chandeliers, delicate Italian food, and a crisp house rosé.

"I can't believe I still haven't said anything. It's been *weeks* since Ken gave me the counselor's contact info. Why can't I just tell Carl how I'm feeling? He is my husband, after all."

"Do you really want me to answer that?" Max teased.

Sarah giggled. "You are incorrigible! You really do hold a very low opinion of my husband. That should have been my first clue all those years ago."

Max sighed. "Sarah, it's not that I loathe Carl. I just know that you deserve better. You always have. Hell, as far as I'm concerned, there probably isn't a man out there worthy of you. Well, except maybe Harry Aiken," he laughed.

"Oh no, Langmore. We agreed not to mention that name. I cannot be distracted by Harry while I try to fix my marriage. You promised."

"On another topic, are you actually going to share your drama with your mother today?" asked Max. "I may need to jump in a cab and rush up there just to watch her reaction, and then witness the copious amount of wine she'll guzzle. It's going to be epic. You must call me as soon as you leave!"

Sarah laughed. "I'm planning on asking for a little motherly advice. But I'll see what type of mood she's in when she gets here. If it's a wine-by-the-glass day, then I'll tell her. If it's a bottle-of-wine day, then I'll probably wait."

"Listen, I've got to run," Max said. "I have a Zoom call with the Egyptologist who is giving next month's lecture to discuss what she needs for the event. You're coming, right?"

Sarah flagged the waiter as she answered, "Absolutely. I've been to Egypt before for work, but I think your new archeological excursion sounds amazing! Is it a singles trip? Sign me up." She moaned again. "What am I saying?" This is no time for jokes!"

"Shame on you!" Max cackled. "Gotta scoot. Don't forget to call me afterward!"

The sun through the picture window felt warm and comforting. It was a surprisingly mild day for February in New York, and everyone seemed to be in a better mood because of it. Hopefully her mother would be in a good mood as well.

The long weekend in Vermont had been fun—great skiing, fabulous meals, games, movies, and lots of laughs. There was no question she loved her little family unit. On Tuesday, at her last appointment with Ken, she'd tried to suggest that there might not be a need to tell Carl about her doubts. Maybe she'd gotten past the worst of what she was calling her "mood."

But Ken reminded her that her concerns had been present for years, not just months, and they would come back around. She was sick of the merry-go-round of emotions; it had been so much easier to ignore them or throw herself into work or the kids. *I am so tired of giving all of my mental real estate to this,* she thought.

She felt a tap on her shoulder. "Hello, dear. Why are you staring into space?"

"Forgive me, Mom. I have a lot on my mind. It's good to see you." She reached forward and squeezed her mother's hand.

Her mother squeezed back. "You look tired. You're working too hard. You really must prioritize rest, Sarah. A lack of sleep ages a woman by ten years—and you're now in your forties."

Sarah sighed. Some battles just weren't worth the effort.

The waiter greeted them. "Good afternoon, Mrs. Fuller. Hello, Miss Sarah. It is always lovely to have you with us."

Sarah looked up and smiled. "Thank you, Enzo. Lunch with you is always a highlight of my day."

Enzo bowed slightly in appreciation. "May I start you ladies with a beverage? Mrs. Fuller, would you like a glass of your favorite Sangiovese?"

Sarah's mother was still staring at her, probably pondering her "tired" face.

"Mother," Sarah urged, "a glass of the house rosé?"

"What? Oh goodness, my apologies, Enzo. Please bring us a bottle on ice. By the look on my daughter's face, I am going to need it."

"Mom, what do you mean? I'm fine, honestly."

"Darling, I am your mother. I might not have your grandmother's psychic powers, but you cannot hide your thoughts from me. Something is weighing heavily on your mind, and it's showing on your face. So unless you want to continue adding to those bags under your eyes, you'd better tell me what's going on."

Sarah sat back in her chair and sighed. "Has it become that obvious? I guess that's not a huge surprise. I've had a lot on my mind of late. I'm not sleeping well."

Her mother reached out her hand again and took Sarah's. "Tell me, dear. What is it that has you so worked up?"

Sarah closed her eyes and whispered. "I'm having some marital problems. I feel so lonely in my marriage. Empty. Lost.

I know, I know, everyone goes through it, but I'm feeling a little hopeless. Ken thinks we should go to marriage counseling, which I am okay with. But I feel overwhelmed."

Her mother sat back. "And Carl? What does Carl say?"

Sarah took a deep breath.

"Well . . . I haven't found the right moment to tell him how I feel."

Now it was her mother's turn to gaze out the window. Thankfully Enzo returned with the wine. He told them about the specials as he filled their glasses. "I knew a bottle was a good idea," her mother nodded, taking a generous sip from her glass.

After they'd placed their orders, her mother leaned back in and said, "Now, look at me and listen, really listen, to what I am about to say."

Sarah sat up straight.

"Every marriage gets to the point where it's basically dead in the water. It's unfortunate, but it is what it is. However, that is no reason to leave the relationship or the family. That is reckless and frankly beneath you and the Fuller name. No. We are friends with Carl's parents and have been for years. You have the kids. You have a business to think about. Now is the time to branch out and find new purpose or hobbies in life. Go out and meet new people and get involved in something that's meaningful to you. What about your new foundation?"

Sarah tried to interject, but her mother held up her index finger. "Why don't we plan a fundraiser for the Arcanum Foundation? Wouldn't it be *gorgeous* in Central Park in the spring? I could make a call and make that happen for you."

"Mother. . . ." Sarah tried again to speak but was given the raised finger.

"Or you should go visit Uncle Pierre and Dr. Brisbois? It's been years since you've been back to France. My point is, you must turn your attention to new pursuits in order to find joy and some meaning. It saddens me that you are now at the inevitable moment when a marriage basically dies, but that only means you have to adapt. And you will find that the marriage then adapts with you into a different cadence. Do yourself a favor: *do not tell Carl.* Do not tell anyone ever again. Bury this feeling deep inside of you and simply carry on."

Sarah stared down at her place setting. When Enzo delivered their plates, she automatically picked up her knife and fork to cut into the chicken piccata, but she realized she couldn't even taste it. Numb. All she felt was numb. As the tears began to well in her eyes, she stood up and excused herself.

After washing her hands and splashing water on her face, she stared into the bathroom mirror and searched for an emotion. But she felt nothing. *Huh, this is new.* She made her way back to the table, feeling flat, and resumed eating.

"Well, darling? Have you nothing to say?"

Sarah looked at her mother again, but it was as if she were looking at a stranger.

"Mother, what would you like me to say? Would a simple 'Yes, mother dear' satisfy you? Or perhaps, 'Of course you are correct, Mother. You are always right.' Or 'Great advice, Mother. Thanks for teaching me to live with loneliness and emptiness in the name of saving face. That's great parenting advice and I'm so grateful.' How does that sound?" she asked, her voice raised slightly.

"Don't make a scene, Sarah. You are not a child, so stop acting like one. Goodness, you always did have a penchant for drama. You become more like my mother every day."

Sarah's breath caught, and she reached for her wine glass. After a hearty gulp, she looked up.

"I'm sorry I brought this up, Mother. Let's just enjoy our meal. I'll figure it out. I always do. Now, about that fund-raiser. . . ."

CHAPTER NINETEEN

Sarah walked home through Central Park to clear her mind, but she kept hearing her mother's words over and over in her head. A deep sadness was setting in—sadness for her mother and father, sadness for herself, sadness for Carl, sadness for any marriage that had no life or love left in it.

No, she thought. *No way, Sarah. That life is not for you.*

Well, the moment had arrived. It was time to tell Carl.

She strode into her building and greeted the doorman. "How's your afternoon going, Lenny?" she asked.

"Oh, you know, Ms. Fuller, just another day in paradise."

Sarah smiled as she walked toward the elevator. "Do you happen to know if my husband is upstairs?"

"I'm not sure. I haven't seen him since I came on at noon," he said.

She stabbed the elevator button, feeling annoyed. *What the hell does that man do all day? I swear, if he's on the sofa, I'm going to lose it.*

Sarah knew she needed to take a breath and calm down before the doors opened into her foyer. She paced the small space just to center herself. *You've got this, Sarah. Just go in there and rip off the Band-Aid.*

She found Carl at the kitchen table reading the *Wall Street Journal*, the remnants of his lunch on a plate in front of him. He looked up as she walked in and smiled.

"There's my girl," he chimed. "How was lunch with your mom? Was it a one-glass-of-wine lunch or a full-bottle afternoon?"

Sarah rolled her eyes and sat down on the stool across from Carl. "Mother was in rare form today, that's for sure. I had hoped the beautiful weather would soften her demeanor, but no such luck."

She picked at the edge of the placemat, gathering her resolve.

"Carl, lunch was actually quite draining, and I need to talk to you about it."

He leaned forward and grabbed Sarah's hand. "Babe, nobody riles you up like your mom. When are you going to learn to just *ignore* her? I do, and it works like a charm." He sat back, a smug grin on his face, as if he'd solved all the world's problems in one fell swoop.

"For the record, it wasn't Mother who caused the issues today. I asked her for motherly advice about something, which unfortunately led to the most awful conversation. Frankly, she scared the shit out of me today."

"Okay, honey, you're clearly worked up. What exactly happened?"

Sarah saw the concern on Carl's face. *Here goes nothing.*

"I told her that I'm not happy in our marriage. I think we need counseling. I know I should have talked to you about my feelings months ago, but life has been so busy, and I just didn't know how to bring it up."

The words kept spilling out; she was afraid to stop.

"Ken has been a help, especially recently, but lunch with Mother today made me realize that we can't just keep treading water. We owe it to our marriage and the kids to get help. Please tell me that you're willing to go see a counselor—I have a good recommendation."

Carl stared at Sarah for an uncomfortable amount of time. Out of nervous energy, she started to clear his dishes, rinsing them and placing them in the dishwasher. When she returned to her seat, she saw his jaw grinding. Finally she had to speak. "Do you have anything to say? I'm sorry I just dumped all of this on you, but I couldn't keep it bottled up anymore."

Carl raised his hand. "Let me get this straight. You have been unhappy in our marriage for what sounds like a very long time, and rather than speak to me privately about your feelings, you have discussed them with Ken, with your mother, and I have no doubt with Max, who's probably loving every minute of it. Damn it, Sarah, I feel ambushed. This is utter *bullshit!*"

He slammed his fist against the table, then ran his hands through his hair.

"Nice, Carl. Really nice. Did you ever think that calling how I feel 'utter bullshit' is why I'm sitting here unhappy? Why I haven't said anything to you?"

Carl shook his head. "That's not what I meant, and you know it. The way this is *happening* is utter bullshit, Sarah. The fact that there are so many other people that know about our marital issues while I *don't* is utter bullshit. I gotta go."

With that, he stood up, knocking over his chair in the process. She heard the elevator open and close. He was gone.

Fuller, you did it. You didn't do it well, but you did it.

She folded her arms on the table and laid her head down on them.

God, what have I done?

———

Sarah woke up to Carl gently nudging her shoulder. "Sarah. Sarah, honey, wake up," he whispered.

She sat up and looked around. She'd fallen asleep on the bedroom sofa. It was dark. "Do you want some dinner?" she asked, gingerly standing up.

"I'm sorry I didn't call or say goodnight to the kids, but I needed to walk and go get a drink by myself," he said. "Are you awake enough to listen?"

She plopped back down on the sofa and pulled the blanket over herself again. "Of course, Carl. Would you get me a glass of water?"

He returned with two glasses and handed one to Sarah. She made room for him on the sofa, but he sat on the bench at the end of the bed.

"Please don't say anything until I'm done, okay?"

She nodded.

"To say I felt sucker-punched by what you said earlier is an understatement. To be honest, I had no idea you were so unhappy. Sure, I know we haven't been as close or as intimate as we once were. But I figured that was normal because of where we are in life. The kids demand a lot of time, your work requires a lot of attention, and my projects keep me busy. But never once have I really worried about our marriage."

He looked at Sarah. "So it makes me wonder if what's really going on here is more of a *burnout* than a *breakdown*. You carry all these commitments on your back—me, the kids, our home, your company, your family, your foundation, your workouts, your friendships, your causes. I honestly marvel at your endurance and abilities, Sarah. But maybe it's gotten to be too much. I'm sorry if I haven't stepped in to make it easier for you. Maybe I've become complacent, just letting you handle everything. I'm sorry about that. But I honestly don't believe our marriage is irrevocably broken."

He got up and sat next to her on the sofa.

"I have an idea. Stuart has been asking you all winter to fly out and visit Walter and him in Aspen. I know I hemmed and hawed about it. The truth is, I didn't really want to stay home alone with the kids and miss my squash games and stuff, and I'm embarrassed about how selfish that was. But now I think that you *definitely* should go. They'll spoil you rotten, and you can get in some skiing *and* some rest. And you and Stuart can work on the budget for the foundation. I can only imagine that as your treasurer he'd be grateful to get a jump start on that."

Sarah hesitated. "Carl, I don't think one long weekend in Aspen can fix what you call my 'burnout,' but I must admit I'm grateful for the idea, and I appreciate your honesty. I'll agree to head out to Aspen on one condition. If I'm still feeling unsettled when I get back, we'll make an appointment with the marriage counselor. Deal?"

Carl took her hands and kissed them. "Deal."

CHAPTER TWENTY

February 17

"Let me get this straight. You finally find the courage to share your feelings with your husband and he makes it all about himself?" Max almost shrieked. "That guy makes me so outraged! I mean, it's you, Miss Sensitive, Miss People Pleaser, Miss Put Myself Last. He ought to know better than anyone how hard that conversation was for you!"

They were seated in his office. His assistants were used to ignoring Max's histrionics by now, and anyway they were busy scurrying down the hallways, trying to ready the offices for the event that night. Sarah took a stress ball from Max's marble desk and tossed it at him.

"*Shhh!* Please don't start in on Carl. You're being unfair and overdramatic. I can see how he felt that it was a surprise attack. I'm actually grateful that he walked away for a while to collect his thoughts. I was impressed."

Max rolled his eyes.

"Max, I'll do whatever's necessary to try and make this marriage work. Even if it's just for the kids, I owe it to my family to try. If Carl is willing to begin couples counseling after my weekend in Aspen, then I'm going to work with that. I need your support on this, Max, not your disapproval."

He came around the desk and leaned over to hug her. "I'm sorry, love. How ironic that here I am, making this moment all about me, when it needs to be all about *you*. Forgive me?"

"You know I always forgive you, but let's be real," she said. "You can't go more than an hour without making things about you. It's part of your charm."

Max clutched his heart as if he'd been stabbed. *"Moi?* Never. I have no idea what you are talking about. I can easily go for *two* hours."

Sarah rolled her eyes as she stood and made her way to the door.

"On another note," she said, "tell me more about tonight's speaker. I can't believe you got Dr. Delilah Salah to come and speak about her new discovery in Egypt. What a coup!"

"It shows you the popularity of high-end concierge travel," said Max. "Wealthy people are crazy for experiences that money can't buy. My invitation-only trips have been selling out for years. I'm extremely choosy when I curate the guest list. Masters of the universe don't want to share a private jet and dinner tables with just *anyone* for two weeks."

He led Sarah down the hall to his "conference room." With its needlepoint rugs, stuccoed walls, oil paintings, and fully stocked bar, it seemed more like the receiving room of a British country house than a meeting room in a Wall Street high-rise. A few rows of chairs were set up, and a bartender was busy chopping limes and icing champagne.

"To be honest, I invited Delilah to accompany us on the Egypt trip on a whim. I knew adding her as a guest expert would make the excursion even more desirable. The media can't resist a ground-breaking archaeologist who happens to look like Angelina Jolie," he said.

"Well, every scientist has to sing for their supper, even the hot ones," joked Sarah. "I think this lecture is a win-win for her, too. You'll sell out the rest of the tour, and she'll fund her next dig tonight."

"This is why I'm always telling you to network more and travel more. I met Delilah at a dinner when I was leading that trip to Jordan a couple of years ago. One of my members asked if she could invite her to join us. You know me—the more the merrier! We just hit it off. I had her sit next to me, and I was mesmerized by her passion for her work. The artifacts that she'll talk about tonight and that we'll see on the trip haven't been seen by human eyes for millennia."

"*Please* tell me you didn't seduce her. I know you, and you're a scalawag."

Max laughed. "God, I tried, but she's happily married and virtuous to a tee. Such a waste."

"Well, I like her even more after hearing that," said Sarah. "It's not an easy feat to turn down the charismatic Max Langmore when he sets his laser beams on you."

The lecture was to begin in about thirty minutes. They returned to Max's office. "Before I practice my introduction on you, please tell me that you're okay with what happened with Carl," he said. "I know I always overreact, but I'm worried that this will take a toll on you. Whatever you ultimately decide, I'll support you."

Sarah hugged him tightly. "Thanks, babe. I know you will. To be honest, I don't feel much of anything right now. But I'm over-the-moon psyched to be going to Aspen. Does that make me a horrible person?"

"Hell no, Fuller. That means you've been paying attention to everything I've been teaching you."

"Twenty minutes. You didn't even make it *twenty minutes* keeping it about me."

Max shrugged. "Now shut up and listen to my speech."

Sarah took her glass of white wine and leaned against the bar, quietly observing the gathering. She recognized a few people from some of Max's previous events, but she still felt a bit like a fish out of water. These were New York's best and brightest—or at least two dozen people who didn't mind dropping the cost of a luxury car on a two-week vacation.

She walked over to grab a seat and was delighted to see Leyla sitting in the second row, front and center.

"Care for some company?" Sarah asked.

"Sarah! How great to see you. I didn't realize you'd be here tonight. Please join me." Leyla gestured toward the seat next to her. Sarah draped her coat over the back of the chair and sat down. "So," Leyla began, "I assume from the fact that your birthday party was in the Temple of Dendur that you have a true interest in ancient Egypt."

Sarah smiled. "You have no idea. Ever since my fourth-grade class trip to the Met, I've been drawn to their Egyptian collection. I can't explain it. In a way, it's like visiting an old friend. Weird, I know."

Leyla leaned in. "You forget who you're talking to. I live and breathe weird," she said with a wink. "There have been a few places, be it actual cities and towns or just being in the presence of certain artifacts and art, that so deeply resonate with me that I know I've spent time there in a past life."

"Well, I've built a business based on that feeling," Sarah said. "My fragrances are inspired by turning my instincts about places into scents. I call it instinct—but do you believe that we've all lived past lives? As in reincarnation? Is that really a thing?"

Leyla's tone turned serious. "As far as I am concerned, I am absolutely positive that it's a thing. In my work and with everything I've witnessed in this lifetime, these past-life experiences are often a large part of how we respond to our present lives and all the events that take place in them."

"Let me ask you a question," she continued. "You say the Egyptian Wing was like an old friend. Besides your draw to Egyptian art, has there ever been a person, place, or object that totally gripped you, as if you were in some sort of time warp or spell?"

Meeting Harry Aiken, she thought.

"I'm not sure," Sarah said. "I guess so. I mean, I call Max my brother from another mother, so would that be what you're describing?"

Leyla shook her head. "Not exactly. I'm in no way diminishing your deep friendship. But this is different. It's as if you are looking at or into your very soul through the beauty of someone or something else. Time seems to stop. It can be very powerful and—trust me—quite memorable."

Sarah just nodded and turned toward the dais. *Good lord, is that what happened with Harry? Is it even possible? Leave it to me to find my soulmate from a past life right in the middle of a midlife crisis. Way to go, Fuller.*

Leyla changed the subject to the evening's lecture. The rest of the group took their seats, and the lights dimmed. Max walked to the front and began. "Welcome, everyone. Welcome to INCIO. As you know, it is our goal to not only offer once-in-a-lifetime excursions, but also to offer you once-in-a-lifetime learning opportunities here at home. And do we have an extraordinary treat for you tonight!"

Max introduced Dr. Delilah Salah. Not only was she an Ivy League–trained archaeologist, lauded for her recent TED Talk on the remarkably powerful and liberated position of women in ancient Egyptian society, she was a stunning brunette who seemed wholly unaware of her own beauty. Sarah could practically hear the five-digit checks being written to Max and to Dr. Salah as she spoke.

She roused herself from her daydreaming when some images in the presentation caught her eye. Two years earlier, Dr.

Salah and her team had been excavating an ancient mortuary temple site near the modern city of Memphis when she was summoned to an unusual find in the burial chamber. The walls of the underground room were muraled, as was the custom, with elaborate scenes from the Pharaoh's life. The Pharaoh on horseback, leading his troops into battle. What appeared to be a royal wedding, the buildings adorned with banners and people dancing in the streets. The citizens of a small village, their fields bountiful, with goats being roasted and children playing by the Nile. Scenes of a peaceful and plentiful Egypt.

One painting was unusual. It depicted the Pharoah walking through a garden next to a woman in fine robes. She was holding cuttings of what appeared to be lavender, lotus, and valerian in one hand and a book showing the figure of Heka, god of magic and medicine, in the other.

As the team of archaeologists had measured and photographed each wall of the tomb, removing the dust and gathering scientific data, they were surprised to find that the stone block on which this mural was painted was hollow! In fact, it was removable. As they carefully eased it out of the wall, they discovered a secret compartment containing a richly inlaid gold cuff, the kind often worn on a noblewoman's arm; papyrus sheets illustrated with cuttings of plants and what seemed to be recipes or formulas; finger-size glass flacons containing essential oils; and small clay boxes showing evidence of powdered myrrh and other herbs. *These would have been my trade in another life,* thought Sarah.

The team examined every other section of the wall, but this was the only block that concealed a compartment. How unusual that it was not behind an image of the Pharaoh himself, or his wife or children! This mystic medicine woman or advisor must have been an important person in his life.

"Among the treasures of this secret trove, we found a work of art that is truly remarkable," said Dr. Salah. "It is no larger than a candlestick, but because of its location in this secret compartment, it holds special meaning. This statue is unlike any other you have seen from the era of the Pharaohs, as it depicts the Pharaoh himself—a god among humans—standing intertwined with a woman. Rarely have we discovered a likeness of the Pharaoh immortalized with another person. Not to mention a woman, especially one whom we do not believe to be the Queen."

Dr. Salah reached behind herself and lifted a wooden crate up onto the table. She donned white gloves, carefully raised the lid, and removed the packing material, then reached in and lifted out an object about a foot tall, wrapped in cloth.

Sarah whispered to Leyla. "Wow. This is so exciting! I can't believe we get to be the first people other than her team to see an artifact that's been hidden in the sand for thousands of years."

Dr. Salah removed the cloth so that the statue was standing front and center on the table.

As Sarah turned to the dais, she let out a gasp. Shaking, she clutched Leyla's arm.

"Sarah, are you all right?"

She shook her head. "No. I suddenly don't feel well. Leyla, I recognize that statue. I've touched it with my very hands before. What's happening?" She was having a hard time keeping her voice to a whisper.

Leyla put her arm around her shoulders. "You're shivering. Stay calm. I'll get us out of here."

Sarah nodded. While most of the attendees walked up to the front of the room to get a closer look, blocking the sculpture from view, the two women stood and made their way to the back of the room, then out of INCIO and onto Hanover Square.

Once on the street and into the wintry air, Leyla had Sarah sit down on the steps of the building. "Rest here a moment, Sarah, and take some deep breaths. I haven't seen a reaction like that in many years, but I *have* seen it before."

"So I'm not losing it completely?" Sarah gasped.

Leyla chuckled softly. "No, not in the slightest. Remember what we were talking about earlier? I believe that you just experienced the recognition by a soul of a past life."

"And based on how deeply you were affected, I feel confident that not only have you seen and touched that statue before, but I feel fairly certain that *you* are the woman standing next to the Pharaoh."

Leyla glanced up and down the avenue. "Look, there's a coffee shop. Let's go sit for a moment while you catch your breath, and I'll explain more about what I believe just happened." Sarah rose and nodded automatically, and they walked in silence to the restaurant. They slid into a booth, removed their coats, had a sip of water, ordered coffee. Sarah finally felt able to speak.

"I really appreciate this, Leyla. Thank goodness you were at INCIO tonight. I don't know what I'd have done if I didn't have you as a lifeline."

Leyla shook her head. "It's no trouble at all. I'm happy that I can help you. I know how unsteady you feel right now, but that will fade over the next half hour."

Sarah sighed. "Thank God. I've never felt like this before. I don't feel sick or anything. There's no nausea or lightheadedness or chills; I just feel a bit out of body, if that makes any sense. It's like my body went somewhere without me for a split second and I have some sort of vertigo as a result."

Leyla smiled. "You really do have great instincts. I've never heard it described like that before, but you are closer to the truth of what happened than you realize."

Sarah shrugged. "I don't know what to think, but I'm feeling better now. I'm ready. Tell me more."

"So. It's not a coincidence that we were discussing the concept of past lives right before you saw the statue. And when I told you I felt confident that you were the female form on the statue, I meant it.

"As you know, history holds many different ideas about what is commonly called the soul. Past lives, reincarnation, samsara—the idea that our souls may live multiple lives has intrigued and inspired numerous cultures and religions since the beginning of time."

"Sure, sure, okay," Sarah said. "I was raised to believe in heaven. I took philosophy in college, and I've taken my share of yoga classes. But I can't really say that I've spent much time thinking about what happens after we die."

"Well, let's just say that *I* have," Leyla said. "I know it's a controversial topic, but I've spent my life searching for confirmation of the existence of the soul. And both my channeling and my intellectual research have made me a firm believer.

"I'll try not to get too deep right now, but I don't use the word 'soul.' I prefer the terms 'higher self' or 'divine spark.' Regardless, I simply mean the eternal part of our being that is infinite and is one with the field of consciousness that creates everything.

"Take quantum physics—the study of the nature and behavior of matter and energy on the atomic and subatomic level. There's solid proof that everyone and everything is interconnected. In fact, there's even speculation that memories and experiences from past lives could be encoded and stored at the quantum level in our bodies, allowing glimpses of past-life memories to emerge. Moments of feeling 'broken open,' as you've described to me before. And I do believe this is exactly what just happened to you."

Sarah sat quietly for a moment. She stared down at her hands, then looked up at Leyla.

"Thank you. I'm not sure how you knew to use scientific data rather than religious mumbo-jumbo to explain this feeling, but it calms me down a lot. At the end of the day, I am a scientist by nature and training, so I find that type of explanation—while far-fetched—much more comforting."

All of a sudden, she no longer felt agitated but exhausted.

"I think I ought to just go home, crawl into bed, and get a good night's sleep. My body feels drained. I promise that I'll be open to continuing this conversation at our next appointment."

"I have no doubt you feel a bit like you've been hit by a freight train. I'll take care of these coffees. Go ahead, and we'll talk soon. And Sarah, I hate to remind you, but even science is built on theories. What your *body* is trying to tell you is the truth."

CHAPTER TWENTY-ONE

Memphis, Ancient Egypt, two years later

Sarrah felt annoyed with her handmaidens as they tried to dress and bejewel her for the night's festivities. She'd been feeling out of sorts for months now. A sense of uncertainty had plagued her despite the celebratory energy that had been building in the palace in anticipation of the unveiling of Meti's majestic temple to Ptah.

She dared not share with Meti what she felt, as he was consumed by this long-awaited event. These past two years had gone by so quickly. Under Meti's reign, the city of Memphis had become the true cornerstone of the country, the boundary between Upper and Lower Egypt. All trade, government, and commerce literally flowed up and down the Nile in both directions from the port of Memphis.

The city had become the center of the cult of the god Ptah—a creator god, the begetter of the first beginning, and the patron saint of craftsmen and architects. As the hymn they all sang declared, he "crafted the world in his design and his heart." Ptah was the husband of Sekhmet, and the father of Nefertem and the sage Imhotep. The high priests of Ptah were highly esteemed and sought after by the viziers of Egypt's major cities, serving as chief architects and craftsmen of the country's most important temples, tombs, and funerary complexes.

Khufu, who served as a high priest of Ptah, had played no small role in the city's becoming a living homage to this god. And it was true that Khufu's glorification of Memphis during Meti's reign—its majestic white walls, its technologically advanced streets, buildings, and infrastructure—had made it the jewel of not only Egypt but of the entire region. And for the most part, Sarrah had been able to keep Khufu on task and subject to Meti's wishes.

Along with the city's rise in importance, Meti's star had risen as well. Sarrah marveled at his transformation into a powerful and popular leader. He was decisive, strategic, unafraid. Hotheaded, yes, but that seemed to work in his favor. She knew that her role in his ascendance to supremacy, his maturation as a man, had been pivotal. Meti's reign would be long and legendary, and she would sacrifice her very life to see to that. Tonight was as much her celebration as it was his. So why the trepidation?

Sarrah had prayed, paced her garden, even sought solace through meditations to Heka and a visit to the heterae, but she was unable to find the cause of her unease. It was as if there was a veil around tonight's gala that denied Sarrah her usual foresight. She felt as if she were lost in a maze, with every corner she turned revealing only a dead end. She knew that something unfamiliar held her in its grip, yet she was unable to determine what or who it was. She felt great distress and growing fear with this loss of insight and intuition. What was happening to her?

She returned to her reflection in the mirror. Who was this queenlike vision? She was more comfortable behind the throne than on it; public adoration or validation had never been her goal. But here she was. The maids had brushed her hair to its most radiant shine and were preparing to secure her new gift from Meti upon it.

Last night Sarrah and Meti had finished their lovemaking in an unusually quick fashion. Afterward he hopped up from the bed and summoned his valet. The servant brought in a box that Sarrah hadn't seen before—a beautiful ebony case inlaid with ivory and red wood. Meti took the box and presented it shyly to her with a boyishness she hadn't seen from him in years.

"For you," he said, as he sat down next to her.

Sarrah suddenly felt cold and sweaty, as if a fever had taken her in its grip.

"My lord," she whispered. "Your ability to surprise me endures." She raised the lid and gasped when she saw the headdress within. She carefully lifted it out of the cushioned case and reverently spun it around in her hands. It was a gold headdress inlaid with jewels that glinted in the candlelight. From the intricate handiwork, she knew that it had taken months to create this piece. A fringe of azure, ivory, and crimson beads falling from the band would frame the wearer's face. Were these rubies? Sapphires? Garnets? Pearls? These jewels must have been sourced and traded from far and wide.

But Sarrah couldn't take her eyes off the feature in the center of the headdress—nor would anyone else be able to ignore it. This was *meant* to be regarded. Rising from the crown were two intertwined gold serpents, the sacred symbol of Heka. Sarrah knew what Meti meant by this glittering iconography. The two encircled powers featured so prominently were his answer to the sculpture she'd commissioned in his honor. And while hers had been a private offering meant to show reverence, his was a public proclamation meant to be seen by the masses.

She lowered the headdress and bowed at Meti's feet. "My king, this is too much. I am not worthy to wear such a crown."

Meti didn't reply for some time. Then he said, "Rise, Sarrah. I am Pharaoh. I give you this gift with gratitude for all that you have taught and given me these past seven years. You are the only person worthy of this honor. You will wear it tomorrow as you accompany me to my glorification."

Sarrah stood and nodded her head in acknowledgment. She hugged Meti, holding the headdress and pretending to admire it. Yet inside she felt only foreboding.

Sarrah was rattled by an encounter she'd had with Nour a few days ago. The two friends had rare occasion to see each other, so she was surprised when Nour passed through the gate one morning as she tended to her private garden.

"I knew I could find you here," said Nour, breathless. She looked around at Sarrah's personal masterpiece—the rows of flowers, the citrus trees, the lotus pond. "It's just as beautiful as I had heard it was," she said. "Sarrah, you are truly blessed by the gods."

Sarrah brought her friend into a tight embrace. "Nour! I am so happy to see you, I've wanted to share this with you many times. But what are you doing here? How did you get through the palace security?"

Nour gave her a knowing look. "I have my ways." She was as mischievous as ever.

The two walked for a bit, arm in arm. Then Sarrah turned to her, looking confused.

"Wait—you said you'd heard the garden was beautiful. Who told you that? No one is allowed here without my knowing it."

They came to a stop by the sculpture of Meti and Sarrah entwined. Nour regarded it, then looked at her gravely. "Khufu told me. That is why I am here."

"*Khufu?* Oh, please. Don't tell me, he was bragging about something or other."

"Sarrah, for several months Khufu has requested me as his hetaera and no one else. I think he knows that you and I are friends, and he wanted to see if you had entrusted me with se-crets. But I told him that we almost never see each other. That I'd be the *last* person to know your secrets."

Sarrah looked at her childhood friend. "Nour, the day will come when we are reunited in friendship. When we will share all our stories again."

"I don't have your gift of second sight," said Nour, "though I trust that you would not raise my hopes if it weren't true. But anyway, I think once Khufu realized I was of no use to him, he started to—yes—brag about his stature in the court, how he'd one day make me his own personal companion. He even gave me this gold cuff."

She raised her sleeve. Sarah recognized the same piece he'd given to her when she was still a girl, that day they'd sailed to the palace. But she didn't say a word.

Nour continued. "Khufu tells me how you've changed since we were children, and how you couldn't be trusted to look out for me or the Pharaoh or anyone else. But that I shouldn't worry—you had underestimated his powers. One day *he* would be at the helm of Egypt."

"Nour, is that true?" Sarrah asked. "But why would he confide in you or anyone in that way?"

"I'm good at what I do." Nour smiled. "Don't underestimate *my* powers."

Sarrah shook her head. "Nour, you are still my dearest friend. Thank you for telling all of this to me and risking coming here. But I've been battling Khufu my whole life. I know my powers are stronger than his. Meti is wrapped around my finger. See this sculpture?"

Nour grasped her friend's arms. "Sarrah, are you absolutely certain? I'm telling you, Khufu is awfully confident. Watch yourself. Something has changed."

Sarrah hugged her. "I hear what you are saying. I promise you, I am devoted to Meti and our mother Egypt. Khufu is right where I want him. There is nothing to fear."

She couldn't risk telling her oldest friend that yes, perhaps for the past two years she had put herself in a precarious position. A little voice in her head had been saying the same thing, but listening to it wasn't something she was prepared to do.

———

She was roused from her thoughts by her handmaidens, who'd finally secured the headdress with elaborate braids. Their fussing and flitting about only added to the rising panic within her. It finally became too much to bear. "Leave me," she commanded.

Sarrah walked out onto her balcony and took a few deep breaths. On the streets below, the city was abuzz with preparation and anticipation. It had been many years since the last dedication of a new temple. Everywhere she looked, she saw richness and promise. Egypt had never been more beautiful. It seemed as if the city had been bathed in jasmine, as if it had been ordered to bloom on cue. The cypress trees and flowering shrubs that had been planted in the past few months looked utterly breathtaking against the limestone structures and sandy streets. Enterprising food vendors fried breads, roasted meats, and cut up melons for the coming onslaught of crowds. It was a joyous sight, yet Sarrah was unable to feel her country's elation.

She looked to the gods for guidance, to clarify the message. At her deepest core, she knew that Khufu had something to do with her sense of unease. He'd been spending a great deal of time with Meti these past months, while the final details of the temple were being completed. Sarrah knew her uncle was up to something. She also knew that he had assigned a few spies to monitor her every move, both inside the palace and outside in the city. But those fools were easy to evade—or were they?

Was it possible that one of Khufu's men had seen Sarrah with Hasim? The two of them had become more and more reckless since becoming secret lovers. She shivered at the thought, as that would mean death for both of them. *Stop this, Sarrah,* she chastised herself. *You are the most powerful person in the kingdom after Meti. You are the one who has his ear. Khufu is nothing compared to you. There is no need to be frightened.* She continued to bolster herself with these thoughts. But as she gazed in the mirror, lining her eyes in kohl, she knew that she was wrong.

The architecture of this temple had been entrusted by Meti to Khufu. Under his decades of service to first one Pharaoh and now the son, Khufu had ensured that Memphis—the city of Ptah—had become the center of architecture and civilization. The temple would be its crowning jewel. However, the temple gardens would symbolize Meti's command of the natural world, of the Nile itself. They would feature an irrigation system and network of canals, pools, and fountains that would take other cultures decades to equal. Meti had entrusted the design of the garden to Sarrah.

To translate Egypt's primacy into a language of plants, Sarrah had proposed including a specimen of every tree, flower, bush, and herb native to Egypt. The temple gardens wouldn't be only a visual splendor but also a working resource. Sarrah envisioned people from villages and cities a day's journey from Memphis—or even farther—traveling here for a cutting of yarrow or a cherry tree to bring to their city or village. The temple garden would be a hub of agricultural and natural abundance, from which spokes of bounty extended. If certain regions of the country were lay fallow or were cursed with drought, citizens from other regions could travel home with seedlings of the endangered crops. It was a grand vision, yes, and would take decades to reach maturity, but Meti praised Sarrah for this initiative and foresight. The power of the plant world and its connection to the gods, prized by Sarrah, was something that Meti had come to appreciate as well. It was theirs now.

For this garden to truly reflect the landscape of Egypt required a knowledge not only of the Nile Delta but of lands farther afield. Of course, Sarrah knew the native crops of her own village, and those along the way to the white walls of Memphis—but she also wanted to see the palm dates of Alexandria, the henna vines of Saqqara, the herb gardens of Heliopolis, the apple orchards of Karnak, the olive groves of Luxor. She wanted to have all these riches represented in the temple garden.

Sarrah would have to learn and catalogue a variety of native terrains. To recreate them in the temple garden, she would create a series of floodplains, wells, and irrigation that would mirror the varying landscape of Egypt. How better to please Ptah?

————

Sarrah was consumed with her new project. Of course, her first obligation was to the daily (and nightly) needs of her Pharaoh. When in Memphis she was never far from Meti's side.

However, she began to travel to other regions of Egypt to complete her research. Meti was young and needed occasional periods of rest (and revelry). Sarrah would hastily gather a small crew to accompany her: slaves to set up camp, maids to pack and cook, and soldiers to protect them.

They knew there were rebels in this generally peaceful country who would like nothing better than to hold hostage the right-hand advisor to the Pharaoh. They were careful to travel lightly and unassumingly, free of any visible sign that they were palace sentries. They wore villagers' rough robes, slept in small tents, cooked simple meals. Even their horses and saddles were inconspicuous. Anyone who passed this band of travelers would have thought the encampment was a group of rug merchants or tradesmen.

For better or worse, these trips offered cover for what was a wildly satisfying yet shamefully ill-advised series of rendezvous with Hasim. As general of the armies, Hasim was required to travel from one military outpost to another, overseeing the training of soldiers and the building of fortresses and suppressing the occasional rebel skirmish. Egypt was generally a peaceful country, but the richer it grew, the more fortified it had to become.

Meti seemed more than happy to have Hasim as his military adviser, so long as he was generally out of his sight. He'd sensed something between Hasim and Sarrah years ago. The partnership between Meti and Hasim was a tenuous one, though Hasim had proven time and time again that he was an even greater proponent of Meti's reign than he had been of his father's. Despite Meti's lifelong insecurity that Hasim was his father's "favorite son," he seemed mollified by Hasim's loyalty.

And yet—with all her powers of foresight, wisdom, and sense—Sarrah kept a secret. Under cover of night, her camp bed was often shared by this swarthy, handsome, brilliant general. Who would think that Hasim, military commander of Egypt, would bother to visit their modest encampment? When in their travels her team found themselves pitching camp with Hasim's army, under a starlit sky they would meet while the two groups reveled into the night or slept soundly in their tents. With Sarrah in her humble linen tunic and Hasim free of his helmet and sword, in the moonlight they looked like just another couple making love under a palm tree, swathed in blankets.

Their love—or was it lust?—was so forbidden, so doomed, that they both had to have taken complete leave of their senses to enjoy these stolen moments. And yet: their senses were so alive when they made love. She breathed in this man until she was drunk on his virile scent. His touch was so different from Meti's—the way he was hungry for her, as if he'd sworn off every mortal pleasure to enjoy this one with her. He knew what he wanted, and he took it. He knew what she wanted, and he gave it.

———

Meti had sought Sarrah's counsel on all aspects of the planning for the unveiling of the Temple and Temple Garden of Ptah. They'd spent countless hours imagining an event that the people of Egypt would remember for the next fifty years. Their most creative moments blossomed after their lovemaking, when they were both spent, sweaty, and breathless. It was just the two of them then, holding each other and whispering about all the possibilities and fantasies that seemed too outlandish to mention aloud during the day. It was in these intimate moments that the best ideas were born to honor and glorify Meti and his reign.

————

Sarrah was overcome as she realized that the moment had finally arrived. She was ready. One last glance in the mirror showed that her headdress, hair, makeup, and robes were all resplendent. The only jewelry she wore other than her crown was her prized gold cuff. She donned the essential oil blend she'd mixed just for this day—sage and peppermint to bring clarity and strength. She walked to meet Meti, surrounded by advisors and servants, in the central hall.

"Ready?" she asked. Though hubbub swirled around them, their eyes locked. He looked so regal—tall, with lustrous skin and robes woven with gold.

He smiled. "Yes."

They would walk from the palace in a royal parade toward the new temple, a ceremonial passage of power. As she strode behind Meti through the triumphal arch built just for this evening, she had to stop for a moment to take it all in. It was unlike anything Egypt had ever seen before. As Meti walked, the crowds fell in behind him. The heady aromas of incense, flowers, and food permeated the evening air. Musicians played traditional hymns on lyres, lutes, and drums, and people hummed and sang.

Sarrah leaned in close to Meti and whispered, "My Pharaoh, while this celebration is marvelous, it does not even touch your brilliance and beauty. It is a triumph."

Meti grabbed her hand and squeezed as he continued to

lead the cavalcade onward. When they rounded the corner, he whispered, "Look up."

Sarrah gasped. Meti had forbidden her to visit the building for nine months. She had objected greatly but nonetheless had obeyed. Her objection wasn't about being left out of the temple design—she had no intuition about architecture. She was concerned, however, that Khufu had had so much alone time with Meti without her presence to provide a counterbalance. Sarrah knew she could never drop her guard when it came to her uncle's schemes and intrigues. But she had to admit, grudgingly, that her uncle had outdone himself.

The crowds cheered and sang and availed themselves of the massive banquet tables of food and refreshments provided by the Pharaoh. Slaves served dishes piled high with fowl, beef, lentils, fruits, and breads. Ewers of beer, juice, water, and wine were poured until empty, while runners hustled for more. As people gathered to dance, sing, and carry on, it was clear that the revelry would go on for hours.

But Sarrah's eyes were fixed only on the monument to Ptah, rising several stories high at the entrance to the temple. The carved sandstone figure bore a specific likeness to Meti, the serene face gazing omnipotently over the kingdom. The four limestone columns on either side of the figure must have been eight feet in diameter. Two majestic sphinxes flanking the entrance into the temple chamber each had the body of a lion and the head of Meti himself. Sarrah doubted that the sphinx heads were Meti's idea—the required hubris seemed uncharacteristic, and she assumed that Khufu had outdone himself with this overweening deference.

She had to know.

"My lord," she said into Meti's ear, "your likeness on the sphinxes is breathtaking. I did not realize you created the guardians in your image."

"That was Khufu and Khepri's idea," he replied. "Khufu and I got on quite well with the design of the monument. I was impressed with his loyalty. He said that he believed I was even more of a natural-born leader than my father."

Meti beamed with pride while Sarrah felt a creeping sense of dread. In that instant she knew that her luck had somehow changed.

Sarrah knew better than to engage Meti further about Khufu, so she dutifully followed him up the grand marble stairs. At the top she saw her uncle presiding as if he himself were the king of Egypt, receiving tribal leaders and the highest members of society.

As they approached, Khufu bowed flamboyantly and said, "Welcome to your temple, my Pharaoh. It will forever be a beacon to all other nations of your eminence and the greatness of Egypt."

Meti slapped Khufu on the back. "Stand, my friend. Stand and accept your just rewards for a job well done." The two men proceeded to enter the temple together, leaving Sarrah alone on the top step. She knew she couldn't enter without the express permission of the Pharaoh, so she simply stood there and watched them recede into the candlelit chamber. Soon she could no longer make out their figures. She felt as if Meti had just abandoned her forever.

Sarrah had put all her eggs into one basket—the one she had felt destined to carry. Her path to where she stood now had been relatively smooth. But had she reached a dead end? The incongruity between her dark mood and the celebrations around her was making her head spin. To be less recognizable, she removed her golden headdress and tucked it into her corded belt. She lifted a glass of wine from a banquet table and began to make her way into the gardens, where the citizens of Memphis were marveling at this new addition to their already majestic city. The air would do her good.

Hasim. She could feel his eyes upon her. As every soul in Egypt was here tonight, of course he would be, too. She didn't try to find him; she wasn't in charge of what happened. She knew he would make his move soon enough, and she was thrilled at the thought of being with him again.

With glass in hand, Sarrah allowed herself to wander freely throughout the gardens, marveling at the canals, the wells, and the variety of ecosystems. As she looked around at the revelers, she envied their gaiety and ease. The weight of her life and her role had never felt heavier than it did right now. *What must it be like to live a simple life?* The allure of an uncomplicated existence consumed her for a moment. But then she noticed their threadbare garments, their bare feet, their body odor, their poor teeth. Sarrah was suddenly grateful for her life at the palace in a way she hadn't felt for years. *I could never survive in poverty,* she mused. *It may be shallow of me, but I love my power and status.* She wove her way deeper into the vast garden rows.

Sarrah turned a corner and came into a clearing where a small band of musicians had set up. She was swept into the crowd of dancing men, women, and children, and she found herself smiling and laughing for the first time in months. She closed her eyes and moved to the music. She felt connected to her people in a way she hadn't since she was a young girl. What if she just disappeared into this crowd and never went back to the palace?

The hand on her waist jolted her out of her reverie as a strong male body pressed up against her back.

"Do not turn around, my beauty," Hasim ordered. "I have been watching you for some time and could not stay away any longer. You captivate my very soul."

Sarrah slowed her movements. Their bodies fell into perfect cadence. "Do you feel it, Hasim?" Sarrah asked quietly. "It's as if we are joined as one in all ways. I could just disappear into you."

Hasim turned her around gently and cupped her face in his hands. "Yes, my love. Yes, I feel it. I have felt it from the very moment I laid eyes on you. You have been with me every moment since."

He leaned in and kissed her passionately. Sarrah threw her arms around his neck. They were utterly lost in each other. They didn't see the crowd part as the Pharaoh strode into the plaza with fury in his eyes.

Meti. Sarrah felt a bolt of terror run down her spine. She jolted back from Hasim. The music stopped. No laughter. It seemed no one was even breathing. She looked into Hasim's eyes right before she turned to face her king; in a split second she knew she might never see him again. Hasim tried to step in front of her, but she stopped him with her hand and an imperceptible nod. She knew she needed to handle Meti herself.

"So Khufu was speaking the truth all these years," Meti began. "I kept telling that wretched fool that my Sarrah vowed to never betray me. That she belonged to me and only me, body and soul. Yet he continued to plant seeds of doubt at every turn."

He took a step toward Sarrah. "How dare you look me in the eye, woman," he said evenly. "You will show your respect by lying on the ground before me."

Sarrah kneeled on the terrace that she herself had designed, surrounded by trees she'd worked so hard to procure and plant, and she lay down prostrate before her Pharaoh. The dread that had plagued her was now coursing through her veins. Her head was spinning, and she was beginning to hyperventilate. It dawned on her that her uncle must have cast some sort of dark spell around her to prevent her from seeing the reality that was now playing out. Still, she cursed herself for not being more diligent about staying close to Meti during the past year. Her complacency and entitlement may have just cost her and her beloved Hasim their lives.

"Hasim, you will remove your sword and kneel before me,"

Meti ordered. With a wave of his hand, a battalion of guards appeared and circled Hasim.

Meti walked toward him and picked up his sword. As he unsheathed it, he said, "Perhaps I shall slice off your head right here and now with your own blade. Your betrayal to Egypt itself is complete. There is no hope for you."

Meti nodded and the guards began to drag Hasim by his arms from the plaza. He screamed over his shoulder, *"Sarrah is innocent! Sarrah is innocent!"* But in a matter of moments he and the guards were out of sight.

Khufu sidled up to Meti and whispered—so that everyone could hear. "Sire, I am humiliated that my niece has betrayed and embarrassed you so deeply. But I am grateful the truth has been revealed, and you now can see her for the hypocrite that she is. May I suggest a public punishment at this very moment, to send the message to all of Egypt about what happens if you are crossed?"

Meti shut his eyes as if he were in pain. "Khufu," he demanded, "I advise you to hold your tongue, or I shall have it cut out."

He shook his head as if he couldn't process what was happening. "Guards!" he shouted. "Remove this slave and place her in the palace dungeon."

As Sarrah rose, she locked eyes with Meti. "My king," she pleaded. "Please give me an opportunity to explain everything. There is a treacherous shadow around you right now, and you are in danger." She saw the deep pain in Meti's eyes and reached out a hand, quivering.

"Woman," Meti growled. *"Do. Not. Touch. Me."*

Then he whispered, his voice cracking, "Why, Sarrah?" He looked at her with both confusion and agony.

"Meti, my beloved—" Sarrah began, then gasped as he brought Hasim's sword up to her neck. In his eyes, she saw the Meti she knew and loved disappearing behind a veil of anger and rage. Her Meti was gone, and it was she who had broken him. He lowered the sword slowly, and with disgust he grabbed the priceless headdress she'd hung from her belt.

What have I done? she thought as she was hustled away. Out of the majestic garden that was her pride and joy. Out of the life that she'd worked so hard to create.

# CHAPTER TWENTY-TWO

Sarrah had lost all sense of time. Her cell had no window and only torches for light, so she couldn't tell how long she'd been imprisoned. She felt it must have been at least a month since that fateful evening at the Temple of Ptah, but in her weakening state she couldn't be sure. Meti had clearly ordered her to be treated as a common thief. Her only interaction with life outside the prison was the woman who delivered her food and water. Sarrah had finally begun keeping count of her visits to get a sense of the passage of time. Given her declining health, she deduced that she received a meal only once a day. By her count, twenty days had passed. She knew that if her imprisonment continued much longer, she'd soon lose consciousness and slowly slip into the afterlife.

Thankfully, Sarrah's intuitive gifts had fully returned. Whatever black magic Khufu had engaged in to keep her in darkness had lifted. He must have presumed that Sarrah was no longer a threat to him. She vowed to see Khufu suffer before she took her last breath. Sarrah tried to channel what Meti's plans were, and where Hasim was being held. She could sense that he was still alive, and she was gripped with fear for his well-being.

"My beloved Heka," she chanted to the god of magic and medicine, weak with fear. "Please cast a protective shield around my Hasim. Keep him safe from all harm, known and unknown, until I am free of this prison and able to get to him."

Though she blamed herself for falling prey to her very human needs, she could feel Heka's wrath at the circumstances Sarrah had been manipulated into. Balance must be restored. Sarrah knew she would have the protection of the gods to call on when she needed it as the coming days and months unfolded.

Her future was not bright, nor was it certain. She could sense Meti's rage and heartbreak over her betrayal. This was not the same Meti she'd last kissed or caressed, or with whom she'd glorified Egypt. The man she now channeled was full of anger and revenge and pain, determined to spread those dark emotions over everyone and everything that crossed his path. Her king was being guided by fury, not magnanimity. Night after night Sarrah appealed to any spirits who were listening, promising that if she were to make it out of this situation alive and regain Meti's trust, she would never leave him again.

A year passed. The country of Egypt, it seemed, had settled into a period of darkness since Sarrah's arrest. She could sense it every day as she was led in heavy chains from the palace prison into the gates of the palace itself. People rushed from place to place, heads down. There was little street life; no music being performed, no market stalls of fresh fruit and bread, no children at play. Soldiers walked the streets, now under Khufu's command. It seemed as if Meti had lost faith in the loyalty of not only Sarrah but of the entire population of Egypt. He ruled with punishment and revenge instead of law and reason.

It hadn't been enough for Meti to let Sarrah rot in her cell. Now on most days—or even in the middle of the night—he would have her bound in chains and brought to him, to stand next to the throne for hours while he exploited her psychic powers. Meti's council of advisors, once a balanced group of elders, military strategists, and loyalists, was now reduced to just Khufu—and Khufu's ambition had expanded with his ego. Having designed the finest city in Egypt's history to honor his Pharaoh, he would not rest until they had conquered neighboring countries and built temples there to glorify him as well.

She didn't see what purpose she served by being here. Frail beneath her shackles, she would try to respond to Meti's barked questions to the best of her powers. The Throne Room was empty but for her, Meti, Khufu, and a phalanx of guards. She summoned as much courage and determination as she could to show Meti reason, foresight, the path of least resistance. But after days of verbal assaults, he finally broke her spirit.

"If you believe that violent overthrows of allied governments are what the gods want, then I suppose you must be right," Sarrah cried. She felt faint and sank to the ground, weeping.

A guard stepped in to catch her fall. "I'll take her back to the prison," he said to Khufu.

"Please do, Asum. Clearly she is no good to us here."

Asum, she thought as she fell weakly into his arms. Hasim's second in command. He carried her out through the halls of the palace and into the street. The prison guards waved them past. Asum lowered Sarrah onto the cot in her cell.

"I am sorry to see you like this," he whispered. "I tried to get you out of there as soon as I could."

"Thank you, Asum," she said weakly. "This is my fate right now. Don't worry, I am stronger than I look."

"I have news of Hasim," he said quietly. "I must speak quickly because I don't want the guards to get suspicious. I just returned from a mission to supervise the prisoners building the trading posts along the nomadic trail across the desert. This is a mission that no one wants to do; it's godforsaken territory. But I volunteered for it."

Asum checked the hallway again to ensure that they were alone, then continued.

"I don't agree with how Khufu conducts the military close to home, so I was anxious to leave the city for my own purposes. Soldiers are uneasy under Khufu's leadership. The prisoners are carried to these remote work sites on wagons if they are lucky; some have to walk, and the weak don't make it. They work from dawn until dusk, sleep on mats, and of course are given very little food and water. It's hundreds of miles, back-breaking labor.

"I have been looking for Hasim at each of these outposts. Just when I had almost lost hope, I found him at a small military outpost in the Kharga Oasis in the western desert. He was difficult to recognize. His hair and beard are long and matted. He has lost weight, and his skin is the dark bronze of a Bedouin Arab, not an elite soldier. Meti had sentenced him to spend the rest of his days there, mining sandstone. He wasn't sure how long he'd been there, but he knew it had been more than a year."

"How is he?" Sarrah asked, softly crying.

"He is as you would imagine—thin and tired. His spirit is low, but he is alive. He doesn't cause trouble, and he hopes for the day he can return to Memphis. But this seems impossible."

Asum took a crumpled paper from his robe. "I have a note for you. I was not sure I would see you, but I told him I'd take it. Read it quickly."

Sarrah's hands shook as she read the note:

Sarrah—Just the thought of you fills me with the will to live and somehow return home. I pray to the gods each day that no harm has come to you. I will never forget the look on Meti's face when he found us—the look of a young boy who has just lost his mother. He is dangerous and vengeful, as he should be. If there is a way I can set the path straight again, for us and for Egypt, I will try until I die. Yours, Hasim

It was more than she could bear. She closed her eyes and feebly handed it back to Asum, who held the note over a torch until ashes filled the air.

CHAPTER TWENTY-THREE

One year later

Sarrah didn't know if she could continue at this pace much longer. She had been channeling for four days straight and was beginning to lose hold of her senses. The borders of space and time no longer existed for her, and she feared she might soon lose the ability to return to reality.

At least she was no longer in the prison. After enduring more than a year of pure torture and humiliation, Sarrah had decided to change tactics and position herself as an ally to this new Meti rather than a defender of the old one. She began to offer hints of mystic insight and encouragement for his upcoming siege of Babylon. Her intuition had shown Sarrah why this campaign was so important—but not for the reasons Meti and Khufu believed. With this knowledge safely tucked in the deepest recesses of her being, she donned the mask of compliant military advisor and strategist. Sarrah knew she was taking a great risk, but she had to install herself as invaluable in the coming war efforts. Khufu seemed suspicious of allowing her such access to Meti, but he was confident that they'd broken her spirit. And they had.

Sarrah tried to put Hasim out of her mind, but the connection that had existed between them was not easily broken. Previously when she'd channeled visions of him lying in her prison cell, it was much as Asum had described to her. She'd seen flashes of desert, heard the noise of a mallet cracking sandstone, felt bitter thirst. But when she tried to channel him now, she sensed that Hasim was closer. She saw images of tunnels, candlelight, maps. She hoped he wasn't somehow within the city of Memphis, because if Meti or his spies found out they would certainly kill him—very publicly. They wouldn't chance banishing him to the desert again.

———

Meti barged into her chamber and slammed the door behind him. He'd moved all her belongings to a suite of rooms on the highest floor of the palace. Sarrah had freedom within these rooms but was placed in manacles whenever she was summoned outside of them. *Progress,* she thought as she watched Meti walk over to the window.

"My Pharaoh," Sarrah began, as she kneeled and bowed to him. Their dynamic was still badly broken, and Sarrah knew better than to ever presume her position again. Any resolution to their relationship had to be instigated by Meti himself.

"Mystic," Meti said, looking out toward the horizon, "I grow weary of waiting for more guidance from you and the gods. My patience is thin. Khufu has presented a new seer at court, a young priest. I am on the verge of having you killed and installing that young man in your place."

Sarrah dared not move. She had seen this moment coming but hadn't expected it so soon.

"What say you, witch?" Meti barked. He hadn't once called her by her name since she'd been imprisoned more than a year ago. Eyes trained at the ground, Sarrah spoke.

"My king, I have foreseen the arrival of this boy for some

time now. Khufu is a fool to think he can find someone who can supersede my abilities. But I welcome the challenge."

She paused for a moment and then continued. "I offer this possibility to help you make your decision. Put me up against the child in a contest of sorts. Put me up against every mystic in the kingdom if you like. Through these trials, I will prove once and for all not only my superiority as the most powerful seer in Egypt, but also my determination to gain back your trust."

Sarrah wished she could look up and see the expression on Meti's face as her words sank in, but she dared not. She remained kneeling, eyes down. After a long silence, she finally heard him move away from the window. She watched as his feet strode past her, then heard him stop.

"Sarrah, look at me."

She shivered at hearing her name on Meti's lips after so long, but she remained expressionless as she lifted her head to meet his gaze.

"You mean nothing to me. Do not doubt that I will kill you the moment you fail in this challenge." He turned and left the room.

Sarrah rose, a rare smile on her face. *Oh, Meti,* she said to herself. *You are so wrong. But fear not. I am coming for you, dear one. I am coming.*

————

Sarrah woke from a brief but deep sleep and felt the exhaustion in her bones. Meti had taken her words quite literally, summoning every known seer in the kingdom over the past few months. Their reputations or status didn't matter. If they were rumored to have any gifts, they were brought to the palace to challenge her. At first Sarrah was amused by it all. But then she realized Meti's strategy.

Meti had every intention of depleting her so completely that she would have no energy left to face Nakia, the psychic that Khufu had discovered in the desert. Through palace gossip, Sarrah had learned that Nakia was indeed powerful. His abilities ranged from reading people's minds to predicting the future with extreme accuracy. He had a host of impressive gifts that seemed to match Sarrah's—but for one. And if Sarrah could get Meti to command a test of that skill, then she knew she would succeed.

Sarrah entered the Throne Room. It was the same scenario as it had been over the past weeks—a small group of onlookers to witness this test of skills. She heard a commotion behind her and turned to see Khufu escorting Nakia into the room. What a public rebuke; so much for family loyalty.

So be it, Uncle, Sarrah mused, staring unabashedly at Khufu. *You will rue the day you ever brought me to court.* She then turned her back on them and faced the throne.

Meti had not yet arrived, so Sarrah took a moment to regard the majestic royal throne she had helped design, with the secret space behind his seat just for her so that she could advise him without being detected. Those days of absolute power and passion at her Pharaoh's side seemed a lifetime ago. Had she really condemned people to death with a thrill in her heart? Had she participated in such cruel and selfish atrocities? How life and the passage of time had changed her.

Sarrah and Meti had had good intentions, but more than once their human failings had caused them to feel quite god-like. Once she was back in Meti's trust, she would never again allow such deadly sins to occur in Egypt. She would refocus on her original intention to return Egypt to its glorified state of power and dominance—but not through fear. A golden age was Egypt's destiny. And this battle was the next great trial she'd have to endure to bring it about.

The gongs sounded, and all those present knelt and bowed their heads. Meti entered from behind the throne and took the steps up to his seat. Once in place, he ordered all to rise.

"The final contest has come," he began. "Sarrah and Nakia, you both understand what is at stake. You will both be put through various challenges to test whose powers are strongest. Each of you will take turns deciding which trial will be undertaken. I will be the final judge." He then tapped his scepter on the floor three times and announced, "Begin."

After several trials put to them by the elders, Nakia seemed as fresh as a lotus blossom, while Sarrah was clearly withering. Thankfully, it was her turn to choose the test. She knew that she must choose a challenge that exploited not only her psychic abilities but those that she'd been taught by her mother and had sharpened herself over time—the magical properties of the natural world. A young man like Nakia would have honed skills that made him popular and rich—fortune telling, finding hidden objects, predicting the outcome of games—but he wouldn't have bothered to venture into the complex alchemy of herbs, trees, and flowers. Sarrah had kept herself occupied in prison by retracing the steps of her private garden in her mind, recounting potions and recipes of her own design, and creating new experiments to try should she ever be free. Even Khufu and Meti didn't know the depth of her knowledge in this field.

Sarrah turned toward Meti and declared, "I request a trial of Sekhmet, goddess of health and healing. I challenge Nakia to save a body just before the moment of death."

The audience erupted in murmurs and chatter, as such a contest had never before been waged. Khufu stood, laughing dismissively.

"My lord, you must not entertain such a notion. Sarrah is clearly delusional in her exhaustion."

Meti slammed down his scepter and roared, "Silence! How dare you speak when none of this concerns you, Khufu. Guards, remove him from the room."

Finally, a win, Sarrah thought. *Khufu will be unable to assist Nakia from afar.*

She dared not look at Meti as she awaited his decision. He rose and addressed the room. "This woman has requested a risky and dangerous test of skill and abilities. However, I allow this challenge. Guards, find two children to be the volunteers."

Sarrah blanched. "No, sire! Please, no. Are there not some prisoners who can be sacrificed?"

Meti turned to her with a sinister look that she didn't recognize. "You should have foreseen that, seer. Not another word or I will name Nakia the winner."

Sarrah was desperate. She would sooner die herself than allow an innocent child to be killed. *I may be the one to die today,* she thought.

One glance at Nakia revealed his own terror at losing this battle and therefore his life. Sarrah realized she had to time the next few minutes to precision in order to save them all.

The terrified screams of children echoed from the hallway, and a doctor brought in a tray, his shaking hands causing the two metal cups to rattle. Two girls around the age of seven were forced by two guards into a kneeling position in front of the Pharaoh. His face devoid of emotion, Meti ordered, "Administer the poison."

The crowd dared not move as the guards handed each child a cup, then raised their daggers to the girls' throats. With tears streaming down their cheeks, they drank the liquid and burst into tears, then passed out on the ground.

Nakia flailed and gestured erratically as he tried to physically revive the first girl, shaking her dying body and breathing into her mouth. He, too, started crying and begging the gods for intercession on his behalf. Sadly, the little girl appeared to pass away in his arms.

Sarrah didn't see any of this happen. She was deep in meditation, channeling Sekhmet—as she had since she was a child—to revive the other girl, whose heartbeat was imperceptible. Voicing an incantation handed down from her mother and never spoken by any man, she repeated and repeated it until moments later the girl gasped, then opened her eyes.

"Bring this girl some water!" Sarrah cried. She was a dead woman, so why not take command of her last moments? The gathered elders rushed around the awakened girl, and Sarrah bolted up the steps to the throne.

"Stand down!" Meti started to say—but she looked at him and he softened. She raced behind the throne to her old hiding place, where there was a compartment even Meti didn't know about. She removed the false panel. *Yes, it was still there!* She grabbed the miniature vial and raced down the steps, taking in her arms the dead girl lying at Nakia's feet.

"Get back from her!" Meti shouted at the crowd that had gathered around the girl. "Give her space!"

Sarrah uncorked the vial and poured a dram of the potion into the girl's bluish lips, then began to pray. Only a few minutes had passed, so perhaps this antidote could still revive her. All those trials and experiments—may this work here as it had in her garden laboratory! She rubbed the girl's forehead, murmuring incantations. She rocked and rocked, warming the girl with her own body, and slowly color returned to her lips and face. She opened her eyes, dazed, and then began to cry. The first girl rushed to her side, and the onlookers shouted with joy. For years to come people would tell the tale of the girls who had come back from the dead, and of the mystic woman who had made it happen.

Meti was aghast. "Are you a woman or a god? Who can bring another mortal back from the dead?"

"My Pharaoh, I spent years experimenting in my garden for antidotes to hemlock poison. I practiced on small animals and birds. I wanted no one to know of the cure but me, your protector. To my knowledge no one on earth knows of it. Should you be poisoned on the throne, I hid a vial of it, not telling anyone, even you, so that I could save you."

"Sarrah, come forward," Meti declared. The room hushed as she walked to the throne. She bowed her head.

"Please look at me," he said, with an unexpected softness in his voice. She raised her gaze to meet his.

"You have proven yourself at every turn and through every challenge. I did my best to defeat you, but you have proven your loyalty to me, which extends farther than even I knew." Meti paused as he looked at the room. "I would be honored if you would rejoin me as my adviser and guide."

Sarrah's eyes filled with tears. She had never been so exhausted in her entire life. She leaned back, weakly. The room began to spin, then went dark.

———

When Sarrah awoke, she was disoriented. She felt the fine, feather-light linens and woven blankets. Next to her bed was a gold-leafed lamp and a glass pitcher. The windows were obscured by heavy curtains. Sandalwood, tobacco, sage—it was a scent she recognized, because she had crafted it herself. For Meti. A lifetime ago.

This was Meti's chamber. As her eyes adjusted to the light, she saw that Meti himself was dozing in a chair in the corner. Her attempt to sit up roused him. "You're awake!" he whispered. "Don't get up. I will bring you some water."

He rushed to the bedside, filled a glass, and lifted it to her lips. She took the glass from him.

"Thank you, I can do it. How long have I been here?"

"You've been unconscious for two days. I carried you here myself after you fainted. Everyone was crowding around you, wanting to touch you, even snip a length of your robe. You are the magic woman who brought two dead children back to life."

"The fragrance I made for you. You kept it, even after everything that happened."

Meti stiffened slightly. "I haven't worn that fragrance since you betrayed me many seasons ago. But the events of the past few days, your brilliance, your loyalty—I would do anything to make sure that you returned to health."

He then stood abruptly, as if remembering his position. Their moment of intimacy came to an end.

"Maid," he called to the hallway. He turned to Sarrah. "Now that you are recovering, I will see to it that you are made comfortable in your own quarters. My maid will help you." He nodded and walked out of the chamber.

"Yes, yes of course. Thank you, my Pharaoh," Sarrah said. *I will settle for this polite interchange until I can regain your trust,* she thought.

As the maid helped Sarrah eat, bathe, dress, and make her way to her own bedroom, she confided that Meti had barely left her side as she'd lain unconscious. He sat with her and stroked her hand, recalling memories of their past successes, their history together, his plans for Egypt. He helped bathe her alongside the maids. He changed the wet cloth on her brow and administered healing tinctures to her skin.

Sarrah was touched by these gestures and heartened that she had made it back into Meti's good graces. Over the next few weeks she returned to full strength. But since the moment she'd watched Meti exit his chambers, she'd not seen him again. She dusted and cleaned her old bedroom, barely touched in two years. She worked in her gardens, which Meti had forbidden anyone to enter. She pruned citrus trees, sowed herbs, and watered scores of plants lying fallow. It felt so good to be outside and free. But where was Meti?

In the evenings, Sarrah took to the library and immersed herself in books of military strategy in order to be better prepared to serve her Pharaoh in the upcoming attack on Babylonia. She meditated and sat in communion with the gods, her mental and physical health restored. Soon she was fit enough to put her gold cuff back around her arm; at first she'd been so frail that it had slid down to her wrist. All the while, she awaited word from Meti. And she secretly wondered about Hasim.

Was it a dream? Was he really close by, or was he hundreds of miles away, or even dead? Sarrah could not be sure. Regardless, she knew their fated union had been a gift. For once she had experienced—could she call it love? But a vow was a vow, and Sarrah knew she had to leave Hasim in her past. She had to focus her entire being on Meti and Egypt. Never again would she risk her position and her dreams. Her love of Egypt and her devotion to Meti were greater than all else.

––––––––

Sarrah paced nervously in the council room, waiting for Meti to arrive. She had finally received a summons to appear before the Pharaoh, and she was eager and excited. As soon as she heard the door open, she knelt on the ground. She was so grateful that the maid had told her of Meti's care and concern during her recuperation, but she didn't know how she would be received now.

Meti entered the room with a few of his military leaders. Sarrah recognized the voice of Ur; she was dismayed that he'd been reinstated as top general. She tried to hide her surprise when Asum entered the room. She was unfamiliar with the others and stayed completely still as she listened and absorbed their plans for the upcoming departure into war.

An hour later the counselors were excused. Meti finally turned his attention to her.

"You may rise, Sarrah," he said curtly.

She stood, gaze to the floor, taking care not to show the stiffness that gripped her body. "You may look at me as I share my plans for you," said Meti, devoid of emotion.

Sarrah looked up into coldhearted eyes that she recognized from that ill-fated day in the Temple Gardens. She felt disappointment course through her body but showed no emotion.

"As I am sure you just heard, we will march for Babylonia within the month. You will escort me and advise me on all the plans and strategies of our enemy. After the display of your gifts during the challenge, I expect full knowledge of every move and countermove before it happens. If any surprise attack befalls our troops, you will be executed on the spot. Do you understand me?"

Sarrah simply nodded briefly and replied, "Yes. It will be done." She then bowed her head once more. But Meti had more to share.

"Your uncle will be joining the entourage as well. The hatred between you two cannot take precedence over Egypt's victory. If I feel that either of you is sacrificing our triumph for personal retribution, I will kill you both.

"Khufu has been made aware of the same and has accepted the terms. He has vowed to work with you to achieve the successful conquest and assimilation of the Babylonian Empire."

Sarrah nearly barked out a laugh. *Khufu's just biding his time until he can have you killed and consolidate power for himself,* she thought. She had to give him credit. Igniting Meti into rage and revenge, and therefore into a state of war, was a brilliant strategy. Killing a Pharaoh on the battlefield was much easier than doing so in a peaceful Memphis.

"I also understand and I vow to do whatever is necessary to assure your victory, my king," said Sarrah.

Then she felt compelled to take a risk and added, eyes still lowered, "And you have my eternal gratitude for your care and concern during my recovery. I am honored. I am feeling quite well now."

Meti stood suddenly and pushed back his chair. "You will not speak of it again, Sarrah. Do not think you can manipulate my emotions with a soft voice, woman. I am no longer the young boy you seduced. I am Pharaoh, and my only love is Egypt." He turned and left the room.

She stood perfectly still until she could hear his footsteps no longer. Slowly she walked out of the council chambers. Asum came out of the shadows.

"Asum, please do not risk either of our lives," she whispered. "Meti, Khufu—there are plenty of people who would be thrilled to have us dead."

"I will be brief. I don't want a surprise on the battlefield. Hasim is with me. I brought him back from the Kharga Oasis. As thin as a reed, with a beard and hair white from stress, he's unrecognizable. This war is a farce, but we need our strongest soldiers. He will be one of my men to march on Babylonia."

"I can see that you have already put not only the two of us but the three of us in danger with your actions," said Sarrah.

"Hasim had nothing to live for out in the desert," said Asum. "At least with my men, death is possible but not certain. I promise that he will not reveal himself or your relationship."

"Please make it clear that I wish Hasim no harm, but I am fully committed to Meti and to Egypt," she said, staring forcefully into Asum's eyes. "There is no hope of a reunion."

"I understand," he replied. "He takes this risk for Egypt and for his Pharaoh as well. When this war is over, he will disappear into obscurity."

CHAPTER TWENTY-FOUR

arrah saw the smoke rising in the distance and knew the Egyptian forces had finally engaged in battle with Babylonia. Here at the camp, at night around the fires, the scuttlebutt among the men was that this was a fool's errand. Every one knew the strength and might of Babylon. It was doubtful that Egypt would return victorious.

The city of Tyre was but the first step in a multiyear campaign of conquest and assimilation. As their armies journeyed further and further from Egyptian soil, the danger and risk grew exponentially. Restocking food, water, and supplies would be more difficult if they found themselves surrounded by the enemy deep within the Babylonian borders. Yet, like all disciplined soldiers, every man was prepared to give his life fighting for his beloved Egypt. As was Sarrah—though she hoped to save her own life as well as those of the men sitting around the fire.

Sarrah had cautioned Meti about launching an attack so quickly, but he seemed to have ears only for Khufu. Khufu swore that the signs and the gods all directed an immediate and swift strike. Sarrah had countered with a strategy of patience and more reconnaissance before entering battle. But Meti's thirst for conquest and bloodshed could not be satisfied soon enough. She watched with that same feeling of dread that she'd felt when Meti's father had entered into battle, leading hundreds of young Egyptian men into harm's way.

To his credit, Meti led the legion on his steed in full Pharaonic regalia. He was utterly breathtaking in his leadership and confidence. But knowing that they were now fully engaged in war, Sarrah sensed the soldiers' collective fear and pain. It was as if she were there, experiencing every strike, every blow, every impalement. She fell to the ground with the enormity of it.

"I beseech you, great Horus, beloved and mighty god of war and triumph," she prayed aloud. "Protect your Pharaoh and the men who serve him. Help them to survive this day so that I may share in your wishes for this crusade."

Sarrah sank into a deep meditation and received visions of all possible outcomes of this engagement. All but one involved humiliating defeat. As she emerged from her communion with the gods, she prayed for the strength to reach Meti in time and convince him of his only chance at victory.

———

Sarrah was startled awake in the middle of the night by the sound of Meti's moaning.

No! Do not take him. It is not time. There is much yet to be done! She battled the voices in her head and the fear in her heart as she rushed around the dark tent, trying to dress and gather her amulets and salves. *Meti is in danger. Meti is in danger,* the voices kept repeating.

She felt the earth tremble, then heard the thunder of hooves and rushed outside. The horses ground to a halt in a cloud of dust and sand.

Sarrah felt him before she saw him. Hasim was here. As the dust settled, there they both were.

Hasim—rangy, silver-haired, covered in dust, sweat, and blood—was sitting atop Meti's stallion with the Pharoah's limp body across his lap. The medicine men helped lower Meti to the ground and gently carried him to his tent. Sarrah watched as Hasim dismounted and walked toward her. She held her breath, frozen in her tracks. She couldn't believe it was really him.

She heard her name—*Sarrah. Help me.* It was Meti. She turned and raced to the royal tent, leaving Hasim standing there.

The following days were a blur. Sarrah spent every minute with Meti, channeling the gods to intercede on his behalf. He had yet to regain consciousness. He had suffered what should have been a fatal sword strike to his torso, but thankfully Hasim had been nearby and had sprung into action. He'd fashioned a tourniquet from his tunic, had the soldiers help lift Meti onto his horse, and brought him to safety. Sarrah shivered at the similarity to the fateful day when Hasim had done the same for Meti's father. She prayed for a different outcome for her king, but the visions that came to her revealed that Meti wasn't out of danger. It was a danger she recognized: Khufu. Had Khufu led Meti into this war to better the chances of his demise? Even more sinister, had Meti's injury been the work of one of Khufu's henchmen?

Khufu was ever present. It was as if Sarrah and her uncle were foes on a psychic battleground, fighting over Meti's survival or demise. Khufu had clearly sharpened his psychic skills during Sarrah's banishment, but he was still no match for his niece. Still, she had to be shrewd in order to get definitive proof of Khufu's duplicity.

———

One morning as she tended to Meti in the hours before dawn, he finally woke. As his eyes slowly came into focus, he whispered, "Sarrah, you found me. I kept looking for you, but it was as if I were looking through fog. I was so frightened." He tried to sit up, so Sarrah quickly arranged his pillows to offer support.

"I remember everything," he said. "Each time I moved toward your voice, something or someone would grab me from behind and pull me further and further away from you. Whatever it was had no heart, no soul. It was as if it were the god Apophis himself." He frantically gripped Sarrah's hand.

"I am here, my Pharaoh," Sarrah said. "I have been here the whole time. There is nothing more to fear."

She leaned in close to his ear and spoke in a whisper. "But your visions were quite correct. I am sorry to tell you that it is Khufu who summoned Apophis and the dark energy of evil and chaos. My uncle wants you dead so he can gain ultimate power. That has been his goal since the day he brought me to you and your father. If you will do me the honor of trusting me a bit longer, I will prove it to you."

Meti looked into her eyes. He then closed his eyes and nodded, still weak. "Do what you wish."

Hours later, as the rays of the sun ushered in a new day, Sarrah burst out of the royal tent, weeping. "He is dying. Our Pharaoh is not going to survive. I beseech all of you to pray to Anubis to offer our king a gentle transition."

Everyone within earshot knelt immediately and began praying and chanting. Sarrah knew this hubbub would garner the attention of her uncle, and right on cue Khufu emerged from his tent and walked up to her. "Stand aside, child, and let me have a few final moments with my lord," he snarled. He brushed past her and into the royal tent, where he remained alone with Meti for a short while.

After Khufu left, Sarah sat with Meti patiently for two hours. That was how long it would take for the sedative she'd administered to him to wear off. The valerian essence had a powerful, hypnotic effect, rendering Meti's mind conscious and aware of all words and movements around him but his body nearly motionless.

Meti awoke; he was still frail, but the fire was back in his eyes. "How do you feel, Meti?" she asked.

"I feel *enraged*," he said. "Sarrah, you were correct. Khufu kneeled over me and whispered curses on not only me but also you. He said he had waited a lifetime for this moment—when he would assume rule of Egypt. He spat on the ground in disgust. Thank the gods I couldn't move a muscle. The coming day will be his last."

———

The following morning, Sarrah emerged from Meti's tent much as she had the day before. She was again weeping, but this time it was tears of joy.

"*Meti!*" she cried to the heavens.

As he walked slowly out of the tent, everyone sank to their knees out of respect.

"Rise, my people. Rise and honor your Pharaoh," Meti exclaimed to the dozens of speechless soldiers and other onlookers.

Khufu ran up, his arms raised in supposed exultation. "It is a miracle, sire. You are alive. I grieved by your bedside only yesterday when your pulse was nonexistent. Praise Sekhmet and all the gods for your miraculous recovery!"

"Kneel beneath me, you fool," Meti commanded.

Khufu, surprised, fell to the ground.

"Sarrah informed me of your true intentions," said Meti in disgust. "I did not want to believe her, but I agreed to drink an essence of valerian that sunk my body into the afterlife while leaving my mind and senses in this dimension. I heard every word you uttered, Khufu."

With a speed that astounded even Sarrah, Meti revealed his dagger. He took Khufu in a headlock, then sliced his neck. Khufu dropped to the ground without a word.

Meti turned to face the crowd. "This traitor will not be granted a burial. I curse him to an eternity of spiritual exile. *Guards!* Dump his corpse far from here so his evil stench does not permeate our encampment."

With that, Meti turned to Sarrah. "Come with me," he said, beckoning her to his tent.

Throughout the following days, Sarrah shared with Meti her insight and visions about winning this war. He spoke only to her, and their thoughts were in communion more powerfully than ever before. Meti had matured into a superior leader. With a new set of strategies, and free of Khufu's vengeful and dangerous counsel, victory in the next skirmish was Egypt's. As the Babylonians retreated, the camp erupted in celebration, giving praise to the gods. Yet Sarrah knew of one final wrong that must be righted.

As the two of them rested on tufted seats in Meti's royal tent, with cheers and music reverberating outside and a grand banquet table being prepared out under the stars, Sarrah spoke carefully.

"Meti," she began, "what do you remember from the day of your injury?"

"Not much," he said. "I was moving swiftly through the enemy; the Babylonian soldiers were no match for our forces. Suddenly someone yelled my name, and as I turned to see who it was, I felt a deep pain in my left abdomen. I felt the wetness of the blood soaking my hands and my tunic. The last thing I remember is falling to the ground."

He looked at Sarrah. "Why do you ask?"

Sarrah answered in a measured tone. "There is a truth you must be made aware of, my king, but it will not be welcome news at first. You see, it seems history has repeated itself, but thankfully this time with a positive outcome."

Meti shifted in his seat.

She paused, uncharacteristically unable to find the right words.

"Just spit it out, woman," Meti ordered.

She leveled her gaze at him. "It was Hasim who saved you, as he saved your father when you were a boy." She dared not continue.

Meti was quiet. After a time, he rose and called for the guards.

"Find Hasim and bring him to me at once," he commanded. "He need not be in chains, but do not leave his side."

Meti turned to Sarrah. "I admit, it took much courage to tell me this. But I must know: Where do your loyalties lie?"

Without hesitation, Sarrah dropped to her knees. "You are my world, Pharaoh," she said. "I pledge my body, mind, and soul to you and to Egypt. This is my solemn vow."

As the guards and Hasim approached, she stood in a corner of the tent, keeping her eyes to the ground. Meti received Hasim formally but graciously, thanking him for saving his life. He did not reinstate his rank of general—that was too much to ask. He would remain a soldier.

"But stay close to camp," Meti said. "I will need you to assist with an important mission."

The next morning Meti summoned all his military counselors and Hasim to the council tent. When Sarrah entered with Meti, Ur was already there, having assumed command after Khufu's demise. Sarrah took a seat off to the left of the table, again keeping her eyes low. She could sense Hasim trying to get her attention, but she focused only on Meti.

"It has come to my attention that the King of Babylonia himself recently arrived in Tyre with his family to oversee the military response against us," said Meti. "But we are no longer going to engage in military combat."

"My king," Ur pleaded. "We are ready and willing to lay down our lives for you and the glory of Egypt. I advise against this plan. I suggest we attack again immediately."

Meti dismissed him with the wave of his hand. "Silence, old man. I never should have given you your position. You failed my father, and I will not allow you to fail me, too." Then he turned toward Hasim.

"Rise, Hasim," he instructed. "Are you ready to hear my plan for you and this war?"

Hasim nodded. "My king. It would be my greatest honor to serve you once more."

"Yes, I have no doubt it would be, given how close you came to death." Meti looked around the table. "Listen closely. Time is of the essence, so I only want to say this once."

———

The waiting was unbearable. Sarrah hadn't enjoyed a good night's rest since Hasim had ridden off with only a few select men to discharge Meti's orders. *He should have returned by now,* she thought as she walked to the royal tent that morning. As she pulled back the tent flaps, she couldn't believe her eyes. There stood Hasim, conferring quietly with the most beautiful woman Sarrah had ever seen.

"You succeeded, Hasim!" Sarrah whispered joyfully, finally addressing him.

Meti turned to Sarrah. "Yes, you are correct. Hasim has done well. My peace treaty was accepted. Princess Lilu of Babylonia is to become my wife."

I know who you are, and I saw you coming for me, Sarrah heard someone say. But the voice was in her head. Lilu! This young princess had psychic gifts.

Lilu moved closer to her. *I am not afraid, and I offer myself to the destiny that has been shown to me.*

Sarrah nodded her head slightly to let Lilu know that she had heard her. She channeled back: *I vow to teach you everything I know so that you may ascend to the great future that awaits you. I pledge my protection and loyalty to you as I do to your future husband, the Pharaoh.*

Sarrah smiled to herself at the intelligence and whimsy of the gods. To advance the primacy and glory of Egypt they looked outside its boundaries—and, of course, to the powers of a *woman!*

CHAPTER TWENTY-FIVE

It was hard to believe that more than a year had passed since the end of the war in Babylonia. Princess Lilu had proven to be a powerful ally in building a strong bond between the two nations. The peace treaty ushered in an era of trade and prosperity for both Babylonia and Egypt. Though a few of the old guard secretly condemned Meti and his decision, one by one those officials were forced into an early retirement in the far corner of the kingdom.

Sarrah reveled in her new mentee, Lilu, who was a quick and intelligent study with both common sense and innate understanding. And her mystic gifts almost rivaled those of Sarrah herself. But Meti was resistant to welcoming Lilu as his betrothed. He was slow to transfer his loyalty to her, having been bruised in the past by his attachment to Sarrah. At first he was happy to keep visiting the heterae for female companionship.

But Sarrah was complimentary of Lilu to Meti. She taught Lilu how to reach out to Meti, how to impress him. She watched with pleasure when she saw Meti soften toward this arranged marriage, and she was delighted when she saw the couple strolling the palace grounds together on a regular basis.

My work here is almost done, Heka. Give me the strength to see it through, Sarrah appealed silently. She had felt the disease in her lungs as soon as it had begun and knew it could spread rapidly, but with salves and incantations she'd been able to slow its progression. While she didn't know exactly how much time she had left, she knew she'd been granted enough to finish what she'd started.

———

It was a perfect late spring evening. As night fell Sarrah wandered the city, enjoying the sights, sounds, and smells of her beloved Memphis. The streets were strewn with decorations from Meti and Lilu's wedding celebration. There were cotton streamers in the dust; the torches burned low, the banquet platters had been removed, and the musicians were packing up their instruments to return to their villages. A small crowd of people, drunk on wine, slow-danced in the square. She hadn't walked so freely through the city since that fateful day five years ago when the Temple of Ptah was dedicated. How much had happened since then!

As she turned a corner, she nearly collided with Hasim. She looked up into the eyes of the only man she'd ever truly loved—the man who had her heart in this life and would in the afterlife. He was greatly changed since their last embrace. His hair was the color of ash; his robes were those of an ordinary soldier. But his skin still had that masculine, regal scent, and his green eyes shone brightly.

His eyes crinkled as he laughed softly. "Of course the gods would bring us together tonight."

"Yes," Sarrah replied. "As hard as I've tried to avoid you, I'm not surprised that tonight nothing can keep us apart."

"Please come sit with me and hear what I have to say." He gestured to the steps of Meti's majestic temple, sweeping a clear seat for them amid the detritus of the parade.

Hasim took her hand. "Sarrah, I love you. I have never stopped, and I never will. I know you love me, too."

She began to reply, but he held his hand to her lips. "Please, Sarrah, let me finish before you speak." She nodded.

"I have been patient these last years," he said, "as I knew you had to get Lilu secure and trained in the mystic arts. I also knew you planned to position her so that Meti couldn't help but fall in love with her. But all of that is now accomplished. Lilu has become not only a powerful visionary but also Queen of Egypt. You succeeded. So now it is *our* turn for happiness and love."

"Hasim, don't," she whispered.

But he forged on. "Will you be mine forever? Will you come away with me from this life and build a home with me in some place where we are both unknown? I may not be able to keep you in the level of comfort you have grown accustomed to, but I am not without means. I vow to keep you safe and loved for the remainder of your days."

Sarrah closed her eyes, her heart beating nearly out of her chest. "My love," she answered. "You ask the impossible. Yes, you have my heart for now and eternity, but Meti and Egypt have my vow. I cannot go with you. But I will ask you this—that you remain nearby, so that we may share moments when we can."

Now it was Hasim's turn to close his eyes and take a few deep breaths. Upon opening them, he leaned in and kissed Sarrah tenderly and with great care.

"That was a goodbye kiss," Sarrah said, with a sob in her throat.

"Yes, my beloved. That was a kiss goodbye." Said Hasim. "I cannot stay, and you cannot leave. This is the end of our story, Sarrah. Perhaps we shall meet again in another life."

With that he stood, descended the steps, and turned the corner. Sarrah rose and tried to follow him, but he had disappeared. This was truly the end. As she walked back to the palace, the only home she would ever again know, her heart broke into a thousand pieces.

Sarrah lifted the curtain and peered out her bedroom window. The streets of Memphis were deserted. It had been one month since she'd seen Hasim that last time, after the royal wedding. Since then she hadn't ventured outside, even to her garden.

Well, not many Egyptians had. These were the doldrums of the dry season; besides the staggering heat, there were sandstorms to contend with. Everything was covered with a dusting of sand—the buildings, the streets, the people, the markets. From her window Memphis looked fuzzy, like a mirage. It dulled the senses.

The clouds of sand could quickly turn a sunny afternoon into dusk. Sarrah ran her finger along the windowsill and it came away with a fine grit. She let the curtain fall, darkening the room further.

Actually, Sarrah didn't mind the darkness. It suited her mood. Over the past few weeks she'd retreated into her thoughts, refusing the company of Meti, Lilu, or anyone else in the palace. She'd even refused food. Whether it was her weakening health or her deep sadness over the finality of the parting with Hasim, these were realities she wasn't ready to face. If she stayed in her chambers, maybe she could stop time.

All the same, she was tempted to just fade away. If this was what it meant to be human, she was happy to leave this life behind. The pain of living out the rest of her mortal days without the one man she had truly loved seemed too much to bear.

She heard a soft knock at the door.

"Sarrah? It's me. I'm alone. Can I come in?"

"Lilu, I'm not feeling especially well. Can it—"

"Sarrah, do not forget that I am your queen, and I'll *order* you to open this door if I have to!" said Lilu in a mock-haughty tone.

Sarrah smiled. This young woman reminded her of herself, or a version of herself from what seemed like a million years ago, when she was full of confidence, and life, and vigor.

"Well then, enter, my Queen," she said. The two women embraced.

Lilu was carrying a lacquered box that looked familiar, but Sarrah couldn't place where she'd seen one like it.

"Come sit," Lilu said, using her sleeve to brush the thin layer of sand off the table. "I want to show you something."

Sarrah sat down, and Lilu opened the box. She lit a candle, then began to remove a set of painted tiles and arrange them face down on the table.

"Ah, I knew I'd seen these before," Sarrah said. "On my very first day in the palace, Amunet, the matron of the hetaerae, read my tiles. She said she could see that I'd come to the palace for good and not for evil. That I should take care to stay humble." She was quiet for several moments. "When she said that I would not be 'here' long, I thought she meant in the chambers of the hetaerae. But now I'm not so sure that she didn't mean the palace." She brushed away a tear.

Lilu looked at her, concerned. "I don't know what has changed for you or about you in the past few weeks, my dear Sarrah, but I would like to try to understand. We're too close now not to share our trials as well as our joys." She finished arranging the seventy-eight tiles. "My grandmother in Babylonia taught me to read the leaves of Thoth. She was my spiritual guide—until I met you. This is her set, one of the few belongings I brought with me when I left my country. Now, please pick ten of them and we'll see what we find."

Sarrah wasn't in the mood to be read or even understood, but it was hopeless to protest to this young queen, so precocious and full of life. She selected ten tiles and handed them to Lilu, who placed them in the same formation as had Amunet those many years ago. Lilu was quiet as she arranged the tiles. Then she stared up at Sarrah with a grave look on her face.

"Sarrah. You *must* be with him. *Whoever* he is. I know that you've always been loyal to Meti, but I see another man, your one true love, in these tiles." She grasped Sarrah's hand. "Do you understand what I'm saying?"

Sarrah tried to pull away but had already weakened, and Lilu wouldn't let go. "Sarrah. I respect that you've never shared any knowledge of this man with me. Meti has told me that you and he were estranged for a time, but he would never tell me why. It was a painful period in his life. But I've gathered most of the details through the palace grapevine."

"It doesn't matter now," Sarrah said, shaking her head, weeping softly. "It was never meant to be. I've given my life to the service of Meti and Egypt. The one time I deviated from that calling was when I let my human frailties guide me. Falling in love was wonderful, but it was a mistake."

"But—"

"And anyway, it's too late. He's gone. We ran into each other in the streets of the city on the evening of your wedding. He asked me to move away with him, and I said I needed to stay here with you. To help you and Meti, and to see this baby be born. This is where I belong."

Lilu looked up in surprise. "Meti doesn't know I am with child," she said. "I wasn't even sure of it myself." The two women hugged again.

"May the gods bless you and your family, and the future rulers of Egypt," Sarrah said.

"My dear friend, you may think that is the end of your love story. But you didn't read far enough." Lilu pointed to the seventh tile. "This is The Tower tile. Here is where you and your soul mate part ways, even though you don't want to."

She pointed at the next tile. "This is The Devil tile. It signals a time of darkness, of drought, of confusion."

She took the next tile and placed it in Sarrah's hand. "But *this* is The Star! Here is where you are *reunited!* Sarrah, you must find this warrior. You must be a warrior, too, and fight for a love like this! Please! The tiles are rarely this decisive!"

Sarrah closed her eyes. But Lilu wouldn't let her rest. "Don't think that I cannot see what else the tiles foretell. Your secrets are yours, and I will not press you. But I do know that time is of the essence, Sarrah. I don't want it to be so, but I see it here. That is the responsibility one accepts as a reader of the tiles."

Lilu raised Sarrah out of her chair. Sarrah didn't resist as Lilu wrapped her in heavy linen robes and bound them tightly. She covered her face and neck in a turban so that only Sarrah's eyes were visible. She lifted the curtain. From the darkening sky it was impossible to tell if it was afternoon or evening.

"Now *go*," Lilu pleaded as she guided Sarrah to the door. "The storm is rising again. Your service to Egypt is complete. As your queen, I thank you. And now, I command you to go."

———

Sarrah stumbled out into the streets of Memphis. The guards at the palace gate didn't recognize her. She was bundled so completely that it was difficult for her to see or be seen. As the wind picked up, merchants bolted their doors and market vendors covered their wares with heavy cloths. Anyone left in the streets gathered their wraps tightly around themselves as protection from the violently blowing sand.

She realized that she was still clutching the tile of The Star in her hand. She leaned her body into the wind and staggered through the winding streets of Hasim's neighborhood. Or was this still where he lived? She'd only been here once, years ago. She cursed herself for how reckless they'd been. She couldn't blame Khufu for her clouded mind at that time. She'd fully chosen to disregard her intuition, her prized gift from the gods— and the gods had punished her for it. But maybe Lilu and the tiles were right—that this was not the end of the story.

The skies were black now. It had taken all her strength to reach Hasim's home. The windows were boarded shut against the sandstorm. Sarrah had nothing left to lose. She raised her fist, still closed around the tile, and rapped on the door. She prayed to the gods for someone to hear her knock over the moaning wind.

A hand unlatched the door, then opened it a few inches to see who could possibly be knocking in these dangerous conditions. She loosened her head wrap and rubbed the sand from her eyes.

It was Asum.

"Sarrah! What are you doing here!" With one strong arm, he swept her into the house, the other arm forcing the door open just enough to do so. The room was dark. As her eyes slowly adjusted, she saw a chair and fell into it. Asum poured her a glass of water, then knelt at her feet, brushing the sand from her robes. She was too weak to take the glass in her hands, but he raised it to her lips. She took a sip, then leaned back and closed her eyes.

"Sarrah, if you are here for Hasim, I am sorry to tell you that he is gone. About a month ago, before the sand rose, he came home and packed his belongings. He said that he had nothing left here, and that he was leaving in search of a place to spend the rest of his days. That I should take this house as my own."

He hesitated, then continued. "Honestly, since Meti has now taken Lilu as his queen, I was certain that you had stolen away *with* him. I was so glad that you would be together and finally be free."

Sarrah shook her head. "No, sadly I did not." She took another sip of water.

"And now there is nothing left for me here, either. Clearly this love is meant for another lifetime. Thank you, Asum. I wish you well. You have always been a loyal friend to us both. I must go."

Over Asum's protests, she unlocked the door and stepped outside despite the howling wind. Her robes flapped loose, and sand whipped her skin from every direction. Still clutching The Star tile, she slowly sank onto the doorstep and fainted.

When Asum found Sarrah the next morning, she was caked with sand. She didn't stir, even as he lifted her limp body onto his horse and carried her through the barren streets to the palace gates.

———

Nine months later

The only moments of joy and reprieve from the pain were the ones Sarrah spent with Lilu and her pregnant belly. There had not been a royal baby since Meti's birth. Sarrah could sense that this child would be a daughter, and that she would inherit Lilu's strength and extraordinary powers.

Lilu passed a boar's-bristle brush through Sarrah's hair as she sat with her on her bed. She'd gathered all of Sarah's favorite items from her chambers to keep her company in her illness—her books, cuttings from her garden, her oils and salves, her handwoven blankets, her treasured gold cuff. She'd also brought the headdress that Meti had restored to her, which Sarrah had lent Lilu to wear at their wedding.

Lilu had also arranged for Nour to be by Sarrah's side until the end. What a bittersweet time it was for the two lifelong friends. Nour had tried to save Sarrah's life those many years ago, and now Sarrah had ensured that Nour's final years would be spent in the private palace quarters. Nour arranged for the royal chef to recreate the soups, teas, and comfort foods of their childhood village for Sarrah—not that she could eat much at this late stage of her illness. But she could still enjoy the smells. They reminded her of happy times in the village—at her mother's table, or playing with Nour at the banks of the Nile, daydreaming about their futures. Once Sarrah passed to the afterlife, Nour would become a nursemaid to the royal baby. Who better to entrust with this blessed child?

"Tell me, Sarrah. What will she be like?" said Lilu.

Nour clasped her hands together. "So it's a *girl!* But how do you know—?"

Sarrah chuckled softly. "So you know that it's a girl. I'm impressed, Lilu. Interaction with unborn souls is quite advanced. But wouldn't you rather be pleasantly surprised by your daughter's personality, beauty, and gifts?" she teased.

Lilu patted Sarrah's shoulder as she, too, giggled. "At least I got you to admit that our daughter will *have* gifts," she said. "That satisfies me. The rest can wait." The women embraced as if they, too, were mother and daughter. Nour dabbed her eyes with a cloth.

"I am going to miss you, my child," Sarrah whispered into Lilu's ear.

Lilu wept quietly. "And I am going to miss you, my Queen."

———

A few weeks later, bells sounded throughout Memphis to announce that an heir had been born to the Pharaoh and his Queen. Sarrah lay in her chamber; she was very close to transitioning into the afterlife, but she had been holding on just to hear those wondrous bells.

"You are here. Welcome, baby," she said aloud.

A few hours later, Meti strode proudly into Sarrah's bedroom, holding his new baby daughter in his arms. Nour put a finger to her lips to quiet him, but the commotion roused Sarrah nonetheless.

Meti stopped short as he looked at her. He could sense death in the room—but then breathed a sigh of relief as Sarrah turned her head and spoke to him.

"Bring her close, Meti. Let me see her finally. I've been waiting."

Meti knelt beside Sarrah's bed and held up his little girl.

"Look, Sarrah. Look what I have created. She is as confident and strong as I am. As intelligent and clever as her mother. And as powerful and intuitive as you."

Meti beamed as he continued. "Lilu and I gave her name much consideration. But she was always going to be named after you." He paused for a moment to be sure he had Sarrah's full attention.

"My beloved, it is my truest honor and privilege to introduce you to my daughter, Sarai."

CHAPTER TWENTY-SIX

New York City, March 17

Never had Sarah been so ready to board a plane. The kids were fine; her husband had kissed her goodbye and told her to enjoy herself. Her "out of office" reply email was on—for the first time ever. She'd packed something besides running gear and mom clothes; sure, they would be skiing and relaxing at the house, but if she knew Stuart, there would be some impossible-to-get reservations for dinner at Matsuhisa and other Aspen nightspots. She'd put on a cashmere sweater, leather pants, and low-heeled boots for the flight—even makeup! She couldn't wait to see Stuart's face when he picked her up.

As she walked down the jetway she left the mental gymnastics of the past few weeks behind her. *I really need to get away by myself more often,* she thought as she stored her bag in the overhead bin and took her window seat. She even accepted the flight attendant's offer of a glass of champagne.

Yes, dammit, she'd sprung for first class. *Let the vacation begin,* she toasted silently. This weekend was her opportunity to enjoy herself. Perhaps the flight would have been the perfect time to sit in deep contemplation about her marriage, even to journal or meditate or something, but she was just in too good a mood. As far as she was concerned, the decision to pursue marriage counseling had been made. If Carl wanted her to go to Aspen and delay that inevitability, who was *she* to argue?

Her self-congratulations were interrupted by the arrival of her seatmate. They exchanged pleasantries as he put his bag away. He was going to Denver on business and seemed rather on edge.

"I'm a nervous flier, so I apologize in advance if I inadvertently grab your arm during any possible turbulence," he said.

Sarah giggled. "My husband also hates to fly, so I'm used to being clung to when it gets bumpy," she said.

"So you're not afraid of flying?" he asked.

"No. I actually love to fly. Even on business trips I always get excited about a plane flight. Excuse me," she called to the flight attendant, tapping her glass. "Can I get another one of these?"

"Sarah?"

She gasped. There was Harry Aiken, standing in the aisle and staring down at her with a mix of wonder and confusion.

"Harry!" Sarah whispered. Her mouth felt dry; her mind was blank. Her seatmate couldn't help but notice the awkward intensity between them and began to stand up.

"Where is your seat, sir?" he asked. Harry was startled, but he looked at the man and said, "I'm two rows back, in 4C."

"Well then, today is your lucky day. Now you're in 2B. I'll move back, and you get the company of this lovely lady." He nodded at Sarah.

Sarah hadn't taken her eyes off Harry, but she was roused back to reality by this exchange. "Thank you, but that's not necessary. I don't want to make you move your things."

"Miss, it's no problem. Besides, the way this guy is looking at you, I don't think I have a *choice*." He winked, collected his belongings, and moved.

"Today is my lucky day," Harry said as he sat down and turned to look at Sarah.

Wow, he regained his composure quickly, she thought. *Buckle up!*

"So—what are *you* doing here?" she asked.

The flight attendant returned with two champagne flutes.

"I'm going out to Denver on some business, and then I'm heading up to Aspen for the weekend to ski and see some friends. What are you doing here?"

"Well, I'm supposed to be getting away from it all," she chuckled. She took a glug of champagne. Was she already tipsy?

"I'm actually flying up to Aspen to spend the weekend with my CFO and his partner. We have a little business to do, but it's mostly for pleasure."

"Oh, it's pleasurable all right," Harry said, looking her up and down. "Do you always wear leather pants to your business meetings?"

Sarah blushed hotly and looked down at her lap.

"I can't do this," she mumbled.

Harry gently took her chin and turned her face to his. "Sarah, take a breath. It's all okay. It's better than okay. We have the next four hours to just talk and get to know each other. It's all I've wanted since the moment I laid eyes on you. I have no idea what this—thing—is between us, but what I do know is that I'm dying to learn all about who the real Sarah Fuller is."

His touch calmed her, and the ever-flowing champagne didn't hurt. They settled into a banter. She couldn't get over how easy it was to talk to him. She'd always prided herself on being a good listener, and she encouraged people to talk about themselves so she wouldn't have to share too much about herself. But here she was, telling Harry everything about her life without any hesitation. Jeez, they were now up to her college years and meeting Carl.

"I really can't believe I am talking this much," she said. "I usually never talk about myself. Except to my psychiatrist. He gets to hear all of it."

Harry leaned in. "Well, I'm honored that you're sharing so much about your life. I can't believe you're an only child. I come from a family of six kids, so I can't imagine the peace and quiet you must have enjoyed. I'm jealous!"

Sarah shook her head. "It was a bit lonely. My parents did their best, but they were both so driven and disciplined. Even their social life wasn't about play, only about work and goals. I always envied friends with siblings. I guess we always want what we can't have."

Harry took Sarah's hand. "You have no idea how much I understand wanting something I can't have."

His words excited her, but they also scared her. She wanted so much to tell him everything she'd been feeling, but an over-developed sense of propriety stopped her. She pulled her hand away and looked at Harry.

"Okay, Mr. Aiken. I've had the floor for the last hour. Now it's your turn to take the mic. Tell me all about these siblings and your childhood."

Harry smiled. "Did you know my real name is Haran?" he asked.

"Haran," she repeated. "What an interesting name. Is it Arabic?"

He nodded. "Close enough. It's a Turkish name. My parents moved to the United States from Istanbul right after they were married. My uncle had moved to Houston a couple of years earlier and opened a bakery. When it began to take off, he asked my dad to come over and help him run it. I was born in the States and spent my childhood in a suburb of Houston."

"Are you the oldest?"

"No. I have an older sister. But I'm the oldest *son,* so my parents had very specific expectations for me."

She took a sip of champagne, settling into her seat. "Boy, do I know about parental expectations."

"Well, I guess that explains why we're both so driven," he said. "When I was ten years old, I started working in the bakery every morning before school, and I didn't stop until I finished college. It was presumed that I'd eventually take over the operations. But I knew that type of business wasn't for me.

"You see, my parents would send me to Turkey every summer to stay with my grandparents and cousins. It was important to them that I be fully immersed in our culture. Sarah, I can't tell you how much I loved my time there as a child. Don't get me wrong—I still love it there, but as a boy Turkey seemed almost *magical*. The sights and smells and colors were so different from urban America. I fell in love with Turkey, and I knew my future was somehow linked to it."

"Is that what motivated you to get into import/export?" Sarah asked.

"Completely. It all started so innocently. During college, I visited Istanbul on a break and decided to buy ten rugs from my cousin's stall at the Grand Bazaar. I figured I'd bring them home and try to sell them for a profit. Well, not only did I sell them in less than a month, but I quadrupled my investment. I'd never made so much money so easily; I was used to working long hours in the bakery for next to nothing. I started importing rugs, and over the years my business grew quite organically into a global entity. I now export jewelry, cosmetics, and of course you know about my essential oils. The common thread is what I feel and know to be truly Turkish and of the best quality."

"How did you get into the essential oil business?" Sarah asked.

"Funnily enough, it was related to the bakery. I wondered why the pastries we made in Houston weren't as extraordinary as the ones I ate in Istanbul. I realized that it was the flavor essences. Every cake, pastry, and cookie in Turkey is laced with rosewater, orange, lemon, almond, vanilla. It's not just about taste; it's about the scent as well; it's a multisensory treat. I think my family had adapted their menu for an American palate. But I vowed that when I grew up, I'd elevate the American perception of Turkish taste—especially pastries!"

"That's so fascinating," said Sarah. "Of course, here in the US, I grew up loving the smell of lavender. It wasn't until I studied in France that I learned there are 47 species of lavender and more than 450 varieties. I couldn't help but fall in love with the complexities of fragrance."

"Not to mention that lavender is delicious on a lemon tart," Harry said with a smile.

"You've got an appetite for the finer things," Sarah teased. "Speaking of which, please ask our flight attendant for two more glasses of champagne."

———

"Oh!" Sarah said, startled. "Are we here already? Has it honestly been four hours?" she asked as the plane taxied toward the airport.

Harry feigned a pout. "I wish it were a twelve-hour flight. I could talk to you all night long."

Sarah blushed and touched Harry's hand lightly. "Which is why it's good that this is just a four-hour flight."

Harry grasped her hand. "May I please have my hand back?" she said.

"On one condition. Promise me that you'll have dinner with me one night in Aspen."

"Please don't ask that of me."

Harry returned Sarah's hand to her lap. "I frighten you, Sarah? I mean you no harm; I promise you that." He began to gather his belongings to disembark.

"Harry, no—that's not what I meant. You don't frighten me. *I* frighten me. I don't trust my self-control when I'm with you. I've never felt this way before."

She felt shy all of a sudden and began to busy herself collecting her things.

"Sarah Fuller," he said, beaming, "I give you my word that nothing inappropriate will happen in Aspen. You are completely safe with me. I simply want to spend more time with you. Please."

Sarah looked up at Harry and saw the sincerity on his face. "Thank you for saying that. I promise I'll think about it."

CHAPTER TWENTY-SEVEN

Stuart was standing in front of his gleaming Range Rover outside the Arrivals exit. He pulled her into a big hug as she walked up, then held her at arm's length. "Look at *you*, Aspen queen! Leather pants? Boots? Loving the fur hat. I wish it hadn't taken three years for you to accept my invitation!"

Sarah twirled for him—then felt a little dizzy. "Whoops, the queen might need a disco nap. I had a few glasses of champagne on the flight to Denver."

Stuart laughed. "Well, you're just *full* of surprises! Nice to meet you, Sarah Fuller! You can nap in front of the fireplace while I make you dinner, m'lady." She hugged him again and sighed a heavy sigh.

Sarah gasped as they pulled up to the house and again as she entered the great room, with its floor-to-ceiling windows overlooking Aspen and the surrounding mountains.

"Oh Stu, look at your home. It's absolutely gorgeous. You can see everything from up here. I may never leave."

Stuart shook his head. "I wanted to get a simple condo in town, but Walter convinced me that Red Mountain is where we belong," he said. "I still refuse to admit to his face that he was right, but I'll tell you in secret that he was spot on. Good thing I married that man. I'd be lost without him."

Sarah smiled as she turned back to the view, but inside she was melancholy. *What must it feel like to be married to someone who makes you feel seen and cared for that way? That's never been my dynamic with Carl. If anything, I'm the North Star in our relationship, and he simply follows my lead. Just once, I want to feel the way Stuart feels.*

Oh, get over yourself.

Sarah shook off her thoughts and followed Stuart to the guest room. "Why don't you get settled in and freshen up?" he said. "I thought we would stay in tonight since you're still on East Coast time. We have to get an early start so we can pick up your ski equipment. Plus, I want you to get a good night's sleep and hydrate. The altitude can be tricky at first."

She squeezed Stuart's arm. "You always take such good care of me, Stu. Thank you."

————

It snowed overnight, so the skiing the next day was utterly ideal. Thankfully Stuart and Walter were also intermediate skiers, so the three of them had a perfect morning on the mountain. They stopped for a quick lunch and got back out on the slopes for another few runs. By the time they returned to the house, Sarah felt more alive than she'd felt in months. She indulged in a long soak in the hot tub out on the deck before crawling into bed for a much-needed nap.

She awoke to a text: "*I'm holding you to our dinner, Sarah. You name the time and place and I will be there. H*"

Her stomach flipped.

Get it together, Fuller. You're not a teenager anymore. In fact, you're a forty-year-old and married, with kids!

She decided to distract herself with a call home. Hearing the kids' voices made her a little homesick, but Carl assured her that everyone was doing just fine. "It's all good here. I'm enjoying having some one-on-one time with them. Who knew nine was such a fun age?"

I did. Involved parents usually find the fun in every age, you lazy shit. Little late to the game there, Carl.

"I'm glad all is well. Thank you for allowing me to really enjoy my time here."

Carl tried to make small talk about the weather and the skiing, but Sarah hustled off the phone, claiming that they were about to leave for an après ski party.

She padded into the living room. True to his word, Stuart handed Sarah a glass of Bordeaux as she sank into an armchair in front of the fireplace. Then he sat next to her in the other armchair.

"Okay, Sarah, tell Papa Stu all about it."

"What do you mean? Everything is *fine*. Honest."

"Don't even try it, young lady. You can't fool me. You've been distracted since you got here. You've never had a poker face, which is why I'm the one who negotiates our deals. Spill it."

Sarah looked into the fire. "What if I told you that I ran into an old friend on the airplane and I'm considering meeting them for dinner?"

Stuart sat quietly for a few minutes as he took his turn staring at the dancing flames.

"Who is this 'old friend'?"

"Someone I've known for a lifetime. Maybe more than one lifetime. Put it this way: I don't even remember how we met."

"Sarah, you're not making sense right now."

She looked at him. "Stuart, the fact that I ran into this old friend this weekend makes no sense. But it's too much of a coincidence not to pursue it."

Stuart leaned forward and put his hand on her knee. "Sarah, you've built an amazing business *entirely* on instinct. It's pure magic to watch you create fragrances, and I feel honored to be a part of bringing them into the world."

She blushed. "Stuart. I'm so lucky to have you."

"I'm not done," he said. "I hope you don't mind my saying this. But I've always been surprised that you don't extend those instincts to your personal life. Instead, it seems like you're generally happy to just keep everyone else happy. To do what's expected."

Sarah was surprised at his candor. "Go on."

"I think you know what I mean. I don't want to say much more, except this. I've lived a bit more life than you, and I know one thing to be true. This life is not a dress rehearsal, Sarah. There's no redo. If your instincts tell you to reconnect with this 'old friend,' then that's good enough for me. Follow your instincts."

Sarah sat back in her chair and absorbed the words of this man she so deeply respected. "Well, we both know it's futile to negotiate with *you*, Stuart. I guess I'll go."

CHAPTER TWENTY-EIGHT

Sarah stepped into the lobby of the Hotel Jerome. She'd taken some care to dress nicely, but she'd also taken care to not look like she'd tried too hard. She'd decided on black jeans, a sleeveless black silk tank, and her gold arm cuff. She looked forward to the moment that she'd slide out of her heavy shearling coat to nonchalantly reveal a barely-there top. Not to mention that she was wearing her signature "evening" fragrance, Memphis. It was muskier and sexier than she thought herself to be, but it always inspired her to live up to its promise. Call it an "aspirational" fragrance.

She cautiously looked around the lobby. The space felt welcoming and cozy yet sophisticated and luxurious. Though the building dated to the 1880s, the interiors were hip and upscale.

The Hotel Jerome was on many a New Yorker's must-visit list for Aspen. Sarah truly didn't want to run into anyone she knew tonight—but if she did, she could always say it was a business meeting, right? A thank-you dinner for Harry's involvement in the Arcanum Foundation.

The concierge pointed her to the restaurant, and even in the low-lit, clubby room she saw him the moment she walked in. He was seated at a corner booth, perfectly tucked away from the central dining area.

Nice job, Harry, she thought. *Very discreet.*

She smiled and waved off the hostess as she walked over. Harry stood to greet her. "Wow, Sarah. The Western look suits you. It beats that boardroom look every day of the week." He gave her a peck on the cheek. "May I take your coat?"

"Gracious, Harry. Such impeccable manners. Thank you, yes."

She turned her back to him, though she wished she could have seen his face when the heavy shearling gave way to bare shoulders. She could have sworn that he craned into her neck for a whiff of perfume.

"I can't remember the last time someone pulled my seat out for me," Sarah said as Harry draped her coat over the back of the chair and eased her gently to the table.

He stood still for a moment, then replied, "That's just not right. Not right at all."

Change the subject, Sarah. "Have you been on the mountain? The skiing has been tremendous. I'd forgotten how much I love being out West in winter." Harry took her lead, and they launched into travelogues of their days in Aspen. "Stuart and Walter have been wonderful hosts," she said. "It will be difficult to leave tomorrow."

Harry leaned forward and said, "I'm glad to hear that Stuart Adler is as good a person as he is a businessman. I hope to get to know him better in the future. He has a spotless reputation."

"You have no idea. I'm so lucky to have him as my right-hand man. He's been an invaluable mentor, but he's been an even better friend. You know, you have him to thank for my agreeing to see you tonight."

Harry raised a brow. "Is that so? I wasn't sure if you'd have told him where you were going. What, pray tell, did he say?"

"Well, I didn't say too much, but he told me to trust my instincts," she said with a smile.

They had an easy dinner, the conversation and wine flowing. As the table was being cleared, Sarah asked, "So where are you staying? Are you with friends, too?"

Harry cleared his throat. "No. I'm not a huge fan of being a house guest. I'm an early riser and like to keep my own schedule. I'm actually staying *here,* so I was delighted when you suggested it as our dinner spot."

Sarah froze. "You mean to tell me you're staying right upstairs?"

Harry reached forward and took her hand.

"Sarah, do you remember what I promised on the plane? That you're completely safe with me? I meant it. Don't get me wrong. I'd love nothing more than to take you upstairs and explore this insane electricity between us. But now is not the time. I just want to be around you for as long as I can before I put you safely into the hotel Suburban to have you driven back to Stuart's."

Sarah didn't dare move.

She whispered, "So you still feel it, too?" she whispered. "What is this thing between us? I've never felt it with anyone before. It's as if I've known you my whole life. Like we have a shared history."

Harry nodded. "It is. I've never felt anything like it, either. I can't tell you what it is, but I *will* say that I look forward to figuring it out."

"How do you intend to do that?" she asked.

Harry laughed softly. "By being a perfect gentleman tonight, so I earn the right to spend more time with you." He rose from his chair and helped slip Sarah's coat onto her shoulders. She could feel his body against hers; this was as close as they'd get tonight. He walked her out to the valet and requested the hotel car.

It had begun snowing, and Sarah felt as if she were in a winter wonderland. "It's just so beautiful; I wish I could bottle it," she smiled wistfully. "The snow falling, the twinkling lights—it's out of a dream."

Harry opened the door and offered her a hand, and she hopped into the car. He leaned in to kiss her cheek.

"Oh, I don't know," he whispered in her ear. "As far as I'm concerned, *you're* the dream."

He stepped back and closed the car door. Then he knocked on the roof and the driver pulled away.

Sarah turned to look out the back of the Suburban and saw Harry standing there. He grew smaller and smaller until he disappeared into the snow. It was warm in the car, but she had the chills.

We've been here before, she knew. *We will be here again.*

It was in the cards.

THE END

EPILOGUE

Forest of Chateau de Fontainebleau, France, 1532

Hooves pounded as the carriage hurtled out the chateau gate and into the dense forest. The carriage was traveling at breakneck speed, swaying precariously as it careened around sharp corners, dodging the mighty oaks and pine trees that Sari knew so well.

Despite the risk, Sari—dressed in a midnight-blue woolen dress and cloak—lifted the panel of the secret compartment in the carriage floor. She gripped the sides and gingerly raised herself into the cab, her eyes just high enough to peer out the window and see the chateau, her home of the past three years, fade away behind her into the darkness until it disappeared. She knew she was being reckless, but she couldn't help herself. She would never see this place again. She prayed that the starless night would protect them.

Sari turned to Marc, crouched in a ball on the floor of the carriage, a rough-spun tunic stretched across his enormous frame. How could such a large man make himself so invisible? But then again, Marc had always had the gift of disappearing in plain sight. It was one of the reasons she'd been drawn to him all those years ago.

Prince Marc, born to aristocracy and privilege, was as handsome as he was strong. He looked like a giant in the court because of his height and powerful build. Too bad his intelligence didn't impress with the same strength. King Francis, Marc's father, had cursed him as an idiot and cast him to the side in disgrace.

As Sari had begun to befriend the dishonored prince, she'd noticed that he might not have the intellect of a scholar or a scientist but was smarter than he let on. No, he hadn't learned to read or write, but he most certainly listened and observed. And as their friendship started to grow and solidify, Sari discovered that he had an extraordinary memory. It was the most remarkable thing she had ever witnessed. Marc could look at something for just a few moments and have perfect recall of it forever. That had most certainly been invaluable during the many months of planning this escape.

As Sari gazed at her friend, she reflected on how they'd bonded over a mutual desire to disappear. They both yearned for privacy and quiet and simplicity—the opposite of the constant public demands of life at court. Marc had literally saved her life; he was the only true connection she had made since the fateful day when she'd first arrived to take her place as a courtesan to King Francis. Never in her wildest dreams could she have imagined that she'd be escaping with the young prince three years later to brave the unknown and fight her way to freedom.

Sari was jolted from her reverie when the coach hit a deep rut, threatening to splinter it into pieces.

"My god," Sari cried, "this is intolerable. We are never going to make it in this ridiculous excuse of a carriage. It's older than I am."

Marc placed a hand on her knee. "You must stay perfectly quiet," he whispered coarsely. "You were made fully aware of the nature of our transportation. You'd better get used to it, as we'll be cramped in here for several days.

"Besides, Pascal is supposedly one of the best smugglers in the region. He knows all the secret routes through the forest. He wouldn't risk his personal coach, regardless of how much we paid him to get us to Le Mans.

"Now crouch down on the floor with me so this journey doesn't end before it has even begun."

ACKNOWLEDGMENTS

There are so many to thank on this extraordinary journey.

First, I want to thank Tripp West for his immeasurable participation, love, and friendship throughout this entire experience. I couldn't have done it without you, "Dad."

I send huge waves of thanks to Kate Hensler Fogarty who has been the best collaborator, sounding board, co-creator, guide, and support system any author could ever dream of having. I am eternally grateful, Kate.

To Paul Carlos and the entire team at Pure + Applied. I could never imagine a greater graphic designer.

To my incredible publicity team at CLC Enterprises. Carol, Keelin, and Anna, you are the best and I thank you for your creative genius.

To my entire publishing team at Mayfly Books, especially Julie and Jess. You made this intimidating self-publishing journey seamless and a pleasure.

To Megan Mulry, who helped me start the engine of my writing career. Love you, sweetie.

To all of my friends and clients who have bathed me in unending support, love, and encouragement. Most especially, Alison, Andrea, Krista, Georgia, Dawn, John, Stacey, Buffy, Marisa, Nori, and Marie. I send all of the love, encouragement, and support right back with huge hugs.

Lastly, to my beautiful family. Ryan and Tyler, thank you for always believing in me and urging me forward. Mom and Dad, I wish you were here to see this but I've taken you with me for all of it and have felt your presence every step of the way. And to my sisters, Meghan and Mary, my brothers-in-law, and my niece and nephews: I love you all so much.

ABOUT THE AUTHOR

Kelly O'Hearn is a master intuitive channeler in high demand for her tarot readings, with clients on every continent but Antartica. Born in New York City, O'Hearn first put her intuitive skills to work as a professional wine taster, instructor, and sommelier in the elite institutions of Manhattan, Portugal, and Aspen. In 2014, she was drawn to begin reading tarot cards, an ancient practice that does not presume to "predict the future" but offers insight through conversation, perspectives, and self-reflections which can guide one to become one's most authentic self. During the Covid pandemic, O'Hearn used the tarot cards to channel her own past lives. Weeks of readings, all captured on video, inspired the time-bending series of novels that is Arcanum. O'Hearn is the mother of two and lives in Florida.

www.ingramcontent.com/pod-product-compliance
Lightning Source LLC
Chambersburg PA
CBHW022111310726
48972CB00007B/1993